SCOTT'S VOICE PIERCED THE SILENCE WITH A SHARP, FRIGHTENED CRY . . .

Chekov clutched the helmet to him again. "Scotty!"

"I've got a suit breach! Ah, DAMN! Chekov! Listen, lad, you've got to—"

Silence engulfed the open channel.

Chekov threw his helmet to the floor and began hastily stripping off his duty jacket.

"Where do you think you're going?" McCoy demanded. "Chekov, don't be an idiot!"

Chekov didn't look up. "I won't leave the lock," he promised. "If I can't see him, I'll come right back."

"We need someone in this shuttle besides me who isn't incapacitated . . ." McCoy began.

"Bones," Kirk said, interrupting the doctor. He turned to Chekov. "Go. But be careful."

Look for STAR TREK Fiction from Pocket Books

Star Trek: The Original Series

Star Trek: The Next Generation

STAR TREK®

THE KOBAYASHI MARU

JULIA ECKLAR

POCKET BOOKS

New York   London   Toronto   Sydney   Tokyo

An *Original* Publication of POCKET BOOKS

POCKET BOOKS, a division of Simon & Schuster Inc.
1230 Avenue of the Americas, New York, NY 10020

ISBN: 0-671-65817-4

First Pocket Books printing December 1989

10 9 8 7 6 5 4 3 2 1

POCKET and colophon are registered trademarks of Simon & Schuster Inc.

Printed in the U.S.A.

Acknowledgments

For all the help and encouragement they've given me, both during the writing of *The Kobayashi Maru* and beside it, this book is dedicated to:

Ann Cecil, friend and editor *nonpareil,* for doing me the very great favor, all those years ago, of reading my first *Star Trek* novel and telling me why it stank.

Jo Ann Baasch, Charlie Terry, Don Wenzel, Kathleen Conat, and, once again, *Ann Cecil,* for proofreading this manuscript to death.

Mitch and *JoAnn, Don* and *Kathleen, Tom* and *Bill, Pam, Sandy, Diana,* both *Joes* and *all the Daves,* and anybody else who sat with us under the fireworks on July 4th and helped me figure out all the ways I could blow up Klingon warships.

Rusty, for (among other things) pushing "G"s.

And, last but greatest of them all, *Don Kosak the Brilliant,* King of Computers, for his valiant battle with and victory over *The Kobayashi Maru.*

If there is anyone I've forgotten (and with all the time and effort that's gone into this thing, I'm sure there's someone), please forgive me. It isn't my intention to slight anyone—I'm just a little hard of remembering at times. But a hearty thank you to everyone, whether mentioned or not. Just as in Starfleet, your contributions to *The Kobayashi Maru* represent the best that is in us all.

Historian's Note

This adventure takes place shortly after the events chronicled in *Star Trek: The Motion Picture*.

Chapter One

HALLEY

"This is *Enterprise* hailing shuttlecraft *Halley*. All frequencies are open to you, *Halley,* and locating circuits are in operation. If you are able, please respond . . . This is *Enterprise* hailing ship's shuttle *Halley*. All frequencies are open to you . . ."

"Chekov, can't you turn that blasted thing off?"

Leonard McCoy's voice was uncharacteristically low, but cut clearly through Uhura's tinny broadcast over the shuttle radio. In the row of seats across from McCoy, James Kirk opened his eyes to darkness.

For a long moment, Captain James T. Kirk was aware of little save that he was hurt, and he was cold. Then the pain took residence somewhere deep in his right knee, and memory came awake with the pain. The remembering made him vaguely sick. He gingerly turned his head, searching the dark shuttle for Scott and Sulu now that the doctor had roused him.

Leonard McCoy occupied the seat just across the shuttle's main aisle from Kirk, one row ahead of where Sulu, propped carefully upright, still slept. The doctor had been in almost the same position when Kirk, drowsy from McCoy's pain medication, slipped into sleep God knew how long ago. McCoy was bundled into a field jacket nearly a size and a half too large, his hands stuffed sullenly under his arms for warmth. The hard, yellow light from an emergency lamp painted his face in bright relief against the cold darkness around him. He hadn't yet realized Kirk was awake; McCoy's attention was fixed on the forward hatch, where Kirk could hear movement, but where the dark was too deep to see.

"Chekov!" McCoy hissed again. "Turn off the radio!"

"I heard you," Chekov called back, sounding more than just mildly annoyed. There was a long pause, then a muted *snap*-slide as the Russian pulled one of the radio's circuit boards. The shuttle fell into dismal silence.

"Don't go getting grouchy on me, Bones," Kirk advised McCoy. "The quarters are cramped enough as it is."

The doctor turned to him, startled. "How long have you been awake?" he asked, avoiding a reply to Kirk's gentle reprimand.

The captain shrugged. "Long enough to hear you snap at my navigator."

McCoy looked embarrassed, and settled back into his seat a bit self-consciously. "Sorry, Jim. It's just . . ." The doctor's ill temper seemed to bleed away with his weary sigh. He didn't look angry then, only tired and old. "It just seemed so pointless," he finished. "That's all."

"I know." Kirk's words puffed out as clouds of white vapor; the shuttle had been losing heat for over an hour now. "But don't give up hope yet, Bones."

McCoy managed a *humph* that sounded so much like his normal crusty self, Kirk had to smile.

"How's your knee?"

"You're the doctor," Kirk replied. "Aren't I supposed to ask you that?"

McCoy favored the captain with an unamused scowl. "You haven't done anything that won't heal, but you'll have to be careful with it for at least a couple weeks. You managed to wrench it pretty good."

Kirk didn't like how that sounded; if nothing else, it meant no movement right now. "'Wrench it'?" he echoed, striving for lightness and (he suspected) failing. "If you keep using these technical terms, Bones, you're going to confuse me!"

"Don't worry about the technical terms," McCoy tossed back, "just tell me if it hurts."

Kirk shrugged again. "A little." In truth, the knee was a solid, steady fist of pain, cramping his thigh muscles until the urge to shift position became almost unbearable. Every time he stirred, though, the joint exploded in violent protest and left him wishing he'd never tried to move at all.

But if McCoy could change the subject, so could he. "How's Sulu holding up?"

Worry flashed across the doctor's face, but, before he could answer, the helmsman volunteered, ". . . I've been better . . ."

McCoy turned in his seat to glare at Sulu. "You're supposed to be asleep, Commander," he reprimanded sternly.

Eyes still closed, Sulu grinned weakly at McCoy over the cervical support holding his head in place. "You've got to be kidding, Doc! My shoulder's killing me!"

"I've got you on a high dosage already," McCoy said, his manner softened. "I don't want to give you anything more just yet."

Kirk thought maybe Sulu tried to nod; the only indication was the tight expression of pain that flitted across the lieutenant commander's face. The helmsman was strapped and belted so firmly into his seat, Kirk was surprised he could move at all. "That's okay, Doc," Sulu said. Even his normally brilliant smile looked only pained and drugged. "I don't want you to O.D. me . . . But I'm not sleeping, either."

Kirk sank back into his seat and tried not to think about his crew or his knee. Neither task was easy. The stale air in the shuttle smelled rankly of burnt circuitry and ozone. Enigmatic sounds and smells wafted into the main compartment from Scott's repair efforts in the rear hatch; in the pilots' hatch, Chekov hadn't so much as cursed as he sifted through the remains of the radio in search of something to repair. At first, Uhura's soothing, velvet voice over their receiver was the only indication that home was still out there somewhere, looking for them. Now, even that ephemeral reassurance was gone. Kirk didn't know whether to be angry at McCoy, or grateful.

We were supposed to go on shore leave in three days. Their first shore leave in four months. It just wasn't fair.

The *Enterprise* wasn't even assigned near the Hohweyn system. Then, just two weeks ago, contact with the Venkatsen Research Group was completely lost, and the *Enterprise* was the only ship in a position to attempt an investigation and recovery. Again.

Failure was a chance the Venkatsen Group and their funders had taken when the Group was first placed on Hohweyn VII. The safest planet in an utterly unsafe system, Hohweyn VII came fully equipped with all the dangers expected in such an arrangement. Hohweyn's forty-seven planets—natural, captured, and rogue—careened about an unstable tertiary sun, creating, destroying, and slinging as incredible an array of astrophysical anomalies as Kirk had ever had the honor to see. Primarily, the Group was there to delve into the secrets of gravitational attraction and repulsion, hoping to better equip modern sensor systems so travelers might discover and avoid gravitic anomalies, rather than stumble into them.

So much for modern research, Kirk reflected glumly. *We've probably got more information on gravitic fluxes than Venkatsen has compiled in a year!* Only they would probably never get home with the data.

One of the unfortunate hazards of the system were several debris clouds and asteroid belts—the remains of the system's more unstable planets and comets. Hohweyn VII spent most of its solar year in the path of one or more of these. Besides the obvious danger of collision, the iron- and nickel-rich asteroids wreaked havoc with sensors.

Upon arriving, Kirk deemed it unnecessary to venture too close to Hohweyn VII with something as large as a starship. The *Enterprise* was left in parking orbit just beyond the path of the debris cloud enveloping Hohweyn VII, and a team was dispatched by shuttlecraft to make contact with Venkatsen and report. Kirk headed the team himself, desperate to be away from the bridge (even if only for a little while), and anxious to have someone of his own tactical skill and diplomacy along. The other five positions were left open to volunteers.

On later reflection, Kirk realized that even if he'd handpicked each member of the shuttle's crew, the results would have been the same. He wasn't sure if he should feel guilty about that, but he did.

Kirk wanted an engineer, in the event some mechanical problem caused the Venkatsen Group's silence. Chief Engineer Montgomery Scott pointed out that the equipment on Hohweyn VII would not be standard, and Kirk would need a top engineer to discern its workings and repairs. When the tally was in, Kirk couldn't argue with Scott's choice for the assignment: himself. The captain had seen Scott puzzle out and repair things Kirk couldn't even recognize as machinery, as well as resurrect equipment other engineers had declared utterly unsalvageable. It sometimes seemed at least half the *Enterprise*'s current engine room was as the designer planned it, the other half Scotty-rigged to do whatever Kirk asked. If the engineer wanted to come play with archaic scientific equipment in the middle of a messed-up star system, who was Kirk to tell him, "No"?

Dr. McCoy didn't offer any explanation for his willingness to tag along, and Kirk didn't ask. The captain suspected the doctor was growing bored with the number of stress-related problems caused by their long stint without shore leave. The Venkatsen rescue was just an excuse to leave the ship in some other doctor's capable hands. Whatever the reason, Kirk harassed McCoy only moderately for his sudden desire to flirt with danger, and silently welcomed his company.

Pavel Chekov's reasons for volunteering were easily the most obvious. Kirk's former navigator, now chief of ship's security, hadn't been the only member of the *Enterprise's* security force to volunteer for the mission. Every crewman in security knew as well as Kirk that it was standard procedure to include at least one armed escort on any investigative team; rank and position mattered very little in the field. Kirk knew, too, that their recent wealth of deep-space runs had provided security with no off-ship time at all, and very few on-ship duties besides trading off at the bridge weapons station. In the end, Kirk looked on in amusement while, at First Officer Spock's suggestion, the fifteen security personnel drew lots for the contested assignment. Kirk always considered it unfortunate that Chekov had been transferred away from navigations (he was by far the best navigator Kirk had ever had), so it was to the captain's advantage that Chekov won the draw. Kirk assigned the lieutenant as both shuttle navigator and team security escort, thus cutting the team's numbers by one.

Lieutenant Commander Sulu was the easiest inclusion of all. Sulu was Kirk's chief helmsman, and the best pilot on the ship (not to mention in Starfleet); Kirk planned to privately ask the small, slender Asian to join the flight. He suspected Sulu could be talked into it, if only to ensure the safety of the others. To his distinct pleasure, however, Kirk never got the chance.

Sulu showed up, as cheerful as if he'd been reporting for a routine practice simulation, while Chekov was still compiling navigational data from the *Enterprise*'s main computer. Within five minutes, it was impossible to tell the two men hadn't worked side by side in several years. "It's like riding a bike," Sulu informed Kirk brightly, obviously aiming the jibe at Chekov. "You never really forget. Besides, I'll make sure he doesn't run us into anything important." As if to prove Sulu's teasing groundless, Chekov reported ready for launch in record time, and they moved the shuttle smoothly into free space.

Halley nosed into the crazy system uneventfully. Scott rode the sensors as if they were a nervous horse, quietly calling off coordinates when the readings warned him of danger. Sulu's skilled and delicate hands laced the tiny shuttle through conflicting gravity wells and any number of tangled lines of force, as calm and unhurried as the plants that shared his cabin back on board the ship. Chekov kept his eyes trained on his own panel, acting on Scott's information as smoothly as Sulu, though less relaxed. Neither of them so much as glanced away from their stations until Scott said quietly, "Mister Sulu, down throttle."

Sulu obeyed without hesitation. Chekov glanced anxiously at Scott, not turning away from his panel. "What's wrong?"

The engineer nursed the readings a moment longer. "The sensors picked up a slight flux just off our starboard bow." A smile that wasn't at all amused crossed his broad, highlander's features. "Don't look now, lads, but I think we've found a gravitic mine."

Sulu groaned. "Lucky for us."

"Can we avoid it?" Kirk asked from the passenger

compartment. No one seemed surprised that he'd been listening.

"We'll find out, Captain," Scott replied. "We're sure as hell not going to try running through it!"

Chekov already worried over his controls, leaning back briefly to steal a look at Scott's sensor readout. "I need more room," he told Sulu shortly. "I can't even turn us at this distance!"

It was serious, Kirk realized then. Sulu could pilot them straight through hell without raising a sweat, but not Chekov. The security chief's irritability was a certain indicator that Chekov was not happy with their predicament. "Take us back about four thousand kilometers," Chekov continued. "Beyond that well at 478 mark—"

"Mother of Christ!" Scott exclaimed suddenly, his voice sharp with fear. "It's moving! The damn thing's *moving!* Nose down, Sulu! Get us under it!"

"Give me a reading!" Chekov twisted about as far as his seat straps would allow. "Scott! A *reading!*"

It wasn't until much later that Kirk realized Chekov wanted the second reading to plot where the mine would be once it passed them. Two points of reference weren't really enough to extrapolate any kind of course, but he was going to try anyway. Like so much else on this disastrous mission, it was a damn fine effort.

The mine struck them broadside, wrenching the tiny shuttle about like a rabbit caught up in a dog's jaws. Kirk slammed hard against the wall, gasping with surprise when the strength of the impact forced the wind from him. All the blood in his body seemed to rush simultaneously into his extremities, swelling them, crowding them. Kirk couldn't tell if the shuttle was under violent acceleration, or merely being torn apart by the gravitic mine's fury. He wondered fleetingly if the horror stories he'd heard in his youth about runaway centrifuges could hold anything to this.

Then Sulu's voice, light and confident: "No—I think I've got it!"

"Sulu!"

Without warning, the engines in the rear compartment fired with a sound like a dragon's roar. A sense of up and down returned abruptly, and Kirk bounced back into his seat so hard his teeth clacked. He'd only just opened his mouth to call for a status report when the suit locker next to the airlock wrenched loose with a squeal of rending metal.

Kirk instinctively bolted toward the sagging cabinet. "Jim, don't!" McCoy called. One of the locker doors bulged, threatening to bury the doctor in an avalanche of heavy suiting and equipment. "We don't even know if we're stable!" But Kirk was already up and moving.

Though there was no more strain on Kirk's body to rush out in all directions, no blood pounding the backs of his eyes into firework displays of light and dark, still, as soon as he was upright, Kirk knew the ship was tumbling. He thought at first he'd hit a slick patch on the deck—and entertained a brief, vicious thought about whoever kept the decks in order until he realized it was Scott—but knew something more was wrong when what should have been a harmless stumble drove him feetfirst against the far bulkhead. He felt his right knee groan with stress, then buckle beneath him in a brilliant, nauseating rush of liquid pain. He twisted his body into the fall and met the bulkhead with his shoulder. That only softened the blow a little. The sympathetic explosion from his knee made him gasp.

The engines coughed again, this time making a guttural, grinding snarl. The outlines of the shuttle interior softened like velvet, then melted into nothing as blackness swept from stem to stern like a thundercloud. Kirk bit his lip hard and watched pain throb and bloom redly in front of his vision. What he feared most happened an instant later—the shuttle settled into a slow, regular tumble, and dropped him from the wall to the deck. He bit his lip harder to keep from crying out, but only half succeeded. The damned locked door held fast, never loosing its load at all. Kirk almost swore aloud.

"Jim?" McCoy's voice, concerned and frightened, came from the doctor's seat.

"I'm here, Bones. I'm all right." That was a lie, and Kirk knew his voice said as much.

"That was damned stupid, Captain!" McCoy began, but Kirk cut him off: "What happened up front?"

"Doctor!" Kirk heard someone stumble over the pilots' seats on their way toward the door. "Doctor McCoy? Are you all right?" It was Chekov.

Kirk could hear McCoy cursing to himself. "Just fine," McCoy growled. "What about you? What the hell happened up there?"

"I'm fine, sir," Chekov reported hastily. "But it's Sulu—he's hurt!"

"Nobody move!" Kirk heard his order stop Chekov only two steps out of the cabin. Beyond the navigator,

Sulu moaned softly, and Scott spoke to him in low, soothing tones. "Nobody's going anywhere until we've got lights," Kirk said.

"But, Jim—!"

"Bones, you can't do anything in the dark!" Kirk twisted about to look back toward the pilots' hatch, forgetting for the moment that he couldn't see anyway. He allowed himself the luxury of an unseen grimace when his knee sang out in protest to the motion. "Scotty?"

"Right here," the engineer answered from near McCoy's seat.

"*Jesus,* Scotty!" McCoy cursed. "You scared me to death!"

"Sorry, Doctor."

"Have we got lamps in the storage cabinet?" Kirk asked, still bent over his throbbing knee.

"Aye," Scott said. "About a dozen. But I'll need some extra hands. Come on, lad—" This apparently to Chekov. "—I think we're the only two still standing."

Kirk sat in tense, painful silence, marveling at how easily he could track their progress in the total darkness. They spoke quietly in the back for a few moments while Scott jimmied open the cabinet, then a fat finger of light sprayed down the center aisle as the first of the emergency lamps was activated.

"Thank God *something* still works," McCoy muttered.

Then the wait began. Chekov helped Kirk back to a seat while McCoy tended to Sulu. Kirk tried putting weight on his leg only once, then was forced to apologize when that nearly toppled both him and

Chekov to the deck. Chekov set about placing lamps throughout the shuttle while Scott shut down the main engines—they were no longer producing anything but noise and would never propel the shuttle another meter. McCoy immobilized everything possible on Sulu, using everything he had on hand, then enlisted Scott and Chekov to help him strap the helmsman into a second row seat. McCoy would have preferred to lay Sulu out flat, but the only space long enough was the center aisle, and that had to be left clear for repair access. Better that he was secure in a reasonably guarded location; they still didn't know how long they would be out here.

Chekov tried signaling the *Enterprise* until it became apparent no one could hear him. Even so, he didn't give up until Kirk told him to. Helm responded to prodding, but was useless without information from the navigational computer. Navigations was destroyed; Scott salvaged what he could from the front to start work on restoring their heat and light. Chekov was left with the radio, an all but hopeless job; Kirk was left to watch McCoy care for Sulu. And to worry.

Sulu's valiant action to fire the engines and blast them free of the mine undoubtedly saved the shuttle from immediate destruction. He'd been forced to unbelt to reach the controls, however; while Kirk was thrown against the bulkhead in the passengers' cabin, Sulu suffered a similar fate up front. The result was a shoulder which hung at an agonizingly wrong angle until McCoy eased it back into place. Torn cartilage, McCoy told Kirk. Severed muscles, damaged nerves. All of it, no doubt, reparable in a starship's sickbay; all of it hopeless in a heatless, lightless, airless shuttle-craft. Kirk watched McCoy wind what seemed like kilometers of translucent bandaging about Sulu's still form, binding his arm fast to his side. *Like a butterfly in a cocoon,* Kirk found himself thinking. *Or a fly wound up in a spider's web, waiting for the inevitable.*

He looked around the crippled shuttle now, wondering how long Spock would search before declaring them dead.

Sulu's voice interrupted Kirk's reverie. "Do you know what this sort of reminds me of? Only a little," the helmsman amended, "but it still reminds me."

Kirk hoped it wasn't anything too dreadful. "What?"

Sulu smiled weakly, and, even though he was ashen, his eyes glittering with pain, the smile brightened his face. "There was a simulation our class ran in command school, where a ship had been disabled by a gravitic mine—"

"Not just your class." Kirk grinned. It was supposed to be kept secret—how else could each class's response be an honest one?—but under the circumstances . . ."All of them."

Chekov groaned inarticulately.

"I remember too. The *Kobayashi Maru.*"

Sulu tried to nod, winced graphically, and instead said, "That's the one." His smile didn't fade.

"What's a *Kobayashi Maru?*" McCoy asked.

"It's a torture device," Chekov volunteered unhelpfully from the front, and Kirk laughed. McCoy glanced up at the hatch, then back at Kirk, looking all the while as if he thought they were trying to pull something over on him. For Kirk, that somehow made it funnier.

"It means 'the ship named *Kobayashi'* in Japanese," Sulu tried to explain. "That was the name . . . of the ship, I mean."

"It was a command scenario," Kirk went on, taking pity on the doctor's obvious confusion. "A command cadet is placed in charge of a simulated starship, then forced to make a decision regarding the rescue of a Federation fuel carrier that's been disabled in Klingon space. The name of the carrier in the scenario is *Kobayashi Maru.*"

McCoy snorted and sat back in his seat. "So what's the big deal about this test?"

"It was a no-win situation," Kirk told him. "No matter what you did, or how hard you tried, you always lost. All the possible decisions were wrong."

McCoy turned, his face a study in indignant disbelief. "Well, that sounds bloody unfair!"

Everyone in the shuttle—even Sulu—laughed.

Kirk said, "That was the whole point, Bones."

McCoy gave up in frustration and settled back into his seat. "I don't understand."

Kirk couldn't help feeling sorry for the doctor, who couldn't realize why his bemusement was so funny. "It was a character test," Kirk explained. "Intended to find out how well you respond to losing."

McCoy surprised Kirk by laughing aloud. "You must have flunked *that* one royally!"

The captain feigned insult. "On the contrary—I actually scored rather high."

"Oh?" McCoy drew back in mock surprise. "I can't wait to hear this!"

Kirk was startled to discover that, even after all this time, the very thought of his private battle with the simulator made him blush furiously. He resisted the temptation to squirm in his seat. "It's a long story, Bones . . ."

McCoy's smile only widened. "We have lots of time . . . Besides," he added, more reasonably, "it'll pass the hours."

The hours they had left before rescue or death. That it would. Kirk's inclination to keep his youthful follies hidden warred with the stronger instinct to somehow serve his men even in this limited capacity. Indeed, if this were not their final wrestle with the *Kobayashi Maru,* what was? At least it was apropos.

"I'm not *supposed* to tell anyone," he said by way of final resistance.

"Our lips are sealed," Sulu promised solemnly, still smiling. "Right, Pavel?"

Chekov stuck his head into the passenger compartment briefly. "I wouldn't even tell my own mother, sir."

"I'll hold you both to that," Kirk promised as Chekov disappeared into the pilots' hatch again. "Because if *anyone* ever tries this stunt again, Starfleet will *know* where they got the idea . . . !"

Chapter Two

THE NO-WIN SCENARIO

CADET JAMES T. KIRK sat cramped inside a rec hall reader terminal, elbows on knees, fists balled up beneath his chin. Thumb-high people scurried about the screen in front of him, running first forward, then backward as Kirk changed the tape's direction with a single whispered word. An on-screen explosion splashed the cubicle with light; darkness rushed in again just as quickly, this time claiming the screen image as well. Only the words KOBAYASHI MARU TEST 463981-009 COMPLETE brightened the black screen, and then only briefly.

I lost.

The thought struck Kirk with numbing incredulity, just as it had five times before. After being accepted into Starfleet at a younger-than-standard age—after testing at the top of his Academy class every single year—Starfleet stuck him in a twelve-meter diameter simulator for less than five minutes, and he failed so miserably not even his classmates had the ill grace to laugh. He signaled the reader to replay the tape again as impotent fury burned his disbelief away.

"Such tenacity should belong to an Andorian, James Kirk."

Kirk jerked upright. Outside the doorway to the reader, Lieutenant Commander Constrev's pale blond hair was the only thing visible through the dark.

"It is after student curfew," he continued complacently. "You should be in the barracks."

Kirk had engaged in late-night discussions with Constrev too frequently to believe the computer expert would report him now. Turning back to the reader and the frantic scenario again filling the tiny screen, he dropped his chin into his hand again. "I wanted to see this one more time." *I want to figure out what the hell I did wrong . . .*

Constrev folded his legs beneath him and sat on the floor outside the cubicle. "The *Kobayashi Maru?*" Kirk flicked a startled glance down at the officer, and Constrev smiled. "It is now almost midnight. I think you have reviewed this tape more than once."

Kirk fixed his attention on the viewer again before Constrev commented on his surprise; he didn't like it that the lieutenant commander could read him so easily. "I'm . . . timing it." He tried to make the admission sound casual. "And I wanted to study the details."

"I see." Constrev watched the screen with him for some time. "Once, nearly fifteen years ago," he remarked, as if Kirk had asked him for the statistic, "a student made the *Kobayashi Maru* test last eleven and one half minutes. My commanding officer, Admiral Howell, told me this," he added parenthetically. "No one has done so since then. Why do you feel the need to succeed where others failed?"

Kirk felt the blood come up into his face and, this time, didn't stop the outburst that followed. "Because I was *stupid!* It took the Klingons less time to destroy me than it takes me to tell about it!" His hands twisted into fists without his thinking about it; he jammed them against his thighs to keep from striking something within the cubicle. "I'm *good* at strategy," he insisted, his voice so soft it was almost a groan. "Damn it, Constrev, I'm a *good* commander!"

Constrev nodded sagely. "Perhaps the Klingons are merely better."

"No." The very thought was too frightening to contemplate. If the Klingons were "better" in this simple classroom exercise, what would they be like out in the real world? "It's just a computer," Kirk finally stated defensively. "I should have been able to beat it."

"Just a computer." Constrev's thin laughter fell dead in the bigness of the empty rec hall. "All the more reason why you could *never* have beaten it."

Kirk fixed him with a wary frown.

Constrev smiled. No one could discuss the intricacies of computer psychology with as much glee and expertise as Constrev; Kirk sometimes thought binary mental functions were his friend's sacred call. "Computers cannot be indecisive," Constrev told him. "Computers can think faster than any biological organism currently known. Computers take their knowledge base from the knowledge of *all* species, not just from the knowledge of one man's experience. They are smarter than you, faster than you, more patient than you."

"They also can't *feel*," Kirk countered. He didn't like being compared to a machine, particularly when the comparison was unfavorable. "They have no instinct—they have no heart!"

Constrev smiled pleasantly. "So you believe spiritually superior biological creatures should triumph over electronics."

Kirk turned back to the reader without dignifying the sarcasm with a reply.

"You should read your philosophy, James Kirk. Earth's Agrippa teaches that all beings are microcosmic representations of the universe around them—a being is born, and grows, and dies. So the universe was once born, grows old, and will someday die. Your failure in this is only a representation of how all things—great and small—suffer failure, until the end of eternity. Accept this, and go on."

Kirk watched as flame swallowed the *Potemkin*'s bridge for the sixth time that evening. He wasn't really interested in what Agrippa thought of the *Kobayashi Maru*—Agrippa's grade didn't depend on it. "How microcosmic can we be," he asked Constrev irritably, "when individual men die every day, but our species continues to thrive?"

"In the end, entropy claims even the most thriving species. We *all* fail in the end."

Kirk slapped off the tape player with an angry swat

of his hand. He'd had too much of philosophy for one night. "Good night, Constrev," he announced shortly.

Constrev stood without protest. "Good night, James."

It was like a bad nightmare.

Smoke obscured Kirk's vision for the second time in as many weeks. Fans roared into life overhead, swirling back the gray-black cloud like a curtain as the simulator cracked open with a loud, hydraulic *hissss*. The students scattered throughout the ruined bridge set looked around in embarrassed confusion. Their grime-smeared faces and averted eyes tore at Kirk's already guilty heart.

I failed them.

He stared fixedly at the navigation-helm console as Admiral Howell stepped onto the bridge. Howell—his dark eyes glittering with sympathy—paused in the arc where the viewscreen once hung, and announced, "The simulation is now over."

Almost as a single body, the cadets exhaled in relief. Kirk couldn't help but marvel, even through his despair, that one calm voice could reassure an entire bridge crew following such a total disaster. He envied Howell that steadiness—a steadiness he was once vain enough to believe he possessed himself.

"You will have thirty minutes to clean up and organize your thoughts," Howell continued, apparently oblivious to Kirk's humiliation. "We'll meet in Kare Conference Hall at ten o'clock to review your performance. Dismissed."

The cadets filed off the simulator in groups of two

and three. Still shaken, their movements too quick and broad, their voices too hushed or too loud, they abandoned Kirk without a backward glance. *As well they should,* he thought bitterly. A second class of cadets, a second starship, a second *Kobayashi Maru.* A second failure. It terrified Kirk to think this might be the beginning of a trend.

"Are you going to join the rest of us, Cadet Kirk? Or wait here until the maintenance crews sweep you away?"

Kirk flashed a look at Howell's smiling eyes, then forced himself not to look away again when he realized he was blushing. "I was . . . reviewing my performance. I think I'm ready to leave now."

Howell waved Kirk back into the command chair when the cadet started to rise. "Reviewing your performance?" the admiral echoed when Kirk stopped and looked at him, but refused to sit back down. "Didn't you get enough of that the other night?"

Kirk snapped his mouth shut the moment he realized it was hanging open. "Constrev—"

"Told me nothing," Howell finished for him. "But I know the tape of your last *Kobayashi Maru* was checked out overnight, you were late for bed check, and Constrev showed up at my office late—and sleepy—for his duties the next day." He stepped forward to lean across the navigation console, chin in hand. "Mister Kirk, do you realize your reaction time to this test was well above average for this kind of encounter? Both times."

Kirk felt his face redden again. "I didn't bother to time myself, Admiral." That wasn't entirely true: He *had* studied his first scenario enough to know it took him four minutes, thirty-seven point zero three seconds to die. He thought it took a little longer this time, but he wasn't sure.

"Both times, you executed flawless approaches. You deviated from the books when applicable, and your crew gave you admirable assistance—especially considering that none of them has actually served on board a starship." Howell cocked one eyebrow and gave Kirk a curious grin. "I didn't expect the Reinhold pirouette this time. I'm not even sure that's *possible* with a *Constitution*-class ship. But Admiral Walgren gave you points for trying. He *isn't* an easy man to impress."

"I lost my ship." The words crept out of Kirk before he could stop them. An agony of shame at his lack of control made him turn to examine the shattered bridge around him. "I lost my crew! *Twice . . .*"

"You did everything you could."

"I should have done more."

Howell shrugged with such infuriating calm that Kirk wanted to hit him. "Maybe. But it wouldn't have made any difference."

Kirk started to protest: He'd studied the great commanders since he was a boy—he knew that Korrd, Garth of Izar, or Shaitani would have wrenched victory from the jaws of even this defeat. God, it was Shaitani he'd tried to emulate in his first scenario, and even then—

Even then, he'd failed.

And that was impossible.

Staring into Howell's seamed face, Kirk looked for some confirmation of what he'd already intuited. He didn't understand why, but he *knew* now. Knew, and hated Howell and all the others for forcing him to face such a scenario.

"You planned this," he accused in a quiet voice. "Both times, you *knew* I was going to lose."

"I know *everyone* is going to lose." Howell pushed himself upright and matched Kirk's glare. "It's the nature of the game, Mister Kirk. No one wins."

Howell didn't seem angry at Kirk or Kirk's newly discerned knowledge. So the ensign didn't interrupt him when he continued.

"The *Kobayashi Maru* is a no-win scenario," Howell explained. "In real life, you only get to face this sort of failure once. But it's something every commander has to be ready for." He gestured toward the smoke-grimed panel in front of him. "No matter what you do, the computer adjusts for it, and compensates. We've drawn knowledge from every commander who ever lived—none of them could beat this computer now. There will *always* be more Klingons, more damage, less time."

Kirk nodded, understanding better than he thought Howell realized. "It cheats."

Howell's laughter surprised him. "Of *course* it cheats! Because the point of the scenario is to not let *you* win! That's all the computer's programmed for. That's all it knows."

"But that isn't fair," Kirk argued. He folded his arms stubbornly across his chest. "When you said I could take this as many times as I wanted, was that a lie, too?"

"No." Howell shook his head. "You can take it until hell freezes over. Or until the end of the semester, whichever comes first. But it won't make any difference."

"Then why tell me this? Why not let me do it and do it and do it, just like everybody else?"

"Because," Howell smiled thinly, "everybody else *doesn't*. No one's taken this test twice in over twenty years." The smile faded, and Kirk thought he sensed true concern in the admiral's dark eyes. "I thought telling you the punch line might change your mind. I didn't want to see such a fine student waste his time on losing."

When he stepped off the dais, Kirk tried to do it with a determination worthy of gods. He wasn't sure if he succeeded; he felt abysmally small. "We'll see," was all he said to Howell as he stepped down.

The World Library annex in Old El Cerrito had nothing on the *Kobayashi Maru*. Not a single book, or article, or footnote reference in even the most obscure journal in the galaxy.

Of course.

Kirk drummed his foot as he waited for the shuttle that would return him to the Academy, damning himself for even hoping write-ups existed (especially after his failure to find any references in the Academy's own library). The fourteen tapes in his jacket pockets clicked like out-of-tune maracas as the December wind whipped all around him. Kirk jerked the front of his windbreaker closed, then crossed his arms in frustration.

The *Kobayashi Maru* didn't exist outside the confines of that damned simulator. No one spoke of it, none of the textbooks mentioned it, none of his exhaustive searches of the Federation computer banks found even the vaguest reference to anything by that name—not even a real spaceship. If it weren't for his own dreams, Kirk could almost imagine he'd never really taken the test at all.

He couldn't count how many times in the last month he'd tossed awake at night, angry and sweating, only to spend the rest of the night in the barracks' bathroom plotting strategies. The fine line between failure and winning had gnawed at his soul; after the failure of his first computer searches, he acquired information on other military defeats. If he couldn't learn success from the masters, he would learn failure from them, instead.

Some of the defeats were foolish, so easy to over-turn that they were hardly worth consideration: Earth's own George Custer at Little Bighorn, who would have slaughtered the Cheyenne if he'd only waited for the rest of his troops; Babin at Rukbat V, who would never have deployed his sixth fleet to the system at all if he hadn't been too obsessed with owning Rukbat to pay attention to the rumors of Romulan ambush. Others were honest defeats that the commanders at the time could never have changed: The Hoshe Offensive throughout the Magellan sector (Earth didn't know about the transporter in those days); Fr'nir at Gast, whose soldiers died slowly from kurite poisoning before anyone knew what kurite was.

After the battles, then, he studied the commanders. Garth, Babin, Shaitani, Hoshe—Igga, Korrd, Friend-ly John, Von. Biographical information and statistics on their battles reeled about his head every waking moment. He dreamed the battle of Tiatris only last night, and he won it, too, despite the odds. Where Friendly John had been food for the *mihka,* Kirk had routed the *mihka* into the sea. He even remembered how—now, when he was awake, he could recount every move he'd made, every order given. And they were brilliant. All of them.

Sitting on the shuttle between the Academy grounds and the library, he sketched and figured and planned, until he could overturn *all* those historic victories as if they were preschool disputes. Some of them he could overturn in less time than it took to enact the original conflict. Some of them he could avoid altogether. Some of them he could end before they would even be considered started.

And on the heels of such successes, his thoughts always turned to *Kobayashi Maru.*

In so many ways, the test was more complex than anything he could find in his historic references. The computer knew *everything,* no matter how obscure or unlikely; Klingon reinforcements could arrive out of nowhere, no matter that the Neutral Zone never hosted more than four unreported Klingon cruisers. Kirk had piles of handwritten notes hidden under his mattress at the barracks—notes that sometimes resembled flowcharts more than battle plans. Twelve times now he'd constructed winnable strategies to the *Kobayashi Maru;* twelve times he'd countered his own schemes by beefing up the computer's knowledge, increasing the Klingon forces. It was like trying to win a war against God—no matter what he conceived of, more Klingons could always converge, or simply not take damage, or fatally damage his own ship with weapons that shouldn't have penetrated the screens.

Kirk was bound by the laws of physics, while nothing bound the computer but some programmer's sadistic imagination; without the framework of reality within which to work, literally *anything* could happen.

So Howell was right: Kirk would lose. Every time. *"It's the nature of the game."*

But it wasn't fair.

When Kirk stepped off the shuttle he found the Academy quad predictably empty. The midwinter rain having chased most of the students inside for the weekend and upcoming finals didn't help. Kirk would have stayed to study himself, but Saturdays were the only time when he could venture off-grounds to the library, and he didn't want to waste what might be his last chance to collect data before the end of the semester.

Halfway across the windy quad, Kirk spotted a solitary figure beneath the arch of one of the elevated walkways. A bulky parka smothered the individual's identity, but the flared black trousers marked him as a member of Starfleet; grinning, Kirk redirected his course to join his snowsuited comrade.

He didn't realize it was Constrev until he stepped up alongside and the lieutenant glanced at him curiously. The computer expert's pale blue eyes looked so appropriately chilled inside the parka hood that Kirk had to laugh. "What are you doing out here?" he asked when Constrev returned to studying the back end of the quad.

"I'm attempting to adjust to the weather," he replied. "I shall be studying at the Academy for two more Earth years, and would like to be able to leave the buildings in the winter." He was trying to sound reasonable, but the defensive edge to his voice betrayed that others had asked him this same question today.

Kirk nodded agreeably, turning to follow Constrev's gaze so that the sight of the parka wouldn't move him to laughter again. "You're lucky the Academy's in San Francisco," he commented. "Most Humans don't even consider the weather here to be cold."

"I am not most Humans." Indeed, it was a very rare Human that was born and raised on Vulcan.

When Constrev volunteered nothing further, Kirk asked, "It doesn't get cold on Vulcan?"

"They have a winter season," Constrev allowed, "but not so severe as this. The summers are much warmer, as well, and approach fifty degrees centigrade when the year is not bad."

Kirk whistled appreciatively. "I thought Humans boiled at that temperature."

"Not me."

They stood, side by side, for several silent minutes; Kirk watched a flock of dry leaves chase themselves across the flat stone, trying not to personify the skittering dervish as some army he should try to outmaneuver. It only half worked, and he made himself look some other way as the leaves settled into a silent pile again.

"Where have you been today?" Constrev asked him. He had been watching the leaves as well, and Kirk couldn't help but wonder if he somehow knew what Kirk was thinking.

"The World Library annex," Kirk admitted. "I was looking for more information on the test." If Constrev knew, there was no sense trying to deny it.

Constrev shook his head, jamming his hands deeper into his parka pockets. "I would never travel so far from the buildings on such a cold day."

"Where I grew up," Kirk told him, "this *isn't* cold. During the winter in Iowa—that's the area of Earth where I grew up—the temperatures can get down to as much as sixty degrees below zero centigrade."

Constrev made a distinctly unhappy noise. "I suppose you have snow as well?"

Kirk sighed. "Where the land is mostly flat, the snow lies across it like icing on a cake. And the morning sunlight turns it so bright it hurts your eyes to look at it—like a whole sheet of stars just packed together on the fields until there isn't even space between them. And you can roll it up into snowmen, or pack it together with your hands to throw at your brother." He smiled in memory of more than a dozen Iowa winters, with his fingers numb and stupid as clay, his breath rushing out of him in feathery clouds of steam. "I couldn't even begin to explain all the things snow can mean to someone who grew up with it. Snow is more than just chemistry. It's a whole part of growing up."

Constrev didn't answer for a long time. After a moment, Kirk glanced over at his friend, surprised to find Constrev staring attentively across the empty quad as though valiantly trying to envision the world Kirk depicted.

"Maybe I'll take you to Iowa someday," Kirk added, feeling suddenly foolish. "It's easier just to show you."

Constrev nodded absently. "You have a poet's soul, James Kirk," he stated seriously. "Why do you wish to spend all your time making war?"

"I *don't* want to make war," Kirk told him.

"You study this test," Constrev pointed out. "You spend more hours in the libraries than you spend in your own bed. You study destruction and tactics. Isn't this war?"

"No," Kirk countered. "It's a principle." He stepped in front of Constrev to break the instructor's eye contact with the nonexistent snow. "I don't believe in the no-win scenario," he told him. "I don't believe it's fair to ask students to accept a concept *I* don't think is valid."

"The no-win scenario is the basis of our universe," Constrev replied. "Depending on which point of view you employ, someone always loses."

"That's garbage."

"If *you* always win, *someone else* must lose. Isn't that so?"

The thought bothered Kirk profoundly. He fingered the computer tapes, suddenly embarrassed and frightened to think that so much of his personal philosophy could be shattered with so simple a statement. "It's not the same thing," he argued, albeit weakly. "Losing and not winning *aren't* the same thing. I believe you can lose. I believe you can die. I *don't* believe there's such a thing as a situation that's impossible to win."

Constrev studied his face for a moment, his pale eyes disconcertingly earnest. Turning away, he stated at last, "Perhaps you are right. But if what you tell me about this test is true, it isn't intended to accurately represent reality. So why concern yourself with it?"

"Because . . ." Kirk stopped, his train of thought suddenly stymied by the idea blossoming in his mind. "Because it *isn't* real," he gasped as the idea took form. "Because it isn't fair. It cheats!" He caught Constrev by the shoulders and shook him joyfully. "It cheats, Constrev! Which means *I* don't have to play by the rules, either!"

Constrev looked uncertain. "I believe tampering with test results is frowned upon."

"Two negatives make a positive, don't they?"

"But cheating twice—"

"Makes for a fair test," Kirk cut him off. "Trust me on this—I'm a command cadet."

Kirk darted into the cadet barracks a breathless seven minutes before the wake-up call. Curled up beneath his bedcovers, fully clothed, he crammed a handful of quilt into his mouth to muffle his panting. *What's happened to me?* he wondered, somewhat horrified. Only a few weeks ago—before the *Kobayashi Maru*—staying out beyond curfew was unthinkable. He'd been the good little soldier, considering without doubting; questioning without disobeying. Now, he felt at war with his superiors over a philosophical issue he'd never even considered before. A war that would end at precisely three minutes after ten today. His heart hammered excitedly at the prospect.

When the wake-up call sounded, Kirk's bunkmate didn't even ask why the young cadet was under his covers, boots and all; Kirk assumed the other man had seen this often enough in the past few days to excuse Kirk's idiosyncratic sleeping habits as beneath mention. *You'll see,* Kirk told him silently as he hastily tucked down the covers on his own bed. *Soon everyone will be able to guess where I've been nights . . .*

His first two classes came and went with all the speed and grace of a dying man dragging himself across the desert. At ten o'clock he was released from class to report to the simulator. Cadets craned in their seats to watch him stride stiffly for the exit; he wondered what they would say if they knew his hands were cold and his mind was numb with indecision. He wondered what admirals Howell and Walgren would say when the test was over.

A collection of students from the security division already milled about the bridge set when Kirk arrived. He reported to the monitoring officers, then took his seat at the command chair. He felt as if he were walking through cold jelly, moving so slowly that everyone *must* see that he was hindered by his vague sense of guilt—that he was actually *afraid* of going through with this, even after investing so much time and scheming. The arms of the command chair were unyielding beneath his grip.

Kirk had the test nearly memorized by now. He watched the cadets around him frown seriously over their instruments until the helmsman turned to request coordinates for avoiding the Klingon Neutral Zone; Kirk could have cued the senior officer who was serving at communications: "Captain . . . I'm receiving something over the distress channel."

The words, "Put it on speakers," sounded clear and confident, even though his mouth felt impossibly dry.

". . . imperative!" a frightened voice whispered through a symphony of static as the comm officer obeyed Kirk's command. "This is the *Kobayashi Maru*, nineteen periods out of Altair VI. We have struck a gravitic mine—"

Kirk didn't wait for the plea to finish—he'd heard it too many times to care for the artifice anymore. A certain amount of cooperation was expected, however, so he pretended concern as he asked, *"Kobayashi Maru*, this is the *U.S.S. Potemkin.* Can you give us your position?"

"Gamma Hydra," the distant voice replied. "Section ten."

"The Neutral Zone," the navigator gasped. Kirk leaned on his fist to hide a smile.

". . . hull penetrated—life support systems failing! Can you assist, *Potemkin?"*

I don't know why I'm smiling, Kirk marveled, still masking his grin. *Flunking out of command school is hardly funny.* He had a dreadful premonition that "out" was exactly where he was headed. So far, nothing about the test had differed—not by a second or a syllable. Had he done it? He was hardly a computer expert.

"Potemkin? We're losing your signal—*can you assist?"*

"Take us in," Kirk ordered, straightening. He didn't even ask to see the stats on the fuel carrier. He'd looked at them the first time he took the test, hoping to gain information; he'd looked at them the second time, hoping to maintain the illusion that he didn't know what to expect; this time, he didn't even care.

"Captain, that would be in direct violation of treaty," the executive officer began.

"I'm well aware of that, thank you." *But if I'm going*

to go down, I may as well go down in flames. "Helm, raise shields. Just in case."

"Aye, aye, sir."

The computer had barely finished warning them that they were now entering the Klingon neutral zone when the communications officer yelped, "I've lost the signal!" and the science officer reported, "Three Klingon cruisers closing on our stern!"

"Evasive action!" Kirk called, gripping the arms of his chair in anticipation of the blow he knew was coming. It jolted the simulator, exploding the helm console into flame, before any of his bridge crew could acknowledge.

"Full power to screens!"

A lithe young woman stepped over the "dead" helmsman to stab at the controls. "Screens are dead, Captain."

Kirk spared only a short glance of irritation at his "dying" navigator. He slammed one hand on the arm of his command chair, wishing he could hurt something besides himself with the gesture. "Contact the Klingon vessels. Tell them we're on a rescue mission!"

He stared accusingly at the viewscreen, knowing Howell and the others were watching, and wanting to burn them with his anger; black space and three gunmetal blue war dragons stared back at him in sinister silence. He didn't even realize the communications officer had never responded until the executive officer prompted, "The captain told you to raise the Klingon commander, Mister."

The communications officer stammered helplessly for a moment. Kirk swung the command chair about in time to see the communications officer close his eyes as if in apologetic prayer and timidly touch a button. "Coming on screen now, sir . . ."

Kirk couldn't help uttering a short cry of surprise.

"This is Commander Kozor," announced a guttural voice, distorted by the intership band, "of the *Kh'yem.*" Behind the rough baritone, Kirk could hear other computer-generated Klingons growling and bustling as they went about their computer-generated duties. "You have entered Federation Neutral Zone against treaty. In name of Klingon Empire, *Kh'yem* declares war!"

Jerking about in his chair, Kirk endeavored to assume what he hoped was an expression of cultured confidence (the Klingons might not be able to see him, but the monitoring officers certainly could). "This is Captain James T. Kirk, of the *U.S.S. Potemkin.*" It was the first time he'd ever said his name that way; the sheer excitement of it made him short of breath. "We are on a rescue mission in search of a civilian freighter registered with the United Federation of Planets. We mean no harm, but we will defend ourselves if necessary."

"Captain Kirk?" the Klingon commander parroted. *"The* Captain Kirk?"

Kirk fought a smile as his bridge crew exclaimed in a single voice, *"The* Captain Kirk?" The "dead" navigator began to laugh.

Kirk cleared his throat and went on. "I'll prove it, if you force me."

The Klingon commander barked to the others in gruff Klingonese. "That will not be necessary," he said in a more subdued tone. "Report coordinates of freighter, and *Kh'yem* will offer all assistance, *Captain Kirk*."

Somehow, the navigator's braying laughter destroyed the solemnity of the moment. Kirk, his head spinning, returned his crew's stunned stares with a smug grin. "Gamma Hydra, section ten. We would greatly appreciate your escort, Kozor."

"Of course, *Captain* Kirk! Whatever you require . . . !"

By the time the test was over, eighteen minutes twenty-seven seconds had elapsed. Kirk commanded the recovery operations in a giddy daze, somewhat amazed to discover that there *was* a *Kobayashi Maru* to be rescued after all. The crew performed beautifully, the Klingons were uncommonly cooperative, and *Kobayashi Maru*'s master, Kojiro Yance, even agreed to have dinner with Kirk that evening.

The simulator still stank of seared wiring and melted plastic when the viewscreen cracked to admit Admiral Howell. Overhead fans vacuumed away the worst of the smoke, but for every whiff whisked away, another rose from the simulated damage. Spidery glimmers of liquid crystal crawled across the soot-streaked floor. Howell paused just inside the starship's viewscreen and shook his head at the laughing, shouting cadets who pushed past him on their way to the conference hall.

Kirk stayed in the command chair, his head angled downward as he stroked the command chair like a prized horse. *We did it,* he thought contently. *We beat the no-win scenario.* Not *specifically* the no-win, since he had changed the conditions, but that seemed a minor technicality at the moment.

"That was an interesting performance," Howell said when the last of the cadets were gone. "Admiral Walgren is talking of having you court-martialed. *I'll* have my hands full trying to dissuade him." He stepped around the helm console to sit.

Kirk grinned and studied the bridge speculatively. "I did succeed."

"What did you prove?" Howell's voice was confused but honestly curious. "That cheating pays off?"

Relegating his solution to the realm of simple cheating stung Kirk's pride. "Consider me a conscientious objector. I don't think of it as cheating when the rules of the game are unfair."

"I explained that to you already," Howell began, but Kirk interrupted, to say again, "I don't believe in the no-win scenario."

"And you think reprogramming the simulation so the Klingons believe you're a famous starship captain proves you're right?" Howell studied Kirk narrowly. "What are you going to do when you run up against Klingons in real life? Convince them all you're Garth of Izar?"

Kirk straightened in the command chair, feeling suddenly protective of some nebulous future ship and career. "I'll deal with that as I come to it, sir," he said stiffly. "I may not have to convince them of anything at all."

Some indefinite emotion flickered through Howell's dark eyes, then was gone before Kirk could identify what he'd seen. When the ensign frowned faintly, the older officer smiled and rose from the helmsman's chair. "Forget I asked," he acquiesced. Stepping to the foot of the dais, he looked up at Kirk like a subordinate reporting for duty. "Let's go see what the rest of the class has to say *this* time," he suggested. "I have a feeling you've got quite a busy time ahead of you."

Kirk stood slowly and joined Howell on the empty deck. "Yes, sir. I guess I deserve whatever they give me."

Howell smiled at him kindly, "Yes, Mister Kirk, I think you probably do."

Somehow, Kirk sensed he wasn't just talking about the rest of the day.

Chapter Three

HALLEY

KIRK HAD SHIFTED POSITION at McCoy's insistence, elevating his knee by sitting with his back to the bulkhead and his leg stretched across the row of empty seats. He sat in that position, drumming his fingers against a seatback, for perhaps a full minute before embarrassed irritation finally moved him to suggest, "It wasn't that funny, Doctor."

McCoy choked his laughter down, 'til it became a sporadic chuckle. "Yes, it is, Jim!" The doctor paused in rummaging through his medikit to lean back in his seat and regain his breath. "It's so *in character!* I'm surprised I didn't just guess it!"

Kirk made a face he didn't think McCoy could see across the half-light between them. Too bad—it seemed a pity to waste such honest annoyance on darkness. "Is that supposed to offend me?"

The doctor shrugged. "It's *your* self-image . . ."

"I don't think I understand . . ." Chekov had joined them from the front hatch partway through

Kirk's narration. He sat now with his back against the airlock doors, his arms folded on his drawn-up knees; lamplight brushed blue highlights into the lieutenant's brown hair, while distance hid his dark-eyed face in shadow. "Are you saying that you cheated?"

"Mister Chekov!" McCoy's tone was mock scolding, his face too studiously serious to be sincere. "'Cheated' is a trite, misapplied word to what our captain accomplished!" Picking something out of his medikit, he tilted it into the light for purposes of identification. "He exercised a commander's prerogative of creativity in the face of adversity!"

"I changed the conditions of the test," Kirk attempted to elaborate, but McCoy overrode him again.

"His solution doesn't even *apply* to the test his classmates took!" Disregarding whatever he'd found, McCoy returned to his rummaging.

Chekov looked from Kirk to the doctor, as though trying to catch some communication between the two that he was missing. "You cheated."

Kirk felt his face twist into a sardonic smile he doubted he would have recognized in a mirror. "I've been cheating my whole life," he said, before he thought better of it. "Fate just never figured it out until now."

Like wax under a particle beam, the tenuous good humor evaporated, leaving only thick, churning silence. Kirk wanted to apologize, but realized that would only make things worse; he listened to McCoy's quiet searching, and Scotty's clatter in the back, and waited for someone to brave another topic.

McCoy, as usual, was the first to break the quiet.

"Come on," the doctor grumbled as he stood,

nudging Chekov with one foot. "Get into a seat! This metal decking'll leech the heat right out your backside; I don't need a hypothermia patient on top of everything else!"

Chekov climbed obediently to his feet; Kirk caught just a glimpse of the lieutenant's troubled, half-angry expression as Chekov passed through the light on his way to an empty seat in the row behind Sulu. "Even the seats won't be safe soon. As long as it's colder out there than it is in here, all the insulation in existence can't keep us alive." He dropped into a center seat and turned hooded, frightened eyes on the encroaching vacuum. "Practical physics in action."

Of course it was Chekov who remained mindful of the death waiting outside the shuttle's doors. Kirk sometimes thought his security chief had spent so much time fighting to stand upright between bludgeoning practicality and blind idealism that he'd finally been torn apart—afraid now to take a step in either direction lest he lose his grasp on the other. Who had done that to him, Kirk sometimes wondered. And why would anyone want to?

"Don't give up," Kirk advised, wishing he could follow his own advice. "We've got quite a few hours before we have to worry about freezing—Scotty could practically build a new ship in that time!"

"If freezing's all you're worried about," Scott volunteered from the rear of the shuttle, "the ship we've got now will suit us fine!"

Kirk's knee barked a protest as he twisted about to face the burly engineer trudging down the center aisle. Equipment belt askew on his hips, Scott passed one hand through his rumpled hair to no particular effect—an afterthought to his physical appearance. He smiled ruefully at Kirk and stepped around the emergency lamp.

"What's the word?" Kirk already knew the answer would not be good.

Scott's initial reply was to pass into the forward hatch and lean across the helmsman's chair. Strong, cool light washed away the darkness as the engineer thumbed a series of toggles; the shuttle itself seemed to heave a grateful sigh. Kirk smiled.

"We've got heat, too," the Scotsman volunteered as he returned to the middle chamber. "We won't be feeling it for another hour or so, but it's working. We won't freeze."

"And we've got more than starlight to see by!" McCoy paused in his examination of Kirk's knee to click off the lamp on the edge of the seat. "This looked better in the dark, Jim."

Kirk grimaced. McCoy had slit his trouser leg clear up to the thigh, and the offending knee had swelled to accommodate. The chemical cold pack draped across Kirk's leg didn't hide the purple-black bruising, or do much to relieve the pain. McCoy tucked the pack under an elbow as he readied another hypo; Kirk listened to Scott with pointed attention so he wouldn't have to observe the injection.

"So we have engine power?" Kirk wanted Scott to keep talking.

"We've got *generator* power," the engineer obliged him, "but no engine ability worth speaking of." Scott leaned back against the bulkhead, stretching his shoulders in a slow, soul-weary motion. "It's like that with gravitic mines," he explained, sighing. "You get what damage the strained engines inflict upon themselves, and then whatever damage the gravitic stress does on top of that! I can hardly track it all down; the damage patterns make that little sense!"

"Does that mean we're still drifting?" McCoy retrieved Kirk's attention and applied the hypospray to his arm just in time for Kirk to notice the doctor.

"Aye, Doctor," Scott admitted. "It means that." McCoy turned away to tend to Sulu, a bit too abruptly, and Scott seemed to feel some need to elaborate. "I've got shunting equipment I can barely identify right now, much less repair. Because of that, the generator and the engines aren't . . ." He waved his hands as if grasping after an appropriate phrase. ". . . Well, aren't on speaking terms, exactly. We can run the lights and heat for another hundred years or so . . . but we canna change our course so much as a centimeter without outside help."

And their only prospect of help came from Spock and the *Enterprise*. Kirk wondered if there was really any chance his starship could save them, or if abandoning what tenuous hope he placed in that chance would be more wise. Like Chekov, torn between placing his faith in what *should* happen or what *would* happen, Kirk decided that miracles were *made*, not waited on; if he wanted to win this scenario, he would just have to cheat again. "Scotty, is there any chance we can salvage the radio?"

Scott looked across the shuttle to Chekov. "Lad?"

The Russian shook his head. "I pulled the master board." He aimed a nod toward the front compartment, and a look of self-reproach so intimate it startled Kirk moved across the lieutenant's face. "It's on my chair, along with what I could remove of the receiver."

Scott disappeared into the forward compartment again, and Kirk heard the engineer make a soft but distinct sound of disgust. When the captain glanced inquiringly at Chekov, the lieutenant volunteered, "Gravitic stress."

"I might be able to cannibalize some of what I have back here . . . !" Scott stomped through on his way back toward the rear, one hand clamped about a shattered, blackened collection of what might once have been circuitry. "It's better than sitting idle!"

"Sitting idle . . ." The phrase stabbed Kirk with gentle guilt, despite the thick pain in his injured leg. *I should be doing more . . . !*

He looked across the aisle at Sulu and McCoy. The helmsman had slipped into waxen unconsciousness a half-hour ago, but McCoy's ministrations roused him now. As he became aware of the lapse, Sulu murmured, "I guess I fell asleep. . . . Sorry, sir . . ."

Kirk shrugged, then realized Sulu wasn't in a position to appreciate the gesture. "You didn't miss much."

"The captain cheated on his *Kobayashi Maru,*" Chekov volunteered from the row behind Sulu.

"Sir?" Sulu asked. Kirk sighed.

McCoy told him.

"I'm not too surprised," the helmsman admitted with a smile when the doctor finished speaking.

McCoy snorted. *"I* said the same thing," he told Sulu. "Only the captain nearly demoted *me!*"

"It's the injury, Doc—it grants me immunity." Sulu dissolved without warning into quiet, pain-filled chuckling. "God protects fools, children, and invalids."

McCoy tossed Kirk a questioning look, and the captain only shrugged. Turning back to the helmsman, the doctor prodded, "Come on, Sulu . . . What's the joke?"

Sulu gathered his breath in a contented sigh. "I was thinking about fools, and the *Kobayashi Maru* . . ."

Before Sulu could elaborate, Chekov suggested from behind him, "You haven't *that* much immunity. . . !" Despite Chekov's threatening tone, the proclamation seemed to amuse Sulu all the more.

"What's this?" McCoy's eyebrows rose in innocent interest. "Someone *else* on this shuttle took the *Kobayashi Maru* test?"

Chekov remained pointedly fixated with whatever was outside his viewport, his face darkening—with embarrassment, or anger, Kirk couldn't tell. When he didn't volunteer a reply, Sulu explained, "We both did." The chuckling overtook him again. "Only *I* left the simulator intact when *I* was done!"

McCoy burst into laughter, and Kirk endeavored to suppress a smile. "Turnabout's fair play, Mister Chekov," Kirk enjoined.

Chekov's resolve buckled slightly. The lieutenant's stubborn ". . . it's *embarrassing . . .*" was so quiet, Kirk almost didn't think he'd heard.

"It's always embarrassing," the captain allowed. "That's part of the test."

"Actually," Sulu allowed, "the *Kobayashi Maru* isn't the embarrassing part."

"Sulu . . . !" Chekov warned again, this time more seriously.

"It's just sort of *set up* for the good part," Sulu persisted despite Chekov's displeasure. "It's a great story—really!"

The Russian heaved a rough sigh of frustration and maintained his study of the stars. "All right, then," he grumbled. *"You* tell them, if you want to. I don't care."

"Come on, Mister Chekov." Kirk felt the need to alleviate a little of the stress building between the two officers. "How bad can it be?"

Sulu giggled. "You'd be surprised."

When Chekov turned a confused, betrayed look on his friend, Kirk echoed McCoy's earlier quip, "It'll pass the hours," and hoped the security officer would understand.

Chekov didn't seem to realize anything fell between the spoken words until Kirk made eye contact with him for a number of seconds. Then the captain saw understanding dawn in the dark Russian eyes, and Chekov nodded faintly, slowly. Somewhere behind his assent, Kirk could see that dim war still going on; he watched practicality win an uneasy victory over whatever Chekov's emotions demanded, and felt both guilty and relieved. "It really *isn't* funny," Chekov insisted. The lieutenant pursed his lips and turned back toward his viewport again. "It's more embarrassing than anything else . . . !"

Chapter Four

HOW YOU PLAY THE GAME

WHEN THE *U.S.S. Yorktown* exploded into a cloud of neutrinos and high frequency light, Cadet Pavel Chekov settled back into his auditorium seat and heaved a contented sigh. The three Klingon vessels surrounding the *Constitution*-class starship followed almost immediately afterward, washing the video screen at the front of the lecture hall an impressive, roaring white. The other students in the hall burst into applause, cheering and laughing like the audience in a theater. Four science cadets in the front row were the only people who looked disgruntled with the proceedings. Chekov noticed Alan Baasch at the center of that group and smiled; if anyone were going to object to a creative finale it would be "By-the-Book" Baasch. It was somehow satisfying to know he'd annoyed the other cadet so thoroughly.

When the auditorium lights came up, cadets blinked like children just out of sleep. Robert Cecil, in the chair next to Chekov, remarked conversationally, "Kramer's gonna kill you."

Chekov leaned forward over his desk again, watching Cecil brush carbon grime out of his dark blond hair. Every cadet in the hall was soot-smeared and smelly from the simulator room. Chekov wondered what his idol, James Kirk, would have thought to see him in such a state of disarray. Chekov had made no secret of his respect for Kirk or his confidence that he would be assigned to the *Enterprise* on graduation.

"What can he do?" Chekov asked the other ensign. "They put me in a simulator and told me to blow up the Klingons—so I blew them up!"

Cecil snorted and settled back into his own seat. "They told you to function as a starship commander," he pointed out. "I don't think they intended you to blow up your own ship in the process."

"Then they should have stressed that before the Klingons arrived." Chekov knew sacrificing the *Yorktown* was quite probably a unique response to a tense command scenario, but he still believed the solution feasible. Commodore Aldous Kramer could strut and fume all he wanted—God knew, that seemed to be the only justification for the man's existence since Chekov entered command school—but it wouldn't change what Chekov had done. And it wouldn't change the fact that they'd been told before entering the simulator that these scenarios were primarily designed to test command *character,* not rules laid out by command school bureaucrats who had never been in the field. If Kramer didn't like Chekov's character, the ensign felt that that was Kramer's problem; Chekov certainly wouldn't waste time liking him.

Kramer stood now at the foot of the floor-to-ceiling video screen. His hair was the color of steel beneath the dismal white overheads, his uninspired eyes nothing but angry black raisins pushed into the white dough of his face. He said nothing to quiet the cadets, did nothing to attract their attention. Instead, he only exuded haughty displeasure until they ceased to rustle in their seats and their busy chatter died away. It didn't take long.

When the lecture hall achieved an acceptable level of order, Kramer stepped neatly to the front of the podium and summoned, "Cadet Chekov!" in a stentorian baritone.

Chekov straightened obediently in his seat. "Sir?"

Kramer angled his head to stare up the length of the auditorium at the young cadet. His mouth twisted slightly, as if he'd just bitten into a particularly tart lemon. Chekov recognized the expression as what Kramer paraded as a smile. "I'd feel more comfortable speaking to you if I could *see* you."

Chekov slid out of his chair before Cecil could surreptitiously nudge him beneath the desk. Cecil apparently feared suffering from the fallout of Kramer's ill-humor; if Chekov didn't leap whenever Kramer commanded, Cecil felt the need to impel him, which frequently led to more embarrassment than Chekov cared to deal with. While disobedience was not something the young Russian would ever consider, Cecil's impatience had still managed to increase his response time a little.

Once Chekov was standing, Kramer linked hands behind his own broad back and said, "Cadet Chekov, you have just reviewed the video record of your

Kobayashi Maru test. Yes?" His words were rounded by a lyric Rhineland accent, the soft tones a sharp contrast to his hard, unimaginative personality.

"Yes, sir," Chekov replied civilly, his own voice accented and firm. "I have."

"And how would you rate your performance on that test?"

Chekov's hesitation was nearly imperceptible. "I feel my performance was quite satisfactory, sir."

Kramer nodded, pacing the podium with slow, measured strides. "A starship captain is sworn to the protection of his ship and crew. Yes?"

"Yes, sir." Chekov tried to ignore the unease dancing about in his stomach.

"And a captain is sworn to uphold and defend the peaceful relations we enjoy with our Klingon neighbors," Kramer continued. "Yes?"

"The Klingons attacked first—!" Chekov interjected.

But before the cadet had a chance to protest further, Kramer pulled to a stop and insisted firmly, "Answer my question, Mister Chekov."

The young Russian clenched his fists at his sides and resigned himself to the verbal beating. "Yes," he finally returned, "he is."

Apparently content with that small victory, Kramer folded his hands across the lectern and didn't resume his pacing. "You violated the Klingon neutral zone. You engaged three Klingon patrol vessels in combat while there was still the potential to retreat. You willfully destroyed a Federation starship worth several *billion* credits, and killed that starship's crew. All to rescue a fuel carrier you cannot prove was indeed in distress at those coordinates! So tell me—*what* about your performance do you consider so 'satisfactory'?"

"If I may, Commodore . . . ?" The politeness was stiff and hard won.

Kramer threw his arms wide in mocking invitation. "By all means, *explain!* I'm very interested."

Chekov tried to ignore the smattering of laughter that passed around the hall. He succeeded only partially. "It is also a starship captain's duty to protect the rights and lives of the civilians in his area of patrol. That includes civilian fuel transports and their crews. We *did* inform the Klingons that we were in the area on a nonhostile rescue mission—they offered no such explanation for their own breach of the Neutral Zone."

"Just because the Klingons violate the rules," Kramer broke in, "does not mean we do."

"I realize that, sir," Chekov allowed. "I only indicate that any large-scale repercussions are unlikely, as the violation was mutual."

Kramer inclined his head, gesturing his consent with one hand. "That being the case," he acknowledged, "we shall only discuss the possibilities of your *posthumous* court-martial." There was laughter again, louder this time.

Chekov held his tongue for a count of three before continuing. "In addition, sir," he went on, "I did *not* kill the *Yorktown*'s crew."

"You," Kramer interjected, "are going to argue that your crew survived because you evacuated the vessel before destroying it, aren't you?"

The sudden perception caught Chekov unprepared.

He hesitated before he could instruct himself not to. "Well . . . yes, sir . . ."

Kramer heaved a sigh so deep, Chekov marveled at the older man's lung capacity. "You physically collided a *Constitution*-class starship with a squad of Klingon cruisers," the commodore spelled out with painful patience. "That means you obliterated four— do you understand me?—*four* antimatter drive vessels, each with a full battery of photon torpedoes and plasma devices! The Federation will be lucky to transmit *radio messages* through that sector of space in the next hundred years, much less move people through it!"

Chekov felt a blush spread from the collar of his uniform upward.

"You didn't think of that, did you, Cadet?"

Lying was not even an option. His face still burning, Chekov shook his head shortly, and said in as firm a voice as he possessed, "No, sir . . . I did not."

"Of course not." And Kramer took up his notes as if that ended the matter.

"But if I may, sir . . . ?"

The commodore paused with his hands full of paper, his head still bent as though studying something astonishing amidst the lecture notes.

"I still believe that destruction of the *Yorktown* was a viable alternative to capture," Chekov pressed when Kramer finally raised his eyes again. "Even if the crew was forfeit, sir. Retreat was not feasible. The Klingons had already fired upon us, and our warp drive *and* our weapons systems were inoperative. It's difficult enough to outpilot a Klingon war cruiser in a *function-*

al vessel, commodore—the *Yorktown* didn't stand a chance."

Kramer, studying him across the distance, didn't interrupt, so Chekov went on. "The possibility of the *Yorktown,* with or without her crew, being taken by the Klingons also existed. Rather than allow them access to our top-of-the-line designs, I opted for destruction of the vessel."

"I see," the instructor said coldly, his tone of voice making it clear he did nothing of the kind.

The flush burned again in his cheeks, but this time not from embarrassment. "I did what I could for the crew," Chekov insisted. "They would have been captured and questioned had any of the Klingon vessels survived." He swallowed hard, and considered briefly not finishing his thought. But anger won out over common sense. "I've read accounts of what goes on during Klingon torture, Commodore. I believe that my crew would rather have died."

No one was laughing now. Kramer's voice, almost too calm to carry across the tall lecture hall, questioned slowly, "Are you quite through?"

Chekov suddenly wanted very much to sit down and direct attention away from himself again. "Yes, sir . . . That's all."

The commodore rounded the lectern with stiff, short strides. "Mr. Chekov," Kramer said, in a tone as devoid of color as his stare, "I will not tolerate another such disruption of this classroom. In the future, if your explanations are required, I will ask for them. Is that clear?"

"Aye, sir."

Chekov held Kramer's gaze with as impassive and hard a stare as he could command, then his teeth clenched so hard his jaw ached. He asked, "May I return to my seat, sir?" in a tone that sounded more subdued than he liked.

"You may." Chekov felt the commodore's eyes track him as he took his seat. Then, without warning, the commodore asked, "Mister Chekov, do you play solitaire?"

Chekov heard another meaning in the question, but the sense of it eluded him. "I know how," he admitted warily. "But, no, sir, I don't play."

Kramer shook his head. "I thought not." His eyes danced away to take in the rest of the class; Chekov recognized it as the dismissal it was. "Would anyone else like to add something regarding Mister Chekov's performance?"

The first volunteer, of course, was Alan Baasch. "Will the entire class grade be based on Mister Chekov's actions, Commodore?"

Kramer smiled thinly. "Of course, Mister Baasch! A captain speaks and acts for his entire crew. Or had you forgotten?"

"But that isn't fair!" Baasch retorted indignantly. "*I* wouldn't have kamikazed the Klingons!"

The commodore shrugged. "But you also were not the captain. Anyone else?"

Chekov had spent enough of his Academy time studying up on Klingons and their war tactics—too much time to care very much about advice offered from station-bound cadets. Instead, he brooded at the back of the room, arms folded perhaps too tightly across his chest, and stared at Aldous Kramer, all the while wondering what a disinterest in solitaire had to do with anything.

The siren tore Chekov out of sleep like a cold hand about his heart. On some distant speaker, a woman's voice lilted calm instructions; Chekov struggled upright in bed, trying to remember if the ship had been on yellow alert when his watch retired. He was still disentangling himself from his bedclothes when the sound of sleepy voices and equipment locker doors penetrated his dream-fuddled panic. Not a red alert siren, but a wake-up call. Suddenly aware that he'd only dreamed about being on board a starship, he heaved a slow, unsteady sigh.

". . . Cadet Bloc G, report to Shuttlepad 7 . . . Cadet Bloc G, report to Shuttlepad 7 . . ."

Cecil, already stepping into his scarlet-and-black cadet uniform, grinned at his friend as Chekov kicked the blankets to the foot of his bunk. "Do you know what time it is?" Chekov was still attempting to shake the sleep from his eyes when Cecil supplied, "0400. They're sending us to the shuttlepad at 0400! Here . . ."

Chekov caught the singlet Cecil tossed at him. His hands still shook as he pulled on the uniform and fastened the front; the dream-need to race for a starship bridge and report didn't fade, even after they hurried into the corridor that led toward the shuttlepad.

They were among the first in G Bloc to leave the bunkard. "I wonder where they're taking us?" Cecil didn't interrupt his efforts to finger comb order into his ash blond hair, even as he and Chekov caught up with the fifteen women already on their way to the shuttlepad. "It could be anywhere, I suppose—that kind of seems the point of being a cadet."

Chekov scanned the people ahead of them for the distinctive flash of Sasha Charles's red-gold hair, spotting her just as Cecil reflected, "God, this might even be important, Pavel!"

Cecil's tone said it was a joke, but the very thought jolted Chekov into breathlessness too reminiscent of his earlier anxiety to make light of. "Don't worry," he encouraged, for both Cecil's benefit and his own. "They'd probably send for *real* officers if it were . . ." It didn't quiet his reawakened nerves.

Sasha Charles glanced back at the sound of their voices. When Chekov and Cecil both hailed her with waves, she stepped against the bulkhead to allow the cadets between them to filter by. She slipped into step with them as they approached and fitted an arm possessively around Chekov's middle. "So what gives?"

"We were speculating," Cecil told her, grinning. "The current favorite is an atmosphere breach on Luna."

A rude noise bespoke Sasha's disbelief. "So what's runner-up?"

When Cecil—for the first time in Chekov's memory—didn't immediately suggest an alternative, Chekov stated simply, "*I* think it's Kramer."

Sasha briefly cinched her arm tighter about his waist, but didn't reply. It was Cecil who cuffed him on the shoulder and complained, "You Russians make me nuts sometimes, you know that?"

Chekov pulled away from the other man's swat,

swallowing a harsh comment with some difficulty. Cecil's pale eyes glittered in annoyance both too friendly and too sincere to interrupt. "You get a bug up your nose about something, and it's like trying to reason with the rain!"

Cecil was from Ohio, in North America, and frequently said the most incomprehensible things. "What's that supposed to mean?" Chekov demanded.

"It means Kramer barely knows you exist," Cecil said. But he'd lowered his voice so no one else could overhear. "It means not everything he does is some direct reflection of his attitude toward you!"

"I didn't say it was." Chekov was distinctly ill at ease with this subject—the fact that he couldn't discern if embarrassment or indignation made his face burn only heightened his discomfort. "But you can't tell me he doesn't enjoy pointing out my errors."

"He's trying to make you a better officer."

Chekov scowled. "Better than whom? He's an academician! What does he know about being a line officer besides what he's read in a book?"

"That's your problem!" Cecil ducked back against the wall, dragging on Chekov's elbow until the other cadet grudgingly halted as well. Chekov, in turn, caught Sasha's hand when she would have continued, staggering the three of them down the hall at irregular intervals. "We're going to be late," he reminded Cecil testily.

A dismissive wave was Cecil's only acknowledgment of that fact. "Remember I wanted to go look up the service records on our instructors at the beginning of the year?"

Chekov nodded; he hadn't seen anything to be

gained by Cecil's search at the time, and still didn't. "I remember."

"Well, Kramer's got a record as long as your name! He was weapons defense officer on the *Farragut* for *fourteen years,* and assistant to the Starfleet Chief Administrator for another seven before he started teaching."

Chekov blinked, honestly surprised. "Who would have guessed?"

"I would have," Sasha volunteered. When Chekov tossed an inquisitive glance in her direction, she shrugged and moved back to stand with them. "I just assumed anybody teaching in command school would have to have *some* experience."

"Why?" Chekov asked her. "Ninety percent of the cadets will never serve on board a starship." The fact that Chekov confidently maintained that he would get such an assignment, and on the *Enterprise* no less, had at first earned him jeers and then suspicious looks.

"That's not all." Cecil caught their attention again just as the last of their bloc passed by. "Kramer also knows your hero Kirk. They go way back, as it were. I'll bet he's the one who convinced Kirk to come give that talk last month."

A month ago, Chekov thought Kirk's visit to the Academy would be his only chance to meet the man in person—and it took less than a half hour for him to decide he would follow Kirk into hell without question. Thinking that Kirk might know—and possibly even *like*—Kramer butted a stubborn fist of rejection against Chekov's opinion of his instructor. "That can't be correct," was all he said aloud.

"When Kirk was a lieutenant," Cecil explained, "he

saved nine people after a premature weapon detonation that took out most of the *Farragut's* starboard pod. Kramer was one of those nine! *Kramer* recommended Kirk for conspicuous gallantry, and then presented the citation when Starfleet granted it."

Sasha nudged Chekov with her elbow. "I'm impressed—you certainly intend to serve with the best!"

"I know . . ." But thinking of Kramer in association with Kirk troubled Chekov's perceptions of both men. Perhaps that explained the commodore's hounding—not jealousy or rancor toward Chekov, but toward *Kirk*, with Chekov the only convenient repository. The realization kindled new anger and frustration, enforcing what he already knew: that he was being treated unfairly.

"We should hurry." He ended the discussion by nodding down the hall, then following his gesture. "Whatever Kramer thinks of Captain Kirk, or of me, won't help us if we're tardy."

Chekov watched a string of emotions chase each other across Cecil's mobile face, but turned away before Cecil could object.

A damp, gusty San Francisco wind skated across the bare shuttlepad, weaving sea salt and winter throughout Chekov's clothes and hair. Waiting beneath the white moonlight was a scarred intrasystem shuttle. Kramer stood at the foot of its hatch, a blue-shadowed sculpture with wild, windswept gray hair; he nodded vague satisfaction as the cadets assembled before him.

"As many of you know," the commodore began, his cool voice in perfect harmony with the seasonal weather, "the Aslan Industrial Station has been abandoned for the past seven months due to bulkhead repairs."

Sasha sputtered a laugh, and Cecil gasped, "I *knew* it!" in a loud, half-serious whisper. Chekov hissed him into silence.

"Aslan does not intend to reclaim the station until after the beginning of the year," Kramer went on. "Until that time, the station has been leased to Starfleet for the use of our officers' training school." He smiled thinly. "That's you."

Cecil made a small, strangled sound. "But is there *air?*" he whispered between his teeth.

Kramer's smile flickered away, and he darted an icy glare at Cecil and Chekov. "Yes, Mister Cecil, there is air." Cecil pulled even more severely upright, his eyes locked on the distance in blind embarrassment. "I was not assigned to this Academy to kill my cadets."

I had wondered, Chekov's mind supplied against his will. He was rewarded by a wash of mixed humor and resentment, and hoped Kramer wouldn't see his expression through the darkness.

If the commodore noticed, he continued without commenting. "For the next three days," Kramer explained, "you will be involved in a training scenario designed to test your aptitude at individual achievement." He didn't direct his attention toward Chekov, but the Russian could almost sense the shift of Kramer's thoughts. "Something of a three-dimensional solitaire, if you will—yourself against yourself.

"In the *Kobayashi Maru* scenario, you were a starship commander; in this test, you are simply a Starfleet officer, stranded on a station that has suffered a crippling hull breach at the hands of an assassin committed to killing you. The goal of the scenario is simple: You must stay alive."

No one said anything for a time, then a woman at the front ventured, "Sir, who is the assassin?"

Kramer's smile was somehow particularly aggravating as he sketched an elegant shrug. "One of you. It would defeat the purpose to tell you who, as that is a step on your path of discovery, as well. I think you will all be surprised." An enigmatic expression softened his entire face for an instant, then vanished so completely Chekov wasn't sure what he had seen.

"You will be outfitted with phasers, unalterably set for stun, and transmitters to inform a neutral monitor of when you have been 'killed.' You can also trigger the transmitters if a problem develops. Food can be obtained through the processors on the station, and sleeping and bathroom facilities are available." Kramer paused to smile at Chekov in paternal condescension. "And, Mister Chekov, much as it may distress you to learn it, destruction of the station *is not* an acceptable solution to this scenario. So, please— endeavor to contain yourself."

G Bloc dissolved into laughter. Chekov tilted his chin fractionally higher, and stared across the bay at nothing as he waited for the jocularity to die.

"Are there any further questions?"

When no one volunteered anything, Kramer called the order to begin on-loading, and disappeared through the shuttle's hatch.

"Honest," Cecil murmured as they performed a smooth left-face, "I don't think he hates you!"

Humiliation burned at the back of Chekov's throat.

He growled a simple, "Shut up!" before following Cecil inside.

"So, are you with us?"

Chekov glanced away from the viewport at Sasha Charles's whispered question. "With you in what?"

"This station thing." She was in the seat directly to Chekov's left, her head tipped back against the headrest and her weapons belt left in a jumble on her lap. "Me, Cece, Westbeld, Cantini, and Gugin are going to try and stick it out together—you know, a cooperative collective. We figured we'd have a better shot at survival that way."

Chekov didn't answer immediately, taking the opportunity to admire the cloud of loose, amber hair that framed Sasha's youthful face, the delicate upward tilt of her aquamarine eyes. While he'd spent more than just a little time with Sasha since arriving in San Francisco (some of it very private), the prospect of teaming up seemed weak; he wasn't certain he wanted to relinquish his solo status so easily, even for her. "I don't know . . ."

"What's there not to know?" Cecil pressed from Sasha's other side. "Either we band together and watch each other's asses, or we sit up all night trying to keep from getting killed." He paused to focus a scholarly frown on something in his phaser. "It's not a hard decision," he continued, apparently dismissing whatever in the weapon had distracted him. "Unless you've got a death wish, or something."

Chekov smiled. "I don't have a death wish. I'm just aware that none of this will be real."

"We're supposed to *pretend* that it is," Sasha pointed out.

Chekov shrugged her qualifier aside. "I just don't think we're supposed to band together," he countered, hoping that would end the discussion.

"Baasch and his cronies are," Sasha argued. "And Kramer never said we couldn't."

"He also didn't say we *could*. It's a test of individual skill, he said—we're to survive on our own."

Cecil shrugged and affixed his phaser to his belt again. "So why can't we survive on our own together?"

A swell of annoyance gnawed at Chekov, and he turned abruptly back to the viewport. *Because I don't NEED you!* he didn't tell them. *Because I can score higher on my own!* Almost immediately, guilt smothered the flames of those feelings; Chekov was embarrassed by his lack of faith in his friends, but no less determined. "What if one of you is the assassin?"

They both laughed. "If either of us were the assassin," Sasha volunteered, "we wouldn't band up with the others."

Chekov looked at her frankly, no laughter in his own dark eyes. "And what if *I* am?"

Sasha searched his face for something—even Chekov wasn't sure what—then pulled away to sink back into her own seat. "You aren't, are you?" Her voice and eyes were now hooded with uncertainty.

Chekov looked back out the viewport without answering.

"You wouldn't kill us in our sleep or anything, though, right? Not if you were working with us."

It's a scenario, he wanted to say as he watched Earth

slide by in marbled, blue-green brilliance. "No," he sighed finally, "I wouldn't." Even that admission seemed weak-willed and unfair.

As the shuttle bumped gently against the Aslan Station's lock, Sasha caught his face in both hands and kissed him briefly. It was her sign that she didn't hate him for being stubborn, even if he drove her crazy every now and again. "Then you're with us?"

Chekov tried to keep the displeasure out of his voice. "I'm with you." It only increased his annoyance when the others reacted with such thrilled disbelief.

Sasha flopped back into her seat, relieved and satisfied. "We'll meet at the station's hub," she announced as Kramer began counting off the groups that would exit. "This level. You think you can find it?"

"I can find it," Chekov told her, then added, "and you'd better wait for me," even though he half-hoped they wouldn't.

Sasha smiled and offered him a secretive wink. "Always."

Kramer made him stay until last.

The cadets, armed with nothing but their phasers, disappeared into the station at irregular intervals. Kramer indicated who could leave apparently at random, sometimes dismissing individuals, sometimes groups as large as four; Sasha's entourage left in three separate migrations. During the next hour and a half, Chekov entertained himself with speculations as to which of them would make it to the rendezvous, then experienced a gnawing dissatisfaction that he'd allowed himself to be chained to them for the next three days.

Cool air from the dimly lit station leaked in through the shuttle's open hatch. Chekov studied the gray-black repair to Aslan's sloping hide through the shuttle's rear viewport; the chill and the dull half-dark within the station were undoubtedly attempts to simulate the eerie symptoms of a distant hull breach. As always, Chekov began unconsciously tallying the errors in the fine details of this command scenario: no "spaceman's breeze" sighing down the empty corridors; no ghost frost hungrily licking the moisture from his lungs; no sirens, no screaming, no distant, desperate cries; no angelic spray of crystal dusting the space just outside a shattered hull; no ice-black eyes crying scarlet from the wrong side of an environmental suit's visor.

The images wrenched up memories from news clips he'd seen of a ruptured deep space passenger liner that a starship had tried unsuccessfully to rescue some years ago. That was the real world, he realized suddenly. That's what serving on a starship was *really* like. Like a bolt of electricity through his insides, Chekov remembered everything about that frosted panorama in a single blinding instant; he pivoted in his seat until the view of the station was out of sight behind him, no longer interested in criticizing accuracy.

Kramer stood guard in the shuttle's empty cockpit. His back was to the twin navigation-helm console, his hands resting on the abandoned chairs, when he caught up Chekov's dark gaze with his own. "You think I keep you here as punishment, don't you?"

Chekov stopped himself before turning to look at the station again.

"Is this the hubris James Kirk inspires?" the commodore went on. "The conviction that every environment you inhabit adapts to encompass your needs, your actions, your beliefs?"

Chekov's hands closed on the weapons belt draped across his knees, and he returned Kramer's gaze with grim propriety. "Captain Kirk is a brilliant officer— there isn't a finer commander in Starfleet."

Kramer came forward three steps—not threatening, but only closing the long distance between them. "I never said he wasn't. I simply questioned the effect he has on cadets who haven't been around him long enough to counteract his charms."

The comment struck deeper than Chekov liked. He felt the warm coil of anger in his chest that sometimes moved him to say things he shouldn't. Standing, he busied himself with the weapons belt so Kramer couldn't see his eyes. "You wouldn't understand . . ."

"Why? Because you don't like me? Because I'm too old?" Chekov shot a startled look up at his commander, and Kramer snorted. "You may hate *me* now," he told Chekov calmly. "But I can guarantee, by the end of this weekend, you'll hate no one but yourself."

Chekov stared at Kramer without speaking. He experienced a moment's discomfort when a search of the older man's eyes revealed only a dim, painful disappointment, and not the jealous rancor Chekov expected to see. He looked away to finish fastening his weapons belt. "Should I enter the scenario now, Commodore?"

Kramer paused only slightly, then stepped between the narrow seats, and waved Chekov down the aisle. "Go on," he said. "Both of us have wasted enough time."

Chekov estimated Aslan's ambient temperature at just under fifteen degrees centigrade; cool enough to chase away a light sweat, as well as make sleeping on the decking a problem. Whether the others would reach the same conclusion couldn't yet be ascertained —Chekov would have to wait until "evening" to see which ones tried sleeping wherever they could find cover, and which ones sought out couches and tables in the labs.

Aslan's corridors proved not as featureless as Chekov expected; works from several artists clung to the sloping walls, and more than one viewscreen reflected gray distortions of his image as he slipped silently past. Damn Kramer for holding him until the end! If Sasha hadn't conspired to ambush him, surely someone else had thought to lay in wait along this central corridor—if not for him, specifically, then merely to eliminate the students forced to travel this route leaving the shuttle. Chekov trailed one hand nervously along the cool metal hull, wondering where the corridor would branch, and how much warning he might have.

When the corridor flared ahead, Chekov noticed the slight whitening of the light long before the opening yawned into view. He eased himself to the floor and belly-crawled the last ten meters. Heat leeched through his uniform to disappear into the decking, reminding him that hypothermia would be a very real danger this weekend. Still, he crawled as far as the entrance to the courtyard, then continued hugging the floor as he listened for an adversary.

No sound filled the alcove but the gentle hum of the kinetic sculpture at the center of the space. The twisted, polished mass of blue-green metal swung slowly on its canted base, strobing the walls with pastel light. Chekov watched the sculpture turn, trying to decide if the constant movement could provide adequate cover for someone plotting an ambush from one of the courtyard's three other exits. He had almost decided it would be more hindrance than help when a pale, blurred face winked at him from one of the sculpture's convex wings.

Chekov held his breath, waiting for the surface to come round again. The smeared reflection sprang into existence just as the sculpture came perpendicular to Chekov's line of sight; it was halfway up the metal leaf, almost too distorted to be recognizably a face. Chekov waited through a third slow rotation to be sure: the reflection didn't move. That meant a fourth exit, barely two meter's to the left of Chekov's current position, with at least one armed cadet securing it.

Chekov drew both arms up under his chin and studied the sculpture as he considered. It was doubtful the other cadet could see him—the angle was in Chekov's favor, and the reflection so meaningless Chekov himself had almost overlooked it. Still, any attempts to move beyond this doorway would doom him, and the sculpture itself prevented a valiant dash for another corridor. He watched the face smear slowly past again.

Slowly, carefully, lifting his boots clear of the floor so as not to scrape against the decking, he rotated himself until he lay lengthwise across the wide doorway. Nearly five minutes were required to gingerly ease himself up onto his knees, another three to silently dog-walk to halfway between his own doorway and the next. All the while, the abstract face winked at him with each passing of the sculpture. His own face had joined it on the bottom quarter of the panel, but the quarry didn't seem to have noticed; that would be his undoing.

Still on one knee, Chekov pressed his left shoulder tight against the bulkhead, held his breath, and raised his arm until he thought it approximated standing-level. Then he gripped his phaser tightly, and eased it around the corner as though probing ahead before turning.

Another phaser flashed into view, also at standing-height, and fired. The beam passed above Chekov's head and spat against the far wall, wasted. Chekov caught the cadet's wrist with his free hand and knocked the phaser free with a single sharp rap against the bulkhead; he was on his feet and around the corner before the other cadet had a chance to do more than swear.

The cadet turned out to be a female—Pamela Spurlock, an engineering/command student who'd be spending time as engineer's assistant on an Earth-based station. Chekov was impressed when the thin, big-eyed woman didn't try to beg for her life.

"How did you know I was here?" she demanded, her voice incredulous and annoyed. "A lucky guess?"

Chekov grinned his apology as he nodded back over

his shoulder. "The sculpture." Then he moved back a step to let her see.

Spurlock's mouth twisted with wry displeasure. "Well, that's real close to brilliant. Damn . . . !"

"I'm sorry."

She shrugged, apparently not holding her failure against him. "Yeah, me too," she sighed congenially. Then she brightened. "Oh, well! I guess I'll see you when the scenario's over?"

Chekov nodded. "I'll see you then." He was just about to stun her when another phaser fired.

They both hit the floor together, instinctively seeking a low position as weapons fired from the three surrounding exits. Chekov didn't even dare raise his head to identify their attackers. "Friends of yours?" he asked Spurlock.

She laughed dryly. "Not hardly! *I* left alone, and *they* must have left ahead of me . . . I've killed everybody else that came through here."

Another barrage of fire answered Spurlock's comments, followed by Baasch's strident voice: "I know you're with her, Chekov!"

Chekov groaned. "Oh, marvelous . . ."

"Get out here and get killed!" Baasch continued. "I'm not going to let you louse up my grade again!"

"He certainly is holding a grudge about this grade average thing," Spurlock commented, apparently not too concerned. "You want to blow him away?"

Chekov tried to remember if Sasha had mentioned how many people Baasch had recruited, or how many he'd seen leave with Baasch. "I think they have us outnumbered," he said at last. "There are at least three of them."

"I counted four phasers," Spurlock added. Then she smiled and elbowed him playfully. "But we're clever! You did a pretty good job with that sculpture, and *I* had a pretty kick-ass trap set up in the first place. Why don't we try to convince them we're coming around either side of the sculpture, then only round on one. We could clear at least one doorway, I'll bet."

Chekov chewed his lower lip and waited for the latest volley of phaser fire to die. "We'll round on the right," he decided finally. Baasch's voice had come from the left. "You fire that way, I'll cover this way." He flashed her a smile, and added, "We'll worry about killing you later."

"Thanks loads."

They fired together, spraying the walls to either side of the sculpture in a futile effort to drive back Baasch's people. The maneuver bought them enough time to dart into the sculpture's cover, then the enemy phasers sounded again; this time, fire was split between the two walls.

Someone poked his head briefly into view from behind the closest doorway. Spurlock took the man down with a single shot, then shouted, "Let's go!" without turning to see if Chekov followed.

Covering their escape with a flurry of rapid shots, he stayed as close to Spurlock as possible. It seemed they'd almost make it—that Baasch would have to wait until later to exact his revenge for Chekov's destruction of the *Yorktown*—then Spurlock staggered and her phaser skittered ahead of her into the body of the man she'd brought down.

Chekov had run into her before he realized she'd been stunned. Looping one arm around her waist, he only just kept her from falling. She was his shield as he stumbled into the hallway and over the body of the "dead" man.

Easing Spurlock to the ground so she wouldn't hit her head on the decking, Chekov stunned another of Baasch's cadets when the woman dared a glance around the doorway to verify his presence. Then he heard someone swear violently, followed by the stealthy sounds of retreat.

Collecting the fallen man's phaser, Chekov quickly patted down the other ensign's body. He wasn't sure what he expected to find, but he knew he'd found it when the man's stomach clacked.

Chekov rapped his knuckles against the front of the other man's singlet, just to make certain, then carefully undid the front of his uniform. Strapped to the man's abdomen with four strips of surgical tape was what looked to be a thin plate, about ten centimeters square. Chekov gently removed the article, refastened the front of the cadet's uniform, and sat back against the wall to examine his prize.

After only a few moments of investigation, Chekov deduced how to unfold the plate into a four-paneled screen that he recognized as a read-only memory display. The activator ran along the right-hand edge; caressing the plate with his thumb immediately produced a sharp, intricate schematic on the face of the screen, complete with reference codes and keys. Chekov smiled, then started to laugh.

A map! A circuitry and layout blueprint for the entire Aslan station! He thumbed through the various screens, taking a quick stock of what information the little device made available. Circuit and computer junctions only took up one subcategory; administrative routing, hub-to-hub referencing, and maintenance access paths were among the others. Chekov was dizzy with all the advantages this blueprint could give him, not to mention the advantage he'd just stolen from Baasch. No wonder his adversary had been willing to risk another soldier to try and retrieve this body. Baasch wasn't the only one who could seek and destroy, however; Chekov intended to make as good a use of this map as Baasch had—probably even better. Referencing the administrative map one last time, he folded the screen to its portable dimensions and fitted it down the front of his own singlet. Then, retrieving the phasers left by Spurlock and Baasch's two comrades, he bid Spurlock a grateful farewell and trotted for the closest stairwell.

The administrative offices were seven levels higher than the docking bay. Chekov traveled the conventional routes long enough to acquire six more phasers, then located a maintenance shaft that took him within two meters of administration. Pausing at the top of the long climb, he waited for his breathing to steady and the corridor to clear before quietly easing himself back into the battlefield.

The door to the administration office was closed, but the jimmied lock was still lodged on the OPEN setting. Inspired by his success with Spurlock, Chekov approached the doorway on his knees, waiting until the last possible moment to key open the door. As the hatch hissed aside, a wild bolt flashed above Chekov's head; the young Oriental at the administrator's desk had only enough time to bark a frustrated curse before Chekov's shot caught him full in the chest.

Chekov scurried into the office on all fours, spinning about to close and lock the door before anyone could be attracted by the noise. The mechanism refused to lock. Chekov jammed it manually; he could always force it open again later.

The Oriental sprawled across the top of the administrator's desk, his face silhouetted against an activated desktop computer screen. Chekov took the young man's phaser, and was just dragging the body out of the chair when he caught sight of the dark yellow screen.

```
>TERTIARY ACCESS ACCEPTED
>LOCKOUT OFF
>DECODE OFF
>
>
>WELCOME, USER 293724443A
```

Chekov nearly dropped his victim. The son of a bitch had broken into Aslan's main computer. Sinking slowly into the chair, he read and reread the screen in awed admiration.

```
>WELCOME, USER 293724443A
```

"Computer . . ." he finally summoned. He wanted desperately to make use of this opportunity, especially since the break-in was something he could never duplicate on his own. "Computer, respond."

Nothing.

Chekov ducked under the desk to retrieve the keyboard from where it had fallen during his attack.

Fitting it across his knees, he considered for a moment before typing:

>VOICE ON

The screen flashed once.

>DO YOU WISH AUDIO OR MANUAL INPUT (A/M)?

Chekov smiled. An admin computer, designed for non-tech users; deciphering such a helpful system might not be as difficult as he'd feared. He chose the audio function, then addressed the computer again.

"Good afternoon, User 293724443A," a sedate contralto voice replied. "How would you prefer to be addressed?"

Chekov searched the other man's uniform until he came up with a tech-rating card (a stunning tech level IX). "Gregory L. Jao," he told the computer, wondering if he pronounced the name correctly.

"Please input your identification manually," the computer requested.

Chekov tapped out Jao's name.

"Thank you, Gregory L. Jao. How may I help you?"

This is it! "I'd like to access your main operating system."

"Main operating system accessed for alteration as of 18:27."

Good. That meant Jao had broken *all* the security, and not just the user code.

"Do you wish to alter my programming?"

For the space of a heartbeat, Chekov wondered who

would be accountable if he crashed Aslan's system; he was willing to take the blame himself, but doubted Jao would be pleased to find out how his tech-rating was used. Remembering Kramer's face after the mess left in the *Kobayashi Maru* test chamber, he doubted the commodore would be pleased, either. Chekov decided it was all part of the risks in the scenario, however, and pushed onward despite the lingering image of Kramer's angry visage. "Yes," he told the computer. "I'd like to alter your programming."

"Please present proof of tech-rating IV-B or higher."

He slipped Jao's card into the reader. The green scanner light flashed, and the computer answered simply, "Thank you."

Faced with all the options a detailed map and a main computer offered, Chekov wasn't sure where to start. There had to be a way to meld both advantages, if only by cross-referencing one against the other. Pulling the map out of his uniform, he spread it across the desk top. "Computer, do you possess schematics of the Aslan Station's circuitry and layout?"

"Yes, Gregory L. Jao."

"Display them, please."

The screen shifted, and a series of blueprints identical to those in the map paraded by. Even the grid referencing was the same. "Can you scan the number of life forms at . . ."—he chose a location at random from his map—". . . coordinates 273-185-55?"

"I'm sorry, I don't have scanner capabilities."

"Damn . . ." Chekov thumbed through the schematics in his map, hoping for inspiration. There seemed to be nothing consistent from map to map, not even from level to level. The only thing all the displays had in common were red coordinate highlighters at some of the circuit junctions. "What is the indicator at coordinates 45-633-33?"

"The red coordinate highlights indicate communication outlets."

He frowned. "Intercoms?"

"Yes."

This had some potential. "Can you monitor the intercom channels on Aslan?"

"I can access all forms of communication on the Aslan Station."

Chekov clapped his fist into his hand in triumph, then remembered that someone might still be outside the door to hear him. "Monitor all intercom outlets," he said, more sedately, "and report the coordinates of any outlets where you hear activity."

A moment of silence followed, then the screen displayed a long list of coordinates corresponding to the precious map. Chekov entertained visions of closing off accessways and bulkheads based on the computer's reports, confining groups of cadets for later disposition. It would limit the amount of physical space he would have to cover, and would greatly simplify his job.

But none of those plans would matter if someone else with an adequate tech-rating (like Cecil) broke into the computer and undermined his plans. Thinking of Cecil reminded him that he was supposed to have gone straight to the hub in search of Sasha and the others; a gust of guilt distracted his tactical strategies. He would only be a bit longer, he promised himself—just long enough to verify his suspicions, and to protect his claim on the main operating system.

Returning his attention to the amber screen, he queried, "Computer, do you speak Russian?"

"Muscovite High Russian, Georgian, or Modern?"

"Modern."

"I speak Modern Russian at a level fifteen fluency."

Chekov folded the map and sat back with a smile. "As of this override, reconfigure your communications system to send and receive exclusively in Modern Russian. All other accesses should be denied."

"As you wish, Gregory L. Jao. Please wait."

Almost immediately, the complex schematic leapt away from the screen, replaced by the message prompts that had originally greeted Chekov. Only this time the prompts were in Cyrillic. *"Pokonchyl."*

Chekov smiled and switched off the screen. *"Prekrasneya,"* he replied softly. "Excellent . . ."

Despite the thundering white noise of Aslan's sleeping generator, the hub was maddeningly quiet. The rumbling was a soothing, subliminal presence coursing like a heatbeat through a great ship's deck, palpable everywhere you stood. It was a vibrant, vital sound, as deep as the Earth; it meant the ship and her crew were cared for, and alive.

Chekov paused to place one hand on the hub's outermost door. If he'd realized the decibel level behind these doors, he wouldn't have instructed the computer to lock the exits. On his way to the hub, it occurred to him that Sasha and Cecil might grow impatient with his tardiness and desert him as a casualty. He ordered the computer to eavesdrop on the area; it reported no success at discerning human activity. He didn't consider that the computer's failure might be because of other noise.

He'd sealed the bulkheads because he didn't want the others to leave him behind. No—because he didn't want them to think he had *failed*. The admission embarrassed him a little, but he would rather they thought he'd abandoned them than know they thought him incapable of joining.

Thumbing the intercom by the huge double door, he leaned close and intoned in Russian, "Computer."

"Da, Gregory L. Jao?"

Hearing the machine answer in Russian still made him smile. Using the same language, he replied, "Open bulkheads at my coordinates."

The computer complied.

Sound poured out at him in a frothing white gale. Chekov stepped through the doors to approach the singing machinery with care. Crannies and cubbyholes littered the ragged room. He couldn't even hear his own breathing above the generator; he only knew the outside door had closed when the ambient light in the room dimmed by half. Sasha and the others were nowhere to be seen.

Pausing by a shunting engine, he eased one of the phaser power packs off his belt and tossed it toward the middle of the room.

It clattered against the gray decking, then lay still.

"You're late!"

Chekov wheeled, phaser drawn. Sasha scowled at the weapon as she stepped from behind the loud generator. Cantini and Gugin peeked out after her, but didn't venture forth. All three cadets were bug-headed with noise-reducing headsets. "Where the hell were you?" Sasha demanded at the top of her lungs, pushing Chekov's phaser away from her with one hand. Chekov returned the weapon to his belt.

"I was attempting to be surreptitious."

She frowned irritably and tapped at her headset. Chekov threw his hands up to indicate that he had no suggestions for better communication. Then he tugged his belt about to let her see the phaser packs there.

She adjusted her headset, but didn't smile. "It's better than collecting scalps, I guess."

Chekov chose not to hear the comment.

Sasha led him around the generator assembly, motioning for Gugin and Cantini to join them. They startled Cecil and Westbeld at the back entrance, and were nearly shot for it. Once everyone was calmed again, Sasha pushed them into the numbing quiet of the corridor beyond.

"I was hoping you would wait," Chekov said when Sasha removed her headset and rubbed at her ears. "I was detained."

"We didn't have a choice." Cecil massaged his own scalp with one hand, twirling the headset on the fingers of the other. "Somebody jammed the doors—we tried to leave almost an hour ago."

Chekov considered explaining the predicament, but decided against it. "Well, I'm here now. We should probably get going before someone finds us in the hallway."

Westbeld laughed once, sourly. "Where are we going to go?" she wanted to know. "What's wrong with just staying here?"

"It isn't secure enough," Chekov informed her. "And it's too loud. We'd never sleep."

"But nobody could ambush us here," Sasha pointed out. "The entrances are easy to guard from the inside. And we've got the headsets." She presented hers to him as though he hadn't noticed them before now.

Chekov pushed the headset back at her. "There are other defensible places—most of them with better acoustics."

Only Cecil looked interested. "Such as?"

"The administrative offices."

Even half-deafened by the generator, Chekov heard Sasha's low laugh. "Sure, us and everybody else in this man's army! Pavel, that's the first place *everybody* will head!"

Chekov flashed her a smug grin. "Of course it is. But *I've* been there already, and I booby-trapped the doors so only *I* can get back in."

The other five stared at him. Westbeld grinned with delight, but the others only toyed with their weapons or headsets and said nothing.

"Is that *legal?*" Gugin finally ventured.

Chekov tried to mask his annoyance. "Is it *illegal?*" he returned. "They told us that we could do anything, so long as we survived. I had spare phasers from three other people I took out of the scenario." He knew now that not mentioning his relationship with the computer had been a wise decision. "Securing administration seemed a prudent course of action," he finished.

"Yeah," Cantini sighed. "I suppose so . . ."

Gugin finally shrugged and tossed her headset back into the supply cabinet by the door. "If you've got it secured already, I guess we may as well use it. Anybody else mind?"

No one voiced an objection. Chekov plucked Gugin's headset out of the cabinet, holding a hand out to stop Cecil from depositing his headset as well. "Take it," Chekov insisted. Then, looking about at the others. "Take all of them—let anyone else who comes here have to fight the noise."

Cecil sighed roughly in frustration. "Why?"

"It'll distract them," Cantini explained, nodding at the headset in his hands. "They'll be easier for somebody else to pick off." He grinned at Chekov. "Good plan." Chekov smiled in reply.

Sasha fidgeted with her headset. "What does making somebody else miserable gain us?" she asked. "I mean, why do we care?"

Chekov shrugged. "If someone else stuns them, that's better odds for us."

Everyone but Sasha took the headsets; Chekov hesitated only briefly, then picked up hers without comment.

Simulated twilight tugged the already inadequate lighting into cold, warped shadows along the reflective floors and walls. Distant phaser fire startled Chekov more than once, pricking him to the alertness of prey for the first time in the scenario; the deck seemed shot through with electricity, making each step both dreadful and exhilarating. He was glad when they finally reached the admin offices.

Jao's body was gone, but a Tseyluri cadet sprawled in the hallway in almost the same position as Chekov had left Jao. He tossed a victorious smile over his shoulder at Sasha as he eased up to the door; she glanced at the Tseyluri and didn't smile back.

Chekov snapped a protractable probe off the clip on his belt and extended it toward the floor. "What are you doing?" Cecil whispered in his ear.

Chekov glanced back at his friend, then returned to his work. "Unboobying the trap," he explained, glad for the distraction after Sasha's obvious displeasure. "Keep everyone away from the door."

The probe was just under a meter in length at its greatest extension. Chekov pressed flat against the bulkhead, placing his feet uncomfortably close together along the wall, and flicked the probe across the sensor governing the access.

The door sighed open and a short, triplicate burst of phaser fire sparked against the far wall. Chekov kicked forward with one foot, propping the door open with his toe, and waited for the barrage to cease.

"It would be easier," Cecil suggested, after Chekov had crossed the threshold to maintain the opening for the others, "to just jam the lock."

Chekov tried for an air of nonchalance as he shrugged the suggestion aside. "I'm not a tech," he rationalized. "I'd probably be unable to open it again." In reality, he'd simply thought the trap a better way to stop Baasch in case the other cadet should follow him here.

Cantini flopped onto a wall-length divan. "Well, it's gonna be more comfortable than the generator room!" He crossed his arms behind his head with a contented sigh.

"As though creature comforts were all that matters to life." Sasha clapped her phaser down on a desktop, then waved off Gugin when the other woman started to speak. Chekov watched as Sasha paced to the other end of the room and stared at the wall.

"Hey, Pavel . . . ?"

Chekov turned to find Cecil bending over the desk that housed the computer terminal. Cocking his head as though trying to read something written there, Cecil asked, "Is this a mainframe terminal?"

"It's down." Cecil frowned at him, and Chekov hoped the answer hadn't come too quickly. "I tried it earlier," Chekov elaborated with a shrug. "The ready screen wouldn't even come up. I guess they've deactivated the system."

Cecil made a face Chekov couldn't interpret at the blank screen. "I guess . . ."

"I'm hungry," Cantini announced abruptly. "Anybody else want to scare up some food?"

Westbeld raised her hand from where she sat in a desk chair across the room. "I will. I haven't eaten since breakfast!"

"See if you can find a rec hall," Sasha instructed without turning around. "They'll have food service there."

"And be careful of traps," Cecil added.

Chekov shot a startled look at the computer tech, but didn't comment. "You can't be the only one to have thought of it," Cecil pointed out, sinking into the desk chair. "We should *all* be careful."

More careful than you know, Chekov thought, turning back to the others. Whether another cadet practiced trapping or not, Chekov had rigged most of the food processors and bathrooms between the administrative offices and the hub; bathrooms and commissaries were the only two places that everyone eventually had to visit. "There's a food service station down that way about four hundred meters," Chekov informed them, pointing. "I think it's the closest." It was also the one he'd left unsabotaged for his own use.

Both cadets nodded understanding before ducking out the door.

Chekov used Westbeld and Cantini's departure to instruct Cecil and Gugin in how to deactivate the door; Sasha, now seated, watched them without interrupting, her displeasure painfully apparent. Chekov was suddenly sorry that they were even involved in this scenario, sorry he'd kept quiet about his involvement with the computer, sorry about his surreptitious bombings. Mostly, he was sorry that this apparently mattered so much to Sasha when it was little more than an elaborate game to him. Her state of pique annoyed him, but he didn't want to alienate her over something that was barely real.

Leaving Cecil to modify the booby trap, Chekov went to sit on the edge of the desk next to Sasha. When she didn't talk to him for a full minute, he asked, "Are you angry with me?"

"I don't want to talk about it here." But her eyes said something different, something furious.

Chekov tugged her to her feet. "There's another office," he said, nodding toward a door at the back of the room. "Let's talk in there."

Cecil looked up in query as they passed; Chekov conveyed his uncertainty with a hopeless shrug, then followed Sasha into the next room.

She crossed to the long, lacquered desk dominating

the far wall, and picked up an amorphous ornament in one hand just to toss it into the other. Chekov watched her fluid movements with attached fascination. Sasha was trained in more forms of barehanded combat than he even knew names for; she could probably kill a Barbarbaar 'yoat assassin a hundred times over with that paperweight alone before the assassin even knew Security was in the room. Well, perhaps she wasn't quite *that* fast. But she was talented, and tempered by a family tradition of martial arts. Chekov had never known her to be timid or circumspect in any aspect of their relationship, professional or personal.

She didn't disappoint him now. "You've turned into a regular Babin the Butcher, haven't you?"

Chekov crossed his arms and leaned back against the wall. "What's that supposed to mean?"

"It means I saw your face in there! It means you booby-trapped the food service centers, probably most of the lifts, and maybe even some of the sleeping quarters." She returned the paperweight to the desk with a startling *clunk*.

"Remember the parameters of the scenario?" Chekov asked. "We're at war."

"So you turn guerrilla?"

The accusation stung more than he'd expected. "I turn practical. We don't know who the assassin is, we don't know what he or she is capable of. If this were real life, you wouldn't be complaining."

She shook her head slowly. "Don't be so sure of that, mister."

Chekov searched her pale eyes for some sign of

uncertainty or weakness, but found none. Finally, he turned away with a frustrated sigh. "You don't understand . . ."

"And don't patronize me! I'm not a child!"

"Then you should know that sometimes the good guys get ugly, too!" he shouted in return.

"But when does it stop? When do we stop fighting fire with fire and decide not to take the easy way out by just killing all our competition? That's not what Starfleet is about and you know it."

"It's a *scenario,* Sasha!" he insisted, resigned to lose this fight no matter what he said. "It's like the *Kobayashi Maru:* It *isn't* real. They're testing our reactions and resourcefulness, not our morality. Whether we're supposed to admit it or not, everyone knows that *no one dies! I* know that—*you* know that! That means we're *all* going to behave differently than we would in real life!" Her jaw muscles twitched as she fingered the paperweight, but she wouldn't look up at him. Taking her chin in one hand, Chekov tipped her eyes into the light and said gently, "Sasha, *in real life,* I wouldn't blow up my own starship just to spite the Klingons!"

She pulled her chin out of his hand and dropped her gaze once again. "I wonder, Pavel," she said, very softly. "Sometimes, I just wonder."

"Sasha . . ."

"I just wish I knew what we were being tested for!" Her voice betrayed something between frustration and anger, but she didn't object when Chekov moved closer to slip an arm about her waist. "It's like the *Kobayashi Maru.* They don't run that test just to find out how long it takes a Klingon war fleet to kick our butts—they run it to find out who gives up, who goes down fighting, who never notices that the battle's over. They want to know everything about us . . ." She sighed, a soft, hollow sound that seemed to echo some insecurity Chekov didn't share. "If I knew what they really wanted," she admitted finally, "I'd feel a lot better about this."

"They want us to be strong," Chekov told her, wishing he could grant her his belief. "Whatever we do—whatever their reasons—they want us to prove that we can deal with anything Starfleet might ask of us. That means we do our best to win, even when our best makes us seem cruel or hard."

She laughed once, and looked at him. "It's the fact that you're so sure you know what winning means," she told him baldly. "It's the fact that you think it's so easy that has me worried most. I think you'll find that you're selling yourself and Starfleet short."

Chekov awoke the next morning to the sound of phaser fire and shouting. Sasha, stretched out beside him on the inner office's only sofa, rolled to her feet with silent grace, her eyes trained, cat-like, on the outside door. Recognizing the voices, Chekov caught her by the shoulder and hissed, "It's Baasch! Lock the door!"

Sasha darted across the room to slap at the door control, twisting the locking mechanism until the status light flashed from green to red. In the office beyond, Cecil's voice could be heard above the others, shouting at Cantini to move something into a more defensible position; Chekov could barely make out the words, and suspected the specifics didn't matter much anyway. Swearing under his breath, he pulled Sasha away from the door, toward the desk on the other end of the room.

"We should go out to them," she insisted in a hoarse stage whisper. "They're going to get slaughtered!"

Chekov's mind still chased itself about, trying to figure out how someone had survived long enough to get past his protection on the door. "We can't help them."

"We should die trying!"

He almost laughed aloud. "And prove what? That we aren't any more serious about this scenario than anyone else on this station?" Besides, he had no desire to grant Baasch his wish by giving himself over to an easy kill.

A phaser bolt landed on the closed door, making the steel and plastic sing. Chekov herded Sasha toward the hollow under the desk as he cast about the room for some escape.

She caught the desktop with one hand and refused to be pushed under. "They're our *friends!*" she insisted. "We can't just leave them out there!"

"Yes, we can." A ventilation grate on the wall above the sofa was the only avenue of escape not involving a rush through the forces outside. Chekov knew from his pilfered map just how erratic and treacherous the ventilation shafts could be; nothing short of impending death of a very real and excruciating nature could inspire him to dare those steep and winding passages.

"You keep insisting that this isn't like real life." Sasha, still standing, looked back and forth across the room as well. "Just keep in mind that everybody will be alive in the real life following this scenario, and they're all going to be *really* ticked off at us!" She hefted the paperweight in one hand. "Use this," she said, handing it across the desk to Chekov. "You can knock out the grate, then we can hide under here. They'll *think* we went through the ventilation system, and we can vacate the offices after they're gone."

Chekov smiled as he took the weight. "You're better at this than you like to admit."

"I don't believe in doing things by halves."

Each of the clips on the ventilation grate shattered after only a single blow. Chekov broke three of them, leaving the grating askew, as though he and Sasha had tried to pull the grate back into place during their hasty departure. The paperweight he left on the sofa.

The hollow beneath the black-and-silver desk was never designed to conceal two Starfleet cadets; they only fit in the space after three minutes of thoroughly embarrassing rearrangement, and that was only when they sat hip-to-hip with their knees in their own ears. Sasha had just adjusted the castered chair across the opening when the door between the two offices blew. Chekov held his breath as light footsteps crossed the room just beyond the desk's outer wall. Every muscle in his legs was suddenly cramped and aching, the need to move almost unbearable as he listened to the intruder step up on the couch and lift away the broken grating. He saw Sasha raise a hand to cover her mouth, her jaw clenched and her eyes closed; apparently, he wasn't alone in his discomfort.

". . . Damn . . ." The voice, soft and muffled, was swallowed almost to nonsense by the ventilation duct. Then the footsteps recrossed the office, and were gone.

Sasha exhaled loudly. "Can I move now?" she whispered.

Chekov shook his head. "Wait a little longer," he whispered in return. "Make sure they're gone."

They waited for nearly an hour. The cramps in Chekov's legs were very real by now; he felt dizzy from their constricted positions. Still, it wasn't until he heard a cleanup crew in the office outside that he deemed it safe to exit.

Sasha fell onto her side in exaggerated agony, pushing the chair away with enough force to bounce it off the wall. "I'm crippled for life! I'll never walk again!"

Chekov crawled out behind her, pleased to hear Sasha's laughter again after her earlier ill humor. He nodded toward the door. "Is the cleanup crew gone?"

She stumbled to her feet and half-ran, half-limped to the exit. Holding herself off to one side as she keyed open the door, she darted a quick look into the other room. "Yeah," she confirmed with a nod. "All clear."

"Good." Chekov terminated his stretching when he felt something twinge in his shoulder. "I may never recover from this."

"I'm not going to live to recover if I don't get to a bathroom!" Sasha glanced into the outer office again. "Pavel, I'm headed for the ladies' room down the hall. Wait for me."

He nodded, still working at his stiff shoulder. "Don't take long—I want to get food, too."

"I'll hurry," she promised. Then she slipped into the next room and disappeared.

Chekov gave her a moment to make it some distance down the hall, then headed into the outer office himself. Nothing of the ambush remained; even the three phasers Chekov had used in the booby trap had been taken by the cleanup crew. He tried not to let their loss annoy him; he could always obtain more.

The desktop computer screen was still dark. Chekov paused on the side of the desk closest to the outside door—wanting to hear Sasha's return in time to terminate the conversation—and powered up the mechanism. "Computer," he summoned, in quiet Russian.

"Good morning, Gregory L. Jao," the computer replied.

"Please monitor all intercom outlets and report coordinates where you detect activity."

"Yes, Gregory L. Jao."

Chekov glanced into the hall for Sasha; there was no sign of anyone in any direction. He ducked back into the office, prepared to wait yet for the computer's response, and was surprised when it greeted him with, "Two beings detected at coordinates 456-779-340, four beings detected at 55-56-47."

Chekov waited for it to continue. When it didn't, he pressed, "Are there any others?"

"Only yourself, at coordinates 147-90-423. Do you wish me to reassess my findings?"

"No . . . No, computer, that's fine." He unfolded the map across the top of the desk. The computer's reported coordinates were several floors apart, both sets quite a distance from his present location. If he and Sasha were survived by only six other students, he could only hope the group of four was Baasch's squad. Tracing a finger along several of the deck plans, he memorized the quickest route between the admin offices and the smaller of the two groups, all the while conscious that Sasha would rejoin him soon. He wasn't certain how she'd respond to discovering his relationship with the computer, but he knew he was going to tell her; the computer offered too many advantages to just abandon it now that the scenario was so close to ending. Besides, having Sasha as a co-victor didn't feel as much like a compromise as he'd expected.

"Computer, isolate floors one through seven, and decks twenty, twenty-two . . ."

In the distance, hollow rumblings heralded the descent of the ponderous bulkhead doors. Chekov left open only a two-deck span on either side of both parties—enough to give them the illusion of freedom, if they chose to migrate. He would worry about confining them further when he and Sasha drew near the sites.

"Will that be all, Gregory L. Jao?"

He nodded as he closed the map, then realized the gesture was lost on the computer. "Yes, computer. Thank you."

"You're welcome."

Smiling at the incongruity of technological courtesy, he leaned over the desk to switch off the screen. Outside, the hallway was still silent and empty.

Chekov trotted down the open corridor without bothering to draw his phaser. He knew the locations of everyone still "alive" on the station; there was no one to defend himself against on this level, as no one was functional here besides himself. That thought carried with it a cold shudder of realization; he slowed his gait to a hesitant walk.

No one. The computer reported no activity on this level except for Chekov in the admin office. That meant Sasha had either departed the level, or was no longer active. He had a feeling he knew which it was.

Dropping to his knees, he dug down the front of his singlet for the map, balancing it on one hand as he flipped the panels apart with the other. The admin level flashed onto the screen, littered with the cobalt blue indicators he'd been setting to highlight his own trap locations. Fifty meters down the hall from the admin office, the women's restroom was littered with flashing blue.

Chekov groaned and buried his face against the map. He was a dead man. Even if Robert and the others never learned that he'd set traps all about the Aslan Station, Sasha had already divined the fact. She would know who booby-trapped the bathroom, and she would kill him.

He scrambled to his feet and ran the last few meters to the bathroom. The door slid aside at the slightest touch; inside was as silent as the hallway. "Sasha?" Unlike admin, he hadn't planned on reentering any of the booby-trapped bathrooms, and so had left no options for bypassing the traps. The phasers fired as soon as someone rounded the first bend in the room. Chekov stayed carefully in the doorway and called her name again.

He retreated to an intercom panel once he was convinced even Sasha wouldn't keep silent so long for the sake of a joke. Thumbing the audio switch, he summoned the computer with a listless sigh.

"Monitor all intercom outlets and report coordinates where you detect activity."

The same groups appeared—two and four—only the two-person group had relocated by a deck; the four-person party still kept to the library.

"Close down the bulkheads to the nineteenth floor," he said. "If the two people at coordinates 425-457-77 move outside the room they currently occupy, seal that room behind them."

"As you wish, Gregory L. Jao."

He headed for a lift without thanking the computer. Less than eighteen hours into this scenario, he planned to finish it before the twenty-four-hour mark arrived, if only he could reach deck nineteen before his quarry found some way to bypass the bulkheads. First, he'd have to stop by the engineering storeroom where he'd pilfered his first collection of timers and triggering devices; he still had seven phasers with which to construct a little insurance.

The two on the nineteenth floor were annoyingly easy to dispatch. Chekov found them arguing in the hallway outside one of the bulwarked rooms, each apparently blaming the other for having locked the door on their way out. Chekov stunned them before they even knew he was there.

He sat on the floor while the cleanup crew came for the bodies, meticulously wiring phasers into a series and affixing them to his belt. One of the cleanup technicians peered at him curiously while lifting a body onto a stretcher. "What're you making? A toy train?"

Chekov didn't look up from his work. "A bomb."

"Ah." The tech nodded sagely at his companion.

"Starfleet's finest," he assured the woman with him. They both giggled as they wheeled the litters away.

Chekov ignored their laughter. He'd told Sasha he wouldn't sacrifice an entire Federation starship just to spite the Klingon Empire, and he still believed that was true. He also believed it was his duty as an officer to make his own death or capture too expensive a goal to be worth the enemy's efforts. In the real world, that might not mean the destruction of a fully crewed *Constitution*-class starship, but it could mean voluntary death in the face of inevitable defeat—death that carried the price of many lives other than his own. Baasch, no doubt, would miss the irony in the gesture, but it wasn't intended as revenge against the other cadet. Not entirely, at least.

Chekov tucked the last phaser into the array, then set about secreting the multicolored wires out of sight behind his belt. With the whole apparatus cinched about his waist again, it looked like nothing more than an equipment belt crowded with a half-dozen extra phasers. Only Chekov knew about the wire threaded down the left sleeve of his singlet, or about the wire loop near his ring finger that he could tug with almost no effort at all. No one else would see the tiny Rube Goldberg that would trigger the first phaser on his belt at almost the same moment it fired the second, and the third . . .

Chekov fingered the wire peeking out of his sleeve. ". . . *boom* . . ." he murmured to himself.

In real life, the enemy would no doubt have circuit detectors, or personnel trained in search and remove. But, as Sasha had so testily reminded him, this wasn't real life. Nor was this real death. It was all a test to which someone else had constructed the rules, but which Chekov didn't intend to lose; even if all he could do was assure no one else won it, either.

The door to the library was locked.

Chekov frowned at the sealed bulkhead, toying with the loop of wire that brushed against his wrist and trying to decide why something as prudent as a locked door should make his spine tingle and his muscles ache as though he were guiding a starship into battle. True, he hadn't instructed the computer to seal this bulkhead; he'd cordoned off the rest of the deck, half hoping this group would show a bit more initiative than the last. They hadn't even left the library, though, and now he'd discovered the door locked from the inside without even a guard placed in the hall. He wondered if Baasch were somehow aware that Chekov was the only one left they had to face—if he were waiting just on the inside for the Russian to override their lock. When Chekov entered, Baasch would shoot him.

Growling low in frustration, Chekov backed away from the door. If there were only some way to force them out, to be more sure where they were, what they were doing. He remembered an intercom only a few meters down the corridor and trotted back to it while still considering his plan. "Computer."

A longer pause than he expected, then: "Yes, Gregory L. Jao?"

"Can you still verify four life forms in the library?"

Another pause, longer this time. "Yes, Gregory L. Jao."

"Can you pinpoint their locations within the library?"

"I'm sorry, Gregory L. Jao, but my audio monitors are not designed for that level of accuracy."

Chekov drummed his fingers against the wall, his thoughts chasing each other round and round like angry birds. If he knew where they were—if he knew what they were doing—if, if, *if!* "Computer," he continued, wrestling his thoughts under control long enough to choose a course of action, "can you override the manual lock on the library door?"

"Of course, Gregory L. Jao. My system is—" An infinitesimal pause in the middle of its answer this time; Chekov wasn't sure why, but the quirk worried him. "—designed for convenient use by administrative personnel. Would you like me to perform such an override now?"

"Yes."

This time the heartbeat of silence was acceptable. Then the indicator light a dozen steps down the hall moved silently from red to green, and the computer announced simply, "Done." Chekov relocated the wire loop in his sleeve, tucking it further out of sight as he returned to the library door.

He shadowed the wall during his approach, triggering the door sensors at the last possible moment. The breathless *hisss* as the door whisked aside seemed almost too loud to bear.

The inside of the library was dark and cavernous. Floor-to-ceiling displays paneled off alcoves where terminals sprouted from the tops of long tables. A maze of shelves—housing a dusty, woody-smelling collection of antique printed paper books—zigged and zagged across the first few meters in front of the door. Chekov crouched lower than the tallest shelving unit and eased his own phaser into his hand.

Well-remembered voices drifted to him from across the abandoned terminals: "—yard looked a lot bigger once we took down the bushes."

"What did you replace them with?" Laurel Gugin wanted to know, sounding more interested in the subject than Chekov would have given her credit for.

"Anne wanted to plant more shrubs," Westbeld replied, "but I talked her into shade flowers and meadow stuff. Actually, she wanted azaleas, too."

Chekov sank back on his heels, suddenly hesitant. Westbeld and Gugin? Here? Had Baasch taken the women prisoner, or had the two groups somehow banded together? Where were Cantini and Cecil? Other sounds came from all over the room: footsteps, dragging and repetitive, like those of a captured lion pacing its habitat from boredom; his own breathing, coming back to him double-loud from the bookshelves to his right and left; the spasmodic click-clacking of a terminal keyboard; an occasional muffled curse.

Robert. Chekov clenched his teeth against a string of angry words as his thoughts leapt up into turmoil again. Robert the computer expert. Robert who was, no doubt, within coding distance of discovering why the computer wasn't as cooperative as it should be. Robert, who had apparently defeated Baasch's squadron after all, then left Chekov and Sasha for dead. Robert, his Achilles' heel.

Chekov decided he'd have to shoot Robert first.

"Where the hell have you been?" The sharp prod of a phaser in the small of his back—not Cantini's voice—stopped him from continuing forward.

"Don't shoot me," Chekov said, trying to hide his annoyance at being caught. "I'm on your side."

Cantini didn't appear to be impressed. "Answer my question," he growled as Chekov turned to face him. "Where have you been?" Chekov heard Westbeld and Gugin's conversation stagger into nonexistence at the sound of Cantini's voice.

"I've been anywhere I could get to," Chekov told Cantini simply. "There aren't many open routes through the station, though—someone's been locking the doors."

"We noticed," Gugin volunteered as she and Westbeld approached their position. They, at least, hadn't drawn their phasers, even if Cantini refused to put his away. "Al tried to leave this level about an hour ago, but he couldn't find an access that would open."

"So where have you been?"

Chekov turned back to Cantini. The smaller man's dark eyes glittered in his round, flat-featured face, somehow accusing Chekov of something too unspecific to state out loud. Chekov wondered how much Cantini had guessed.

"What do you want me to tell you?" he asked. "I've been confined to this damn station, just like you. Trying to keep myself from getting stunned. Just like you."

The anger in Cantini's eyes faltered momentarily. "We left you with Sasha in the admin offices. You ran away when we were attacked—you didn't even come out to help us!"

"We didn't think there was anything we could do," Chekov told him. "By the time we realized what was happening, we thought you'd already been taken out."

Cantini snorted. "So you ran."

Better to repeat a lie they already believed than to muddy the waters with the truth. "Yes," Chekov told him. "We ran."

When Cantini would have said something more, Westbeld interrupted, "So where's Sasha?"

"Out of the scenario," Chekov answered. The mention of her name, and the thought of how angry she would be when he saw her next, made his face burn. "We were surprised by two other cadets on the nineteenth floor." The lies seemed to come awfully easily now.

Keyboard clatter attracted his attention again; he tried to look past the shelving unit between himself and Westbeld, but couldn't see beyond her shoulder. "Where's Robert?" he asked, as casually as he could.

Gugin glanced over her shoulder, as though expecting to see someone there. When there was nothing, she turned back to Chekov with a shrug. "With the computer. Doing something."

Chekov fingered the wire up his sleeve. "Do you know *what* he's doing?"

"Does it matter?" Cantini demanded acidly. Chekov only glanced at him; he knew enough.

"He's trying to break in," Gugin volunteered. She was the first to turn back toward the room, obviously losing interest now that their prowler proved to be friend rather than foe. "He thinks the locked bulk-heads may have been arranged through the main-frame."

Chekov, still under Cantini's watchful eye, stood to follow the women further into the room. "How long has he been working?"

Westbeld settled back into one of the stiff, unpadded seats. "About three hours. He says he almost got it once or twice, but it keeps denying his communications protocol—even in binary."

Chekov nodded vacantly, and played with his wire.

Cantini poked the other ensign in the ribs with his phaser, startling a sharp profanity out of him. "What's the matter?" Cantini asked shrewdly. "You don't look like you think it's a good idea."

"It's just . . ." Chekov made himself stop fingering the trigger wire. "What if he disrupts something? This is a civilian station—they might not take well to having their data corrupted."

"He knows what he's doing," Gugin said without concern. She turned on a reader by her left hand. "Besides, somebody else already broke in once. What more harm can Cece do?"

If only they knew.

"Damn it!"

Only Chekov jumped at Cecil's sharp invective; the others were no doubt inured to his outbursts by now. Pulling away from the table, Chekov started in the direction of his friend's voice, ignoring Cantini's belligerent, "Don't you go *anywhere,* Chekov!"

Cecil crouched over an active terminal, his eyes washed copper by the steady amber light. He didn't look up as Chekov approached, didn't even glance away from whatever his eyes tracked across the tilted screen when Chekov paused at the rear of the monitor to stare at him.

"Robert . . . ?"

"Don't bother me," Cecil muttered distractedly. "I'm busy."

I'll bet you are. "What are you doing?" Chekov pressed. "This isn't our equipment."

Cecil growled inarticulately and punched at a series of buttons. "Yeah, well, tell that to the tech nine who cracked the system." He slapped his hands against his thighs in a fit of frustration.

Cantini materialized at Chekov's shoulder. "Leave him the hell alone!" he grumbled, tugging at Chekov's elbow. "I'm still not convinced you're not Kramer's assassin, so just—"

Chekov jerked his arm away just as Cecil exclaimed, "Pavel!" and Westbeld and Gugin ran up to join them.

"What's going on?"

"Did you get in?"

"Welcome, User 128641937F . . ."

Chekov grabbed the terminal and spun it about before Cecil could respond. "Computer!" he shouted. *"Slushayetye! Otkluchenoe!"*

The terminal went dead.

No one said anything for a moment. Then Cantini caught Chekov by the back of the neck and spun him roughly about. "Why you son of a—!"

Chekov struck the other man's hand away, ducking out of range as Cantini drew back to swing at him. "Remember the beginning of the scenario?" he cautioned. "They told us anything goes!" Westbeld had unlimbered her own phaser, but didn't look as though she knew what she wanted to do with it.

"You aren't a tech nine!" Cecil argued. He still looked vaguely puzzled, not even capable of anger in his confusion. "I've seen you work, damn it—you *didn't* break into this system!"

Chekov half turned to Cecil, glad for the distraction. "I didn't," he admitted. "I took it from the tech nine who *did.*"

Cecil shook his head slowly. *"How?"*

"Who cares how?" Cantini interjected. "He screwed us, Bob! He agreed to work with us, and then he screwed us over!" He swung an angry glare on Chekov again. "Did you set up that ambush, too? How did you *really* kill Sasha?"

"I didn't!" Chekov shot back, furious at the suggestion. "We really thought you were gone—Sasha and I wanted to help you!"

"Well, a fat lot of help you turned out to be!" Westbeld pursed her lips and combed her hair out of her eyes with one hand. Looking at Cecil, she stated, "I say we kill him."

Cecil still stared at the blank screen, occasionally punching a button on the keyboard as though expecting some reply. "I can't believe this . . . !"

"We're gonna kill him, Bob," Cantini said, a bit more loudly. "It's three to one, unless you want to help."

"Laurel didn't vote," Chekov started to point out, but Gugin added, "I want to kill you, too," before he even finished his sentence.

Chekov threw up his arms in exasperation. "You don't understand . . . !"

"I understand enough," Cecil said quietly, evenly, "to know that we six agreed to work as a team." He looked up from the keyboard, his blue eyes hard and bright as ice. "Why didn't you respect that? Why didn't you tell us about the computer, or the traps? What game are we supposed to be playing here?"

Chekov sighed. "That's your problem," he said. "This *isn't* just a game."

"It was a figure of speech," Cecil began, but Chekov cut him off.

"It's more than that. Every step of the way, you've been treating this like real life—as if we were all really in danger of being killed by some desperate situation! But it's a *command scenario,* and the only 'scores' any of us are gathering will be on our records for the rest of our lives." He looked from Cecil's frustrated face to Cantini's angry one and back again. "I've nothing personal against any of you," he insisted. "You're my friends. But this is my *career.* If only one of us can be alive at the end of this scenario . . . then I have to make sure that the one alive is me."

"Why can't we just *all* stay alive?" Cecil sighed. "Band together or something, just the five of us. A passing grade split five ways still has to count for something."

"Yeah," Westbeld said. "Wouldn't they rather have *five* cadets who were good survivors than just one?"

"I don't think it works that way," Chekov admitted. "If *one* of us doesn't win, then none of us does."

"They never said that," Cecil pointed out.

Chekov shrugged. "They never said that they would split the grade, either."

Cecil ran his hands along the top of the terminal,

making the gray-and-white box spin lazily. "So where does that leave us?"

"The way *I* see it," Cantini said, "our buddy, the berserker—" He hooked a thumb in Chekov's direction. "—sees it as his duty to either kill us, or die. The rest of us are willing to take the chance on a split grade. So let's kill him, and get it over with."

Cecil looked at Chekov; the smaller Russian man shrugged. "I don't want to argue with you," Chekov said. "But I don't want to lose, either."

"You set the ground rules," Cecil told him.

Chekov nodded. "I guess I did."

Cecil spun the terminal one last time, then turned his back on the rest of them as though washing his hands of the situation. "Then do it," he instructed Cantini. "I still want to get into this system."

"Robert . . ." Chekov slipped his finger through the loop up his sleeve just as Cecil stopped to face him. "I really do understand your choice. And it's nothing personal." He hoped Cecil would remember that when this was all over.

Cecil's face softened into a faint smile. "No," he said softly. "It's nothing personal."

Before Cecil turned away again, Chekov tugged once on the hidden trigger. He didn't even have a chance to notice Cantini's reaction before the blasts of six widely dispersed phasers "killed" them all.

He awoke with a headache, and muscles so stiff he could barely lift his eyelids to review his surroundings. When he did, he found himself alone in a plain storage room, lying atop a narrow foldaway in a sea of other—although empty—cots. Pushing up onto his elbows, he swung his legs carefully over the side until he could cradle his head in his hands. Then he waited for the pounding to subside, and tried to remember why he was here.

Memory came back quickly. He'd probably been unconscious longer than the others, thanks to his proximity to the phaser fire. That no doubt accounted for his stiffness and headache as well; he'd never been stunned by a phaser before, but had a cousin who always relished passing along such horror stories at family gatherings. Chekov smiled. He'd have something to contribute to those discussions now, if only his headache faded enough for him to stand.

Voices from the next room finally piqued his interest enough to encourage movement. One hand still shielding his eyes from the light, he pushed to his feet and shuffled gingerly toward the door.

The adjoining lounge was dark and vacant. The only light came from the wide-screen monitor set into one wall—the same source of the distant voices. Scenes of various locations on the Aslan Station passed across the screen in increments of thirty to ninety seconds, effectively displaying every square foot of the station over a period of an hour or so. Chekov approached the viewscreen, studying the printed data in the lower right-hand corner. Hours, minutes, seconds, date. He wondered if they had taped the entire weekend.

"Excuse me?"

He turned, finding one of the cleanup crew poised attentively in the doorway behind him.

"The shuttle's loading up, sir, I . . ." The tech paused, then reached around the doorway to key up the lights. Chekov saw something like amusement and delight cross the young man's features. "It's you!"

For the first time that weekend, Chekov felt a whisper of fear. "I beg your pardon?"

The tech recovered quickly; studied politeness replaced his animated expression as he joined Chekov at the viewscreen. "I recognize you from the drill," he explained. "I've been helping with the revival crew—everybody you've met up with this weekend has come through here!"

Chekov followed the tech's broad gesture, staring once about the abandoned lounge, then turning back to the tall screen. "What's this?" he asked.

The tech surprised him by laughing. "Video monitor," he explained. "We used the security pickups to record everything that went on this weekend. Anybody killed early on in the game could sit in here and see what everybody else was doing. Or review all the stuff that had happened before they died."

Chekov's headache settled deep behind his eyes as the tech leaned over to intimate, "You've been a pretty popular viewing subject, my friend."

He could just imagine.

"It was a command scenario," Chekov stated carefully. He was amazed how thin and worn that litany was growing by now. "I did what I was told. That's all."

The tech shrugged. "I suppose." He leaned over to switch off the monitor, then turned a sunny smile on Chekov. "Is that what you're going to tell all the rest of them?"

Chekov opened his mouth, then realized he didn't have the faintest idea what to say. Struggling against panicked thoughts about Sasha, Cantini, and Cecil, he said haltingly, "I . . . they knew what to expect. We're all cadets here."

The tech draped an arm across his shoulders to steer him toward the door. "If that's the best you've got as a defense," he said companionably, "do yourself a favor and take a *civilian* shuttle home . . . !"

This must be what it feels like to drown in liquid nitrogen, Chekov thought as he stepped through the hatchway to the already packed shuttle. No one spoke to him as he walked the interminable distance to the only empty seat. Chekov couldn't very well blame them. He stared out the window, not wanting to face anything living during the hours-long voyage back to Earth.

The pointed silence was maddening. He felt as though he could feel his sixty-four classmates' angry thoughts as keenly as daggers slipped under his skin. He wanted to try and explain, to say that he was sorry. Only he wasn't. Not really. He was sorry that they were angry, and sorry that *he* was going to have to pay the price for their lack of understanding. But that didn't change what he did.

Maybe this was the difference between line officers and desk men, he thought, not without some rancor. The ability to do what's necessary without needing to place blame. Everyone was so ready to condemn him because he had acted quickly—decisively—but no one seemed willing to offer suggestions for what should have been done instead. They all thought exactly the same way: *Run and hide! Protect what you have! Don't try to do too much—you might fail and end up with nothing!* He'd just proven that an officer's response to a threatening situation was not limited to passive defense, and they all hated him because he acted outside their ability. Too bad. They would still be complaining about the *unfairness* of it all long after he was assigned to a starship and gone from their petty little world.

Chekov crossed his arms in a gesture of angry defiance, then sat back in his seat to watch the shuttle deberth.

Forty minutes into the flight, however, some of his hauteur began to fade. The oppressive silence weighed on his spirit like a dead comrade, and Kramer had come to stand, equally uncommunicative, at the front of the aisle. Chekov stared resolutely out his window, but started to consider apologizing again.

"I take it," Kramer began, as though he'd only just arrived on the scene, "that none of you are terribly pleased with the outcome of this maneuver."

A discontented growl boiled from the rear of the shuttle forward. Kramer smiled. "What do you perceive to be the problem?"

Without hesitation, Cantini offered: "Chekov."

Another chorus of growls indicated mass agreement. Chekov clenched his teeth, pretending to ignore them.

"Do you have a comment on that, Ensign Chekov?"

He hated Kramer more intensely than he had ever hated the man before, but didn't turn away from his window. *They're a bunch of goddamned children,* he wanted to say. Instead, he stated simply, "No, sir. I have no comment."

"None?" Kramer frowned faintly, his eyes bright

and attentive. "Cadet Chekov . . . I'm disappointed." If he meant it to be cutting, his tone of voice failed him. "What about someone else?"

Chekov knew the cadets must be bursting with complaints and arguments, but no one volunteered. He didn't care. Not anymore. He thought perhaps if he told himself that often enough, he'd believe it by the time they reached home.

"Very well," Kramer continued. "Then we shall start with my evaluations on your performances." Chekov feigned enough disinterest to make himself feel better about turning to look at the commodore. Kramer waited until everyone's attention was on him before announcing, "You all failed."

"What?" Chekov wasn't the only one to ask the question aloud; he assumed that was why no one turned to scowl at him for speaking.

"What the hell did you want?" Baasch demanded. "We didn't *all* do the same thing!"

"Some of us," another cadet injected, "didn't even kill anybody!"

Kramer stood, unmoving, at the front of the shuttle, not even raising his hands to signal for silence. "Nor did any of you," he told them sternly, "react appropriately to the situation presented." No one interrupted him. "Cadet Nabuda," he summoned. "Explain the objective of the Aslan scenario."

Nabuda frowned, glancing to her left and right as though hoping to gain some insight from her classmates. "We were to stay alive," she said finally. "To avoid being killed."

"I see." Kramer looked from one bewildered face to the next, his gaze resting on Chekov's only long enough for the ensign to understand that he'd been noted. "I needn't ask to know that is what you all believe. I observed enough ambushing and booby-trapping this weekend to know how you were thinking."

"Chekov was the only one setting traps."

Chekov twisted in his seat to face the speaker, alarmed and injured by the bitterness in her words. Sasha kept her eyes pointedly locked on Kramer, not even acknowledging Chekov's attention with a scowl. He felt his heart melt within him.

"He was merely the most creative killer among you. None of you *really* understood the difference between self-defense and command." Kramer crossed his arms and leaned back against the bulkhead. "Many years ago, this same exercise was performed with a class of cadets on an abandoned lunar base. They were told the same things as you—that they were being hunted, that they must survive. Unlike you, however, they had among them a very creative officer who *commanded* in the situation, instead of merely preserving himself.

"The officer in question inferred—correctly—that it made no difference if one or one hundred cadets survived the scenario. What mattered was avoiding the assassin. He secured one of the dining halls and began drafting a security force to guard the entrances. Anyone who wished to enter had to surrender their weapons; they were then guarded by a handful of cadets already known to be trustworthy. In that manner, the scenario concluded without a single casualty, and that student received a high passing grade."

Kramer looked down the aisle at Chekov again.

"Would you care to hypothesize as to that cadet's identity, Cadet Chekov?"

Chekov shook his head, strangling with shame. It was Cecil who spoke the name, "James Kirk."

Kramer nodded. "Command is not a picture drawn in black and white," he told them gently. "Not a game that one can win or lose, depending upon one's decisions. Command is an ongoing struggle. In it, you strive to *maintain*—not win. In the real world, no one is keeping score. I think Mister Chekov can tell you that winning and not losing are not necessarily the same thing."

No one said anything after that. Chekov folded his hands tight in his lap and watched the stars from his window. All his hopes for a brilliant Starfleet career floundered at his feet like dying birds, killed by the realization that he could never hope to live up to the standard James Kirk had set in both Starfleet and Chekov's own life—the realization that Kirk would be ashamed of Chekov, and everything Chekov had accomplished in the past forty-eight hours.

When the shuttle bumped gently to ground several hours later, the coral-pink streamers of sunrise were just caressing the eastern horizon. Chekov stayed in his seat, staring out at the pitted, blasted landing pad as the others filed silently past him. He glanced up only once, to watch Sasha walk away from him as though he meant nothing to her and never had. For a moment, he thought he might cry.

"So, you want to get breakfast?"

Chekov closed his eyes, not wanting to face anyone —even Cecil—just yet. "I'm not hungry," he said softly.

Cecil sat down beside him. "I am. Wanna keep me company?"

"No."

The last of the footsteps retreated to faint, sharp echoes on the slabwork outside. Chekov felt Cecil shift in the seat, then the computer tech said stiffly, "Boy, are *you* a poor sport, or what?"

Chekov laughed without humor. "My career is destroyed in a single weekend, and you expect me to be gracious?"

"You overreact," Cecil scoffed. "Nobody's gonna boot you out of Starfleet for booby-trapping a scenario."

"You don't understand . . ."

"Sure I do." Cecil caught his shoulder and turned Chekov about to face him. "We *all* screwed up," he said simply. "I get the impression that's the actual point of these scenarios—we get to do it here so we don't do it in real life. Kramer even said your Captain Kirk is the only one who *didn't* flunk the damn thing!"

The very mention of Kirk's name wrung his heart with despair. "I should have known better!" he insisted. "I thought I had the right to serve under him, but I don't know *anything!*" He took Cecil's shoulders. "I'm sorry, Robert! I know what I was thinking, only . . . I *don't* know! Not now. It just doesn't make sense anymore . . ." He turned away to the window again. "I feel like such a fool . . . !"

"They've given fools starship commands before," Cecil tried to console him. "They gave out commands before Kirk came along—they can't break the tradition now!"

Chekov smiled ruefully and sat back in his seat. "If

they ever give me a command, I want *you* to be my executive officer. To keep me from getting beyond myself like this . . . to keep me from being stupid."

Cecil shrugged, flushing with pleasure. "After this weekend," he allowed, "I don't think you'll need as much reminding. So . . ." He stood and offered Chekov a hand up. "Do you want to discuss my future vacation pay over breakfast?"

Chekov stood as well, groaning at the very thought of facing the others so soon after his embarrassment. "I can't! If they don't kill me, I'll have to kill myself!"

Laughing, Cecil headed for the hatch. "Okay," he acquiesced. "We'll get civvy food. More carbohydrates—more energy!" He leapt out onto the landing ground with ridiculous enthusiasm. "We'll *need* energy!" he assured Chekov fervently. "We're going to be *heroes!*"

Chekov stepped down more sedately. Cecil's face held such an expression of trust, Chekov didn't know how to tell him that he feared all that trust misplaced. "Are we? I'd forgotten."

Cecil slipped an arm around his friend's shoulders and smiled. *"I* know what you are," he said serenely. "I've always known. And I *never* forgot . . ."

Chapter Five

HALLEY

"I CAN'T BELIEVE Starfleet ever let you two out in the field!"

Chekov rewarded the doctor with a look of profound irritation; Sulu merely started laughing again.

"It isn't that bad, Bones," Kirk volunteered from his own seat. He hadn't missed the depth of displeasure in his security officer's dark eyes, or the embarrassment still evident on the lieutenant's face. "You do a lot of things in command scenarios that don't exactly correspond to your attitudes in real life."

McCoy nodded, obviously unconvinced. "Like making up things so you can talk your way out of a bad situation."

Kirk felt his own cheeks start to burn. "That's different . . ."

"Sure it is." The doctor turned to Sulu long enough to order brusquely, "Stop laughing! It's bad for your shoulder!" then commented to Chekov, "If you feel the need to take direct action in the next hour or so, go into the back or something, okay?"

Chekov continued staring out the window, refusing to produce a reaction. Leaning back with a weary sigh, Kirk hoped the doctor would take the hint and leave Chekov's Academy embarrassments in the past.

An hour later, emergency sirens boiled away Kirk's troubled dreams like a laser through hot wax. He tried to bolt upright, only to discover he was already sitting, his shoulders braced against the shuttle's inner wall. The muscles in his thigh yanked at his swollen knee; he cursed his disability aloud as he gripped the seat back with one hand.

"Scotty?" Light from the forward hatch spilled onto the floor of the passenger area. Kirk could just hear Scott's baritone voice above the buzzing siren, answered by Chekov's lighter tenor. "Scotty! Chekov!" He swore again, knowing they couldn't hear.

McCoy leapt from his own seat as soon as Kirk swung his legs to the deck. "Hold it, Captain! You're not going anywhere!"

"Get out of my way, Bones . . ." Kirk clenched his jaw, settling all his weight onto his left foot as he lurched upright. "I'm going forward."

McCoy caught at his arm to keep him from falling. "Dammit, Jim!"

"Scotty!" Kirk pulled his arm from the doctor's grip, immediately sorry for the action when he nearly overbalanced and fell. Two frantic hops—guided more by luck than skill—collided him with the entrance to the forward section. Kirk clutched at the doorway, ignoring McCoy's glare of disapproval as he dragged himself closer to Scott. "What's wrong?"

The engineer threw a quick glance over his shoulder. "Debris," was all he said as he turned back to where Chekov crouched in the navigator's seat, trying to reach under the shattered panel.

Even without putting weight on his knee, Kirk could feel the joint filling with hot fluid; the climb in pressure made it feel as though the bone would crack. Hobbling unsteadily past Scott, the captain lowered himself into the pilot's chair so he could extend his damaged leg under the panel.

"Got it!" Chekov tugged something loose from deep beneath his console, and the alarm abruptly silenced. Scott was already punching up coordinates on the navigations display as Chekov righted himself in the seat.

"I used the radio to wire up the warning," the engineer explained without looking away from the panel. "I was hoping we wouldn't need it."

"A warning for what?" Kirk asked again.

Scott tapped a display to attract Chekov's attention, then stepped back when the lieutenant nodded and set to work. "Space debris," he answered Kirk. "There's flotsam out here big enough to carve a starship out of—even some of the small stuff could hull a craft this size! I rigged the sensors to warn us about anything that got too close." He squinted past the forward viewport, as if he saw something Kirk couldn't. "Something just got close, it's big and we're in its way. If it were smaller we could try to move out of its path, but as it is . . ." Scotty's voice trailed off.

Kirk followed the engineer's gaze. "How far?"

"Ten thousand kilometers," Chekov supplied. "Off our starboard stern." The Russian frowned at the instruments, his eyes flicking back and forth between columns of numbers. "It's closing quickly though—about two hours until impact."

"And then?"

McCoy's voice from the doorway startled them all. Kirk glanced at the doctor, then back to where Chekov worried over the panels. "Don't worry about it, Bones," Kirk said softly. "We're going to be fine." *Liar!* he chastised himself. *How can you be such a liar?* He opted not to think about it.

"Sir . . . ?"

Sulu's voice barely carried from the passenger cabin into the foredeck. McCoy backed out of the doorway to turn toward the helmsman; Kirk called, "What are you thinking of, Mister Sulu?"

"We could divert it," Sulu answered hoarsely. His eyes were closed, his face drawn and sallow in the half-light. "Isn't the starboard engine nacelle the one that's gone bad?"

Scott nodded, his eyes unfocused with thought. "That it is . . . !"

"Couldn't we use the pile in that nacelle to knock the thing off course?"

"Aye!" The engineer's face brightened. "Or at least use it to blast the rock into pieces small enough for the shields to handle!"

Chekov uttered a short, mirthless laugh, then flushed when Scott glowered down at him. "So we sever the pod," Chekov pointed out. "The pod is tumbling at the same velocity as the shuttle . . ." He covered one column of readings with his hand, as though unable to look at the numbers any longer. "We'd all reach the same point simultaneously."

"Can't we do *something?*" McCoy pressed. "Get out and kick it, at least?"

Chekov looked frustrated to the point of anger, but Scott only laughed. "We can kick it a good sight farther than you might think!"

"With what?" Chekov wanted to know.

Scott clapped the younger man on the shoulder. *"Accelerators!"*

Revelation hit Kirk at the very same moment. "The e-suits! Go to it, Scotty!"

Scott ducked past McCoy into the main section, leaving the doctor to ask no one and everyone, "What have the environmental suits got to do with this?"

"They've got jump packs," Kirk explained, feeling giddy with relief. "Set for continuous burn, we should be able to accelerate the pod to within a half hour of the shuttle."

"That'll knock us about a bit," Scott called from the other chamber, "but it beats the hell out of a collision!"

"It ought to make a good light show, too, shouldn't it?" McCoy glanced about hopefully, actually looking optimistic for the first time since the accident. "Even Spock couldn't miss an explosion like that!"

Kirk nodded; McCoy's faith was infectious. "Let's hope so, Bones." *Let's hope Spock's looking in the right direction.* There were so very many directions to look in space.

A loud *snapt!* pulled Kirk's attention back to the navigation-helm console. Chekov had prized up the panel's face, and now sat with it raised at a seventy-degree angle as he leaned in to inspect the circuits.

Kirk edged forward as well, reminding himself abruptly of his injured knee and limited mobility. He stopped his movement halfway to the console. "What's wrong?"

"Hopefully, sir, nothing . . ." Chekov pulled his head back long enough to call, "Mister Scott, I need to pull the memory!"

Scott reappeared in the doorway. "What're you doing?" he asked with a frown.

Chekov nodded toward the open panel. "I've extrapolated the projectile's course against ours. If you want the nacelle to actually hit it, you're going to need something that can remember a course." He motioned toward the circuitry with his free hand.

Scott grinned and came into the hatch. "Good thinking, lad!"

McCoy leaned over Scott's shoulder as the engineer bent down and began tugging at a circuit panel. "Won't we *miss* that?" the doctor inquired.

Scott shook his head. "With the engines all but out," he finished, "the pilot can't really maneuver, so it's a moot point anyway." He jerked free two interconnected boards, then backed out from under the panel. "That'll do it," he announced. Chekov settled the console back into place.

McCoy turned to follow Scott's progress back toward the suit locker as the engineer left the forward hatch for the second time. "Let's just hope we don't need those suits later."

Kirk sighed. "Bones, you're becoming a doomsayer."

The doctor's half-smile faded. "I worry."

Kirk's first impulse was to tell McCoy that worrying about not having e-suits would be pointless if Scott's hunk of rock hit them broadside. And even if this diversion worked, they were better off suffocating in a shuttle all together than floating away from each other in fragile, one-man life suits with less than six hours of air. Introducing such thoughts was pointless, however; spirits were low enough without Kirk giving them something else to brood over. "Scotty knows what he's doing. If he can't convince seven jump packs to work together, no one can."

"Six." When Kirk frowned at Chekov, the lieutenant said simply, "Six." He turned to stare out the front viewport with a distinctly unhappy air. "Someone still has to wear one of them outside to sever the nacelle."

"It's only logical—*I'm* the most expendable member of this expedition."

Kirk felt a mixture of annoyance and admiration at Chekov's persistence. The lieutenant had been in a foul mood since being coerced into explaining the aftermath of his *Kobayashi Maru,* and Kirk wasn't certain how much to blame that on the impromptu tale-telling or Chekov's usual solemnity. Either way, he didn't like the direction the lieutenant's arguments had taken.

"Mister Chekov," he said aloud, "I'm sure Mister Scott appreciates your willingness to go EV, but I don't think we've reached the point of discussing who's most expendable just yet."

Chekov looked up from where he'd been dogging

Scott as the engineer wired the accelerators. It struck Kirk, for the first time, that Chekov was the only one who hadn't discarded his duty jacket when Scott reinstated the heating; the brass and silver pips at the shoulder and cuffs glinted dully as he stood. "I'm serious, Captain."

"You're not going," Scott stated flatly. The Scotsman's obstinacy surprised Kirk even more than Chekov's.

Chekov glared down at him. "You're our only engineer," he persisted. "If something should happen to you, there isn't anyone else who could repair the systems!"

Scott wouldn't even look up from his repairs. "Nothing's going to break down any more than it already has."

"I was brought along to navigate. We have no navigational abilities, we have no helm. If I die, it won't make any difference."

"Listen to me," Scott overrode him, rocking back on his heels. "There's a laser cutter involved here. There's a lot of connections and conduits that need sealing off if we aren't going to contaminate the whole craft. There's these accelerators to place, and a short-term memory to install. Those are all procedures *I'm* better qualified to perform."

"Then show me how," Chekov insisted. "I've worked with you before—you *know* that I can learn this equipment!"

"Chekov . . . !" Scott sat for a moment in silence. Kirk watched his jaw knot as the Scotsman turned a narrow tool over and over in his hand. "That was a long time ago, lad," Scott said slowly, evenly. "I'm concerned about the safety of the people left in the shuttle. I could show you the equipment, I could drill you on the procedures, but *I'm* the only one who could make *absolutely* certain *everything* was done right! If you missed even one conduit, or slipped and damaged the pile—"

"I'll be careful."

"You won't be *anything!*" Scott exploded, angry and insistent. "Because you're *not going out there!*"

"Why won't you even *talk* to me about it?" Chekov wanted to know.

"Because you're not qualified!" the engineer shot back. Chekov drew back as if struck, his eyes wide and injured. "You haven't logged a single hour with delicate equipment in nigh on five years!" Scott continued. "I'll be *damned* if I depend on you remembering enough of what I once showed you to do this!"

Chekov stared at Scott in brittle silence, his face blank, his back rigid. He reminded Kirk of the antique tin soldiers his grandfather used to have, with their identical stoic expressions, and identical scarlet uniforms. Kirk was immediately embarrassed for the comparison, especially in lieu of Chekov's story and Scott's angry words.

"I'm sorry, lad," Scott said, more gently. "But it's true, and you know it's true. I can't take a risk like that. Not with other people's lives."

No one said anything for a very long time. Kirk finally broke the painful silence. "Scotty, finish what you're doing, then get suited up and out there. Chekov, go up front and monitor that thing's position. We can maintain radio contact with Scotty through the main console."

Chekov hesitated only a heartbeat, then turned and swept into the forward hatch without even acknowledging Kirk's decision. Kirk was still warring with whether he should feel anger or sympathy for the young Russian when he noticed Scott staring after Chekov as well.

"Get to work, Mister Scott," Kirk suggested softly. Scott blinked, flicking a startled, embarrassed glance at his captain, then nodded and bent over the jump packs again.

Settling back in his seat, Kirk listened to Sulu's shallow breathing, to Scott's deft tinkering, and to Chekov's accusatory silence from the front cabin. His own knee sang a waspish song of pain from where McCoy had elevated it again. The doctor had rewrapped his knee with another cold pack and brace, but this dressing was no more comfortable than the first. His body urged him to give in, to go to sleep . . . but his mind refused to desert the four men who depended on his strength even when he couldn't assist them. He forced his eyes open again to find McCoy situated in the row behind him. "I'm fine," he said, more from habit than because it was true.

McCoy's eyes, directed toward the front, shifted to look at him. "We've been stuck in this box too long." His voice was low and concerned. "Startin' to snap at each other . . ."

Kirk glanced to the forward hatch as well. "Yes . . ." Scott was stepping into an e-suit by the lock, his back to them; there was still no sound or sight of Chekov. He thought about the intense young ensign who was his navigator for four years, now his chief of security, and how badly Scotty's words would have stung himself as a young lieutenant, and how vulnerable Chekov must feel after confiding about his Academy days.

Kirk was almost to his feet before McCoy caught his shoulder and insisted, "Where do you think you're going?"

He shook off the doctor's concern when McCoy rose to intercept him. "Into the front," he hedged, not interested in trying to explain further. "I need to talk to Chekov."

"You're his captain," the doctor said, so softly that only Kirk could hear, "not his father."

"That's right," Kirk replied, hopping toward the front hatch. "But I'm his captain, even now." *Even when there's nothing else I can do.* "Just let me talk to him."

McCoy held Kirk's elbow protectively for a moment longer, then nodded. The captain was reassured by the trust in his friend's blue eyes.

The navigator's console was in sorry disarray, a legacy to Scott's heroic repair efforts. Chekov sat with his back to the doorway, staring pensively out at the dusty stars; he didn't even turn when Kirk settled into the helmsman's chair.

"Do you understand why I'm keeping you inside?" the captain asked without prelude. They didn't have time to waste with coddling.

Chekov cast a bleak look over at Kirk, then seemed to catch himself and hardened his expression again as he turned away. "Yes, sir, I think I do."

Kirk knew from his reaction that he didn't. "It has

nothing to do with what you told us, or with what Scotty said." Something that was almost surprise flitted across the lieutenant's face, but he didn't shift his gaze. "I don't care what you did at command school. I *know* how difficult it can be to reconcile what you did as a student to what you want to do now— real life is never quite like what they tested you for, and things that seem obvious to an experienced officer weren't obvious then. Failing a scenario isn't the same thing as failure."

"Isn't it?" Chekov turned to face him, his expression belligerent, but his eyes still hurt. "What Mister Scott said earlier—that I'm not qualified . . . Do you believe him?"

Kirk met the dark Russian eyes earnestly. "You're a good navigator," he said, "and a good security chief." Any truth beyond that was so subjective. "Scotty values technical expertise a great deal—*I* value good officers. You do what you feel you have to, and you do it well. No one can ever fault you for that." He wished he could offer more.

Chekov's expression closed down again, and he turned back to the console to adjust something on the sensors. "I'm sorry if I've disappointed you," he said softly.

Kirk wanted to reassure him somehow—to reach out and touch him, to chase the insecurity away. Nothing he could think of seemed appropriate, though; all over again, he recognized the distance that had developed between himself and the navigator he once thought he knew. "You've never made me anything but proud."

Nothing further was volunteered, and Kirk didn't push the issue. Feeling cold and tired, he limped back to his seat to find McCoy waiting for him. "He'll be all right," he told the doctor quietly. "You'll see."

McCoy scowled, unconvinced. "And so will we?"

Kirk lowered himself into his seat, not meeting the doctor's gaze. "I trust Spock."

"I do, too," McCoy admitted, sitting back. "It's Fate I'm not too keen about." He looked off to starboard. "There seems to be a lot of 'ifs' in Scotty's diversion plan. *If* he can get the pod cut free in time—*if* the jump packs are strong enough—*if* the debris isn't titanium or some blast-resistant alloy." A haunted, frightened expression danced across his seamed features, and he finally averted his eyes. "If we aren't going to be rescued," he confessed, "I'd rather be hulled by Scotty's rock than die of dehydration forty or fifty hours later."

"I'm all set," Scott announced, inadvertently saving Kirk from having to respond to McCoy's disclosure.

The captain nodded once. "Verify the course with Chekov before you leave." And the maneuver was on its way.

Kirk moved into the front hatch while Chekov stood at the airlock to monitor Scott's departure. McCoy hovered over Kirk's left shoulder, pressed into the corner between the pilot's chair and the wall, as out of the way as he could manage. The radio's speaker sat cockeyed atop the helm controls, having been removed from the panel proper by Scott when the engineer jerry-rigged the alarm. Kirk listened for the Scotsman's first transmission, already thinking he might go mad with no visual to keep his eyes occupied.

"I'll be out of the lock in a moment now. Ah, there she goes . . ." Scott's voice rasped out of the damaged speaker just as Chekov returned to the navigator's seat in frigid silence. *"I know you can't confirm hearing me,"* the engineer continued, *"so I'll just have to hope for the best. I'm going to head along the hull until I can belay myself off to that damaged pod. It's pretty mundane until then, so I'll just let you know when I'm in place. Scott out."*

McCoy snorted from behind Kirk. "Just great! If he gets swept away by a stellar wind or something, the first we hear is when he doesn't call in."

"Bones, shut up." The doctor's sarcastic comments were wearing on Kirk's nerves.

"How long do you figure it'll take him to get in place?" McCoy, predictably, ignored Kirk's wishes, but at least changed the subject.

"Five, ten minutes," Chekov answered. His attention remained fixated with the navigation board. "Perhaps not even so long."

"How long before collision?" Kirk asked.

Chekov punched up a reading. "One hour, fifteen minutes."

Not a great margin for error.

It was nearly thirteen minutes before Scott called in again. Kirk traced the outline of every button and light on the helm console with his finger as he waited, wishing a dozen times each minute that someone would think of something to discuss so they could pass the time less painfully. When the radio finally sputtered to life, Kirk jumped so sharply that his knee screamed pain clear up into his skull.

"All right, I'm at the nacelle now . . . Och, what a sorry mess! She's got enough damage back here that we're lucky she didn't go critical five minutes after we hit the mine!"

McCoy leaned over Kirk's shoulder to growl at the speaker, "Forget the editorial, Scotty! *Launch* the thing!"

"He can't hear you," Chekov advised impatiently.

Just at that moment, Scott reported, *"I'm going to place the packs first, then start cutting. I don't know what I can tell you before I'm done, so I'll just work, I guess."*

"Marvelous . . ." Kirk sighed.

"I'll let you know when we're ready to cut free. Scott out." The transmission again went dead.

As Kirk tried to will himself not to drum his fingers, McCoy asked Chekov, "What kind of margin does he have? I mean, how long before it's too late to launch?"

Chekov shrugged, his lips pursed in irritation. "It depends."

"On?"

"On our position in the tumble when he finishes— on how quickly the packs can accelerate the mass." He pushed himself to his feet and stalked into the middle hold. "It just depends."

Kirk stopped McCoy from following. "Let him be, Bones."

"I will." The doctor looked troubled by his inadequacy in this new development. Kirk knew just how McCoy felt. "I'm going to look in on my patient."

Kirk took the hand McCoy offered him to struggle to his own feet. "Which one?" he asked. "The mobile one, or . . . ?"

"The cooperative one," McCoy sniffed. *"Neither* of my patients is *supposed* to be mobile!"

Kirk chuckled, but didn't contradict the older man.

Sulu watched McCoy reposition Kirk in the front aisle, grinning. "And I thought *I* was a lousy patient!"

"You're a saint," McCoy assured him. *"You* at least act as though you understand the English language."

"Now, that's not fair, Bones."

McCoy ignored the captain. "So what about you, Sulu?" he prompted, peeking under Kirk's cold pack before adjusting the brace on the captain's leg. "You took this *Kobayashi Maru* thing, too, didn't you?"

"Like a shot in the arm," the helmsman admitted.

"Well, we've got some more time to fill. I'd say it's your turn to 'fess up'."

Sulu looked suddenly, strangely uncomfortable. "It's not really all that interesting," he hedged. "And it isn't too appropriate, I think." When Chekov grumbled inarticulately from behind him, he insisted, "No, I'm serious."

"The captain cheated, Chekov blew up everyone he knew . . ." The doctor returned to his own seat just in front of Sulu's. "How bad can yours have been?"

Sulu didn't smile. "You might be surprised."

Kirk sensed a tension in the helmsman's usually light tone. "Don't push it, Bones," he suggested. "We're all tired. It can wait for another day."

"If there is one."

The doctor's frankness horrified him. "That's enough, McCoy . . ."

"What I mean," McCoy said, striving for humor, "is that we're all remarkably receptive to disclosing embarrassing anecdotes just now. If he doesn't tell us here, we may never get it out of him. Considering how he insisted with poor Chekov, it seems only fair."

"He's right," Chekov agreed simply.

Kirk looked over at Sulu. "Mister Sulu?"

Sulu sighed and closed his eyes. "It isn't funny," he said tiredly. "It isn't even clever."

"We'll settle," Kirk allowed.

"Although," McCoy intimated, "I find the thought of you devising a boring solution just a little hard to believe."

"It isn't boring," Sulu explained. "I just said it wasn't funny, that's all. And it takes a little extra explaining—to really understand it, I mean. A lot of things went into what I did, not just the decisions I made during the test . . ."

"Well," McCoy said placidly. "We certainly have plenty of time."

Chapter Six

CRANE DANCE

SULU CROUCHED LOW against the boom of the brilliant blue windsailor while it skated like a dragonfly over a bottle-green ocean. Water sluiced up like a shattered, sparkling curtain in the narrow craft's wake, and Sulu whooped with zealous enthusiasm when the sailor leapt for an instant into silence, then crashed down onto water again. Sea salt dusted his face and stung his dark eyes. *If all the happiness and excitement in my whole life,* Sulu thought, *could be jammed into one pure, breathless moment, it would be now!*

"How're we doing, Poppy?" Sulu laughed again to hear how insignificant and fragile his voice became against the sound of a playful sea. When the old man just ahead of him on the craft didn't answer, Sulu leaned forward—rocking the craft—and called again: "Hey, Poppy! Anybody home?"

Tetsuo Inomata twisted as far as his one-hundred-and-three-year-old muscles would allow, but didn't release his hold on the main mast. "You're going to dunk us, boy!" His wrinkled golden face sat atop his orange flotation jacket like a happy, sun-dried apple.

Sulu leaned into the boom, cutting the sailor across a corduroy of swells that made it jump and twitch like a grounded swordfish. "I love this craft! I love this *wind!* How can you not trust wind like this?"

"Never trust wind!" Tetsuo ducked the boom with the grace of an expert as Sulu swung it past him to bring the craft about. "The wind was here long before man was, and it's never much adjusted to man getting in its way."

As if to prove the old man's point, a gust nearly tipped the boat sideways. Sulu rode with it frantically, bothered by the coincidence, but too elated with his success to back down. "One more," Tetsuo informed him sagely, once the craft was righted again. "One more, and we'll both be wet!"

Sulu opened his mouth to scoff Tetsuo's lack of faith, and the wind flicked the sailor's bow with an element's uncaring ease, flipping the sleek craft end over end.

Salt water enveloped Sulu's sun-warmed torso in a rush of stinging, too-cool enthusiasm. He squinted his eyes shut, avoiding most of the pain ocean water could inflict, and rocketed to the surface with a single, powerful kick. Bobbing between the swells like a lazy gull, he caught sight of the blue-and-white sailor not far away; Tetsuo's bald head and orange flotation jacket flashed in and out of his vision just beyond the capsized craft.

After breaking down the sail and righting the board,

Sulu helped his great-grandfather to a seat against the slender mast. "I don't need help," Tetsuo complained. But he didn't push Sulu away.

"You never need help." Sulu lingered with one hand on the older man's wrist, not liking the chill feel to his great-grandfather's skin. He strove to cover his concern with a smile. "I'm heading for shore," he said as he fastened a rope to the craft's tow ring. "It's going to be dark soon, and I've still got to pack for tomorrow!"

"You don't have that much left to pack." Tetsuo shifted position to face Sulu as the lithe Oriental rolled onto his back and started for shore. "You're already taking most of the family heirlooms."

Sulu grinned. "Only some of them—it just seems like all."

Tetsuo made a face that quickly dissolved into chuckling. "You know what I mean!"

"Yeah, I know . . ."

For a while, they said nothing. The ocean whispered soothing secrets to no one, and the waves hissed a distant message to the gray-white sands a hundred meters away. Sulu continued for shore, watching the sky over him darken while the last defiant red rays leapt toward the eastern horizon, as if to hurry the dawn. *Everybody's anxious for tomorrow,* he thought, sighing. *I only want today. Forever and always.*

Because tomorrow, he'd be gone.

It seemed to Sulu not so long ago that Poppy raced him all the way to the old subway station and back, and sometimes even won. They were both much younger then—Sulu all of nine or ten, Tetsuo only just in his nineties—but the fourteen years between had come and gone like the flash of a distant white

gull. Somewhere in the midst of them, Sulu devoted
two carefree terms of his life to Starfleet, and Poppy
began what would be a long, bitter struggle with what
the neurosurgeons called a "grade four glioblastoma."
The man he sailed with today was immeasurably older
than the great-grandfather that his childhood had left
behind.

Most of the medical jargon meant nothing to Sulu.
Still, he understood enough to know that the growth
in Poppy's brain could be controlled with radiation
and chemotherapy, but could never be made to go
away. It had moved in to stay, entwining with healthy
nerves and tissue until removal of the tumor would
require removal of most of what was Poppy. The
doctors had no opinions as to how long the stressful
regime of radiochemicals and toxins could go on; it
would be years before the body's systems finally
broke down—before one-hundred-and-three-year-old
blood vessels refused to tolerate the chemicals that
seared them clear every week. When that finally
happened . . .

Sulu reached for his great-grandfather's hand as
they sailed beneath the gently graying sky, trying to
imagine those once-strong hands crippled and useless.
Without meaning to, he tightened his grip protectively.

"Worried about tomorrow?"

Sulu craned his neck up out of the water to see his
great-grandfather studying him across the gathering
dusk, and noticed his hold on the older man's hand
for the first time. He didn't let go. "A little, I guess,"
he admitted, glad that Tetsuo missed the actual course
of his thoughts. "Command school isn't like the

Academy. They won't let me just be good at what I do—there, I'll have to be good at what everyone *else* does, too! That's kind of the point of being a captain, I guess . . ." His voice trailed away into a sigh. "I don't want to do anything wrong."

Tetsuo made a small noise that Sulu took to signify his displeasure. "How asinine!"

"It's not asinine!" Sulu's cheeks stung as much as his pride. "It's a very serious thing! There's never more than a thousand people in command school at any one time, and they're very picky about who they let stay!"

"And you think they won't let you?"

Sulu paused in his swimming. "I don't know . . . I guess so . . ."

Tetsuo shifted toward the front of the little windsailor. "Listen . . ." he instructed. "Did I ever talk to you about cranes?"

"This is *command school—*" Sulu pitched his voice as a complaint, even though he smiled. "—not a construction company!"

Tetsuo laughed, splashing his great-grandson with a generous handful of water. "I'm talking about birds, not machinery!"

"You showed them to me at the zoo." Sulu returned to his swimming, angling his body to talk as he moved. "They all stood on one leg and stared at us. I bounced peanuts off their heads, and the zoo attendant made us leave."

"You were a terrible child," Tetsuo conceded.

"And you folded me a thousand of them out of the napkins from my seventeenth birthday party." Sulu smiled at the memory. "At least, you *told* me they were cranes—*I* thought they looked like ducks!"

"Those *are* ducks," Tetsuo allowed dryly. "Whoever invented origami just thought cranes would sound more distinguished. You know why I folded you all those cranes?"

"You thought I liked birds?"

"No," Tetsuo told him. "It's because of a Japanese legend."

Sulu rolled his eyes in mock disbelief. "Uh, oh— more Japanese philosophy!" It was a private joke between Sulu and the old man; like Sulu, Tetsuo was born of immigrants, grown old in California without ever having seen the Oriental sun.

"Will you listen to me?" the old man complained. "I was just going to tell you that the old Japanese believed if you folded one thousand origami cranes— preferably while meditating—you could make a miracle happen."

"Did you?"

Tetsuo shrugged. "You got into the Academy, didn't you?"

Sulu made a face, admitting that he'd walked straight into Poppy's verbal trap. "So what has this got to do with me and command school? Did you fold more cranes to make sure I wouldn't flunk out?"

"I didn't think of it. I was actually going to talk to you about *real* cranes, not paper ones."

"Okay," Sulu allowed. "I'm listening."

"Do you know why they all stand on one leg?" Tetsuo asked him.

Sulu shook his head. Then, realizing Tetsuo no

doubt lost the motion in the waves, he added, "No, Poppy. Why?"

"Because they're clumsy as hell," the old man replied. "Nature really blew it when it came to giving cranes virtues beyond their good looks, so whenever the birds put both legs on the ground, they trip over themselves."

Sulu burst into laughter. "I thought you were going to tell me about *biology!*"

"I *am* telling you about biology! Don't you think Nature is part of biology?"

"Are you *sure* I'm not being exposed to Japanese philosophy?" Sulu asked, trying to contain his mirth.

"I don't know any Japanese philosophy," Tetsuo snorted. "Are you going to be quiet and listen?"

"Does this have something to do with why origami cranes look like ducks?" Sulu asked.

"I said be quiet."

Sulu slapped a pleasant, schooled expression on his features. "Okay."

Apparently satisfied, Tetsuo settled back against the mast and went on. "In the hopes of fixing things up, Nature went through and gifted some cranes with the grace she left out of the others. Even the cranes don't know which ones—they can only find out by *trying.*" Purple shadows played across his face as he angled his head to look down at Sulu. "Every crane has to have the courage to put both feet on the ground," he said seriously. "Take a few steps—find out the hard way if you can dance. A dancing crane is a very beautiful thing to see, but it's hell for the cranes that fail, because they have to look at the cranes all dancing and know what they might have been."

Sulu didn't comment. Gulls cursed angrily above them, and, from not so far away, Sulu thought he heard the whooping of a lonely white crane.

"We're just like the cranes, you and me," Tetsuo said finally, softly. "While everybody else is worrying about how to balance on that one safe leg, you and me are out seeing how far the other one will stretch. Even if you fall, you've got to remember that everybody really has two legs after all—even if you stumble, you can always get back up again."

Sulu listened for the crane again, but heard nothing now except the gulls and the sleepy sea. "Does this mean you don't think I should worry about command school?"

Tetsuo smiled down at him. "It means I don't think you should worry about command school. You'll do fine."

He grinned in return and kicked a small spray of water over the prow of the sailor. "And *you* said you didn't know any philosophy!"

Tetsuo shrugged and splashed water back at him. "I don't. I read that in a book a long, long time ago . . ."

Returning the rented windsailor took longer than the commuter shuttle back from L.A.—by the time they reached Oakland, Sulu and Poppy were both still damp from their excursion. Leaving his great-grandfather in the foyer to discard his sandy shirt and footwear, Sulu kicked off his own shoes while padding into the kitchen to turn on the lights.

A piteous howling erupted in answer to Sulu's touch on the light panel; the young cadet cursed shortly and shouted at the plant across the kitchen from him: "Shut up, Filbert!"

Long, fuzzy green tendrils snaked back across the countertop to curl about the meter-long pot as if they'd never strayed. Filbert emitted another wail of despair, and Sulu was forced to cross the kitchen in two hurried strides and clap a hand over the plant's flattened central trunk. Filbert whimpered and fell silent.

"Has nobody fed you today?" Sulu asked, feeling immediately sorry for his harsh tone when the plant gently entwined his hand.

Tetsuo snorted as he shambled into the kitchen and found himself a seat. "It can't answer you," he advised sagely. "And it'll eat your hand if you stand there much longer!"

Sulu disengaged his hand with little effort. "You also said my iguana would eat Mom's parrot."

"Didn't it?"

"The parrot ate the *iguana,* Poppy!" Sulu ducked back into the pantry in search of one of Filbert's mice, but only found dried earthworm left over from his attempt to keep a carnivorous Rosserian ivy. "The Tellurian greencat ate the parrot," he continued upon returning. "That's why I gave it to George Temmu. Remember?"

Tetsuo waved off the details as unimportant. "Did it eat his mother's parrot?"

Sulu dumped a handful of earthworm down Filbert's open throat. "She didn't have a parrot."

"Smart woman."

Sulu dug into the container for another serving of worms, and nearly spilled it all over the floor when the viewer next to him chirped. Jerking his head up in surprise, he called, "Yes?" before even considering whether or not he wanted to answer.

Whatever greetings he normally uttered leapt from his mind the instant he met Arthur Kobrine's stern and stormlike gaze over the viewer. "Where the hell have you two been?"

Kobrine's harsh attitude caught Sulu completely unprepared. He glanced at Poppy, found no help there, and just shrugged stupidly. "Sailing," he said, feeding Filbert again. "Why?"

"How are you doing, Doctor Kobrine?" Poppy called from the kitchen table.

Kobrine shot a glance in that direction, but Sulu knew the angle of the viewer would keep him from seeing Poppy or the table. Sulu pushed Filbert to the back of the counter and stepped forward to turn the viewer slightly. "They've been waiting for you in radiochem since this morning," the neurosurgeon informed Tetsuo with ice in his tone. "They wanted me to send an orderly out for you."

"I'm not a child," Tetsuo told him, with perhaps more force than Sulu thought necessary. The old man's hand found a paper napkin in the table's centerpiece, ripping it into tiny squares without apparent thought. "My great-grandson here's almost a starship pilot—we don't need you chasing around after us as if we were children."

"Then act like an adult!" Kobrine shouted at him. "Act like you understand the responsibility you have, and stop dragging your great-grandson along as if he can keep you from getting in trouble!"

Sulu felt fear's left-handed cousin start to stir inside

his chest, and he pushed in front of the viewphone hastily. "Doctor Kobrine, we were just sailing!" he began, but Kobrine silenced him.

"Ask your great-grandfather why he wasn't at the hospital today."

Sulu blinked at Kobrine, then looked over his shoulder at Tetsuo only to be confused by the old man's reluctance to meet his eyes. "What?"

"Your great-grandfather skipped his therapy," Kobrine clarified. His voice was tight with anger and whatever emotion provoked parental lectures on "disappointment" and "duty." "If radiochem had hounded me—*me,* of all people!—one more time about how important these therapy sessions were, I'd have killed someone!"

"Poppy . . . ?"

The old man reluctantly looked up from the crane he was patiently folding.

"Is that right?" Sulu pressed. "You skipped your therapy?"

Tetsuo made a face and shrugged an indefinite reply as his attention returned to folding. "What are you, Art?" he asked of the neurosurgeon on the screen. "A private detective now, too?"

"I'm a doctor!" he exploded. "I'm supposed to make sure you do what's best for your health! Mister Inomata, I'm supposed to take care of you!"

"What if I don't want to be taken care of?"

Sulu crossed the kitchen to sit in the chair next to Poppy. "Why?" he asked, frightened. "Did you forget?"

"I didn't forget." He seemed offended by the suggestion. He flicked the limp paper crane across the table; it skittered over the edge and out of sight. "It makes me sick," he admitted. "It makes me feel all sunburned, and I figured I'd be getting enough sun as it was." Casting an angry look at Kobrine across the kitchen, he complained, "Being a day late can't make that much difference when you're my age!"

"But after the treatments, you feel better for the rest of the week, don't you?" Kobrine insisted.

When Tetsuo didn't respond immediately, Sulu pressed, "Don't you?"

The old man sighed and started on another square of paper. "For two, maybe three days at the end. Before then my head hurts, and my skin hurts, and sometimes I can barely stand. I go to the bathroom all the time . . ." He paused in his folding, running a hand through Sulu's close-cropped black hair with a smile that nearly made the young man cry. "I wanted to go windsailing with you today! You're going to be gone to command school tomorrow, and I might not get to see you . . ." He swallowed whatever he'd intended to say. "It'll be a long time," he finished. "I didn't want to be throwing up the whole time we were together!"

"It's only across the Bay," Sulu scolded gently. "I'll visit—"

"When they let you!"

Sulu smiled and tousled Tetsuo's thinning hair in kind. "This is Starfleet, Poppy, not jail!"

"I just wanted to go with you," Tetsuo said again.

"Well, you're coming in here now. I'm sending a volunteer to get you." Kobrine gestured at someone off-screen; the doctor's expression made Sulu suddenly want to remind him that Tetsuo was old, not stupid.

He exchanged long-suffering looks with Tetsuo instead, and accepted the half-completed crane his great-grandfather passed him.

"I could bring him in," Sulu volunteered.

Kobrine scowled and shook his head. "Your great-grandfather says you're leaving tomorrow. I don't want to disrupt your schedule any more than it already has been." He seemed to notice Tetsuo's half-clad state for the first time, and added, "Take your great-grandfather upstairs and get him dressed. Someone will be there in about fifteen minutes."

"I'll bet he was a brat when he was little, too," Tetsuo intimated when he and Sulu were halfway up the stairs.

Sulu smothered his laughter, and hugged Tetsuo soundly. "They'll assign me soon," he promised, wishing tomorrow wasn't hurrying upon them so fast. "It'll be on one of the big starships, Poppy, you'll see! . . . I want you to be there when it happens! I want you with me when I go!"

Tetsuo held onto Sulu longer than the young man expected. "I love you," he whispered warmly in Sulu's ear. "And I'll always be with you . . . always!"

When he finally broke the hug, Sulu saw that they had crushed the little half-finished crane.

Sulu pressed back into his aircar seat as the Pacific Ocean caught a great sheet of sunlight and threw it up at the aircar. He squinted his eyes shut against the light, marveling at the people milling about the landing field below him.

Out of the whole galaxy—billions of people!—only a thousand of us are here! The thought made Sulu's stomach crawl up into his windpipe again, and he looked back at the command school landing pad in the hopes that studying the ground would smother some of the panic he felt building inside.

The aircar ahead of them was a commercial transit; no one held up the six cadets who exited with long and tearful goodbyes. Sulu's little aircar landed without having to wait for a window.

"Well, this is it . . ." Sulu's hand was cold and trembling when he closed it on the handle of his carryall. His door was open, his right foot touching the warm landing pad; he missed home already, and was irrationally afraid he might never see his family again. Especially Tetsuo. He knew the old man wanted to drop him off today, but the treatments made him so ill, and Sulu didn't feel he had the right to bring him.

"Excuse me, sir," a polite, computer voice interrupted his thoughts. "We are delaying on a private-access pad."

Embarrassment stung his cheeks momentarily. "Sorry," he murmured, feeling stupid. "Thank you. I'm out." The door closed without a sound, and the aircar climbed into the sunny, salty-smelling air, leaving Sulu alone.

It was a good morning. Sulu tried to distract himself with that knowledge as he headed for the main building, turning his back on the aircar now landing. It was already warm, and uncharacteristically clear for late-summer San Francisco. A hood of mist along the crest of Mount Tam blushed pinkly in the early morning sun, and the Golden Gate Bridge swept across the Bay like a daring ballerina. The bridge's delicate silhouette reminded Sulu of Poppy's dancing cranes. Thinking of his great-grandfather somehow cheered him and hurt him at the same time; he didn't want to leave him behind, but didn't want to be a peg-legged swamp crane either. Grasping for some distant rapport with Tetsuo, Sulu tucked one foot behind the other, hoping to unobtrusively test Poppy's theory of one-footed confidence before leaving these wide open spaces.

He swayed ever so slightly, and bumped into someone behind him.

"Hey! What are you, a no-zee who doesn't know how to walk?"

Sulu botched regaining his footing, and stumbled another few steps before completing his turn. The woman with whom he collided pushed him upright, and demanded acerbically, "Let me guess—you don't speak English either?"

Sulu thought that must be a joke, her own accent was so pronounced. He smiled and extended a hand. "Ah, no—I mean, no, I don't not speak English. My name's Sulu."

She furrowed her brow distrustfully, but accepted his handshake. "You just don't speak English well?"

Sulu fell into step beside her to join the migration toward the main building. "I'm from right around here, actually—I was born in San Francisco!" When she volunteered no reply, he prompted, "I don't think I caught your name . . ."

"Maria Theresa Perez-Salazar," she admitted after a considered pause. Her gold-brown hair was pulled so severely toward the crown of her skull, Sulu found it somewhat amazing she could draw her face down into the expression of displeasure it now wore. He opted not to comment on that, but thought he'd have to watch her to see if her demeanor ever changed. "My friends call me Maté."

Sulu also decided she didn't necessarily consider him among that privileged circle. "I take it you're *not* from around here?"

Perez-Salazar tilted her chin infinitesimally higher, but her expression was etched in titanium. "I'm from Mexico City—I attended the Academy in Tempe."

"You speak English very well."

He'd hoped it would be a compliment—since she seemed as preoccupied with proper English as a high school teacher—but Perez-Salazar only snapped him a cold, lizardine look and reproved, "Of course! Mexico is a very civilized state!"

When she lengthened her stride to outdistance him, Sulu didn't try to keep pace. "Starfleet's finest," he muttered toward her back. "Wow . . ."

He managed to cultivate two more successful conversations in the line leading into the main building, one with an Australian who'd lived on Earth for his entire life. Another with a Human who'd never been to Earth before. It was an interesting comparison of cultures and intellect. He and the Australian were exchanging opinions on the West Coast's best windsailing spots when Sulu's turn at the admission's station came up. The lieutenant on duty had to hail him three times before he realized she was speaking to him.

He swung about guiltily. "I'm sorry, sir—I was talking."

The small lieutenant smiled and pushed a square of

coded tape across the counter at him. "I noticed. Here—you'll need this to find your bag once you get to the billets."

"I thought a computer would be doing this," Sulu admitted as he hefted his carryall onto the counter.

"You'll see enough machines the rest of the time you're here," the lieutenant assured him. "We try to keep things as personal and low-key as we can the first day." The bag disappeared behind the counter. "Around me and to your left, Cadet. You'll be issued your uniform and an agenda for the day. Good luck!"

For the next three hours, Sulu barely had time to blurt out thanks for the instructions and orders he was given, much less converse with the other cadets. He lost the Australian shortly after relinquishing his bag, but Maté Perez-Salazar seemed to cling to his peripheral vision like a berm-runner on an illegal hyperjump. Once he'd changed, logged in, been issued a counselor, a billet number, a class schedule, a bloc, carried about and delivered numerous medical records on himself, identified himself for more computer systems than he'd ever have dreamed, and tried to explain to an indifferent liaison officer that he wasn't Das Res-Pamudan from Isrando-on-Sheshwar, he was pushed down a long, windowless hall and told to "go straight, then left, then left, wait in Sunside until a monitor comes—*Next!*" It was a long, perplexing walk, indeed.

He was perhaps two-thirds of the way to Sunside—studiously mirroring the route indicated on his handsize datex screen—before he considered that anywhere called "Sunside" was perhaps not a preferable place to be. All his imagination could conjure was lurid, molten still shots of Mercury's daylight half; he wondered why anyone would go there, much less name a meeting room after the place. A punishment cubicle, perhaps? *"Here at Starfleet's command school, we believe no raw potential should go undeveloped. For example, impressive disciplinary results can be obtained through the use of pain."*

Sulu grinned, and rounded the last corner before Sunside's entrance. Nearly thirty cadets looked up at his entrance, but no one volunteered a greeting until Sulu released his own grin and waved. "Hi."

"We're taking a poll," called an extremely long-legged youth from the back of the room.

Sulu laughed. "Can I defer my response for an hour?"

"They may kill us before then," someone else suggested. Another replied, "I think that's why he asked."

The conversation spread to another dozen cadets, and several inventive ideas were voiced as to the name's true meaning. Another twenty cadets joined them over the next forty minutes, Perez-Salazar among them, and Sulu was still trying to explain the gist of the guessing game when a small, trim commodore interrupted the discussion.

Her mere entrance proved enough to bring the room to its feet. After accepting a moment of the entire bloc at rigid attention, she called them at ease and sat herself on the edge of a table.

"Well, that was impressive!" Her dark, Mediterranean eyes were quick, and as calm as a midnight sky.

Sulu liked her instantly. "I'm Commodore Rachel Coan, and I'll be your bloc commandant while you're here at the Command School. You are Cadet Bloc W. You're here today because I, personally, wanted to make sure you all understood *why* you're in command school." She nudged a cadet near her with one foot. "How about you? Why are you here?"

She answered without hesitation, "Because I want to command a starship someday."

Coan nodded, turning to the rest of the room. "You—" She singled out another from the rear. "What about you?"

"My parents made me."

Amusement stirred through the bloc at that. "All right . . . That's honest, at least." Then Coan's eyes caught on Sulu's. "And you?"

His mind became a hissing white void. Despite that, he heard his voice say, "To see if I can."

Coan nodded, but didn't comment on his answer. "Okay," she said, standing. "You seem to be an honest bunch. That's good—I like honesty. I expect it. Okay?" Half the gathering expressed confusion, the other half nodded. Coan crossed the room, gesturing as she spoke for various cadets to relocate themselves.

"Right now, we're going to perform the first of many scenarios you'll be forced to endure during your time here. This one's called Galactic Politics!" Groans answered her announcement, and Coan's grin grew wider. "Get used to it," she cautioned. "It's the second oldest profession in the cosmos."

Everyone laughed.

"Now," Coan continued, "when I give the word, each of you is to check your computer to find out which planetary system you represent. Someone will be Earth, someone else Vulcan, someone else Klingon, or Andorian, or Altarian, et cetera, et cetera." A handful of cadets stood to help her drag a table toward the center of the room. "The Klingon and the Romulan empires will sit at this table with the Federation." She pulled a random collection of chairs into a wandering circle farther out from the table. "The Federated planets will sit here. Since the Federation and the Empires control most of the galaxy's resources, those people will get to make decisions regarding the disposition of those resources. The rest of the Federation can help, of course, *but . . ."* And here her eyes glinted with playful malice. "The Federation and the Empires can talk at will. To each other, to anyone else they want to. The Federated planets can talk at will among themselves, and to anyone not seated at the table. *However,* they can't interrupt the three main powers at the table, and they can't take any action without the consent of the leading three."

She retrieved another chair and placed it far away, against a distant corner. "The Vulcans," she went on, "who are frequently viewed as having the answer to most of the galaxy's problems—" This was greeted with mild amusement. "—sit here. They can only interfere with galactic politics once every half hour, but have a wide range of possible activities. Each time another planet requests aid from them, however, their half-hour wait starts anew."

"This sounds pretty complicated," someone ventured, and Coan stretched her hands out to either side in a helpless shrug.

"Real life politics isn't like playing jacks," she explained. "All I'm trying to do is simulate some of the restrictions and tensions existing in the real life arena. You'll find details specific to your own situation in your computer. I'll be here to answer questions. Just stick with me, okay?"

No one said anything. Moving back toward her original seat, Coan nodded. "Everybody check their computer now to get your assignments, objectives, and limitations. This simulation will continue for two hours, or until somebody accomplishes something." She flashed them a sudden, delighted smile. "Let the games begin."

Others about the room were already chuckling or moaning about their assignments by the time Sulu thumbed his retrieval button. The little computer screen flashed a series of code, and a column of print started its slow bottom-to-top scroll.

MENAK III

TECH LEVEL: Three.

Sulu pursed his lips pensively. Tech level three meant no subspace radio capabilities, and no warp drive—rudimentary hyperdrive at best. He hoped his objectives didn't involve any long-distance negotiations or travel.

FEDERATION MEMBERSHIP: Menak is not eligible, due to her current political climate.

AFFILIATIONS: Long-standing trade relations with Carstair's Planet.

Carstair's—a frontier world inhabited by four species' bail jumpers and troublemakers. Sulu sighed.

HISTORY: Mineral-poor Menak III depends heavily on Carstair's for raw materials, interplanetary and interstellar relations with wealthier societies, and infusion of medical and food production technology. Menak III is approaching the end of its second industrial revolution; sweeping political reorganization and economic upheavals are the results. The current parliamentary government is threatened by a separatist religious faction which believes a return to "simpler times" would be in Menak III's best interests. Menak III's political leaders do not agree.

RULES OF PLAY: You can only communicate with the Federation through Carstair's Planet . . .

Sulu looked up from his computer to scan the room. A dozen other cadets craned looks left and right, as though trying to identify their allies by facial feature alone. Sulu noted that two of the table's three inhabitants were in place. Perez-Salazar sat at one end; Sulu felt some sympathy for whomever Fate chose to share that galaxy with her for the next two hours.

"Who's Carstair's Planet?" he called congenially, turning back to his own affairs.

On the floor across the room, sitting with his back

against the wall, a dark-skinned Maori jerked his head up in ill-humored surprise. Glittering black eyes darted left and right. "Who asks?"

Sulu attempted his most disarming grin, and waved. "I'm Menak III." Settling back into his seat, he continued with his reading.

. . . You can only communicate with the Federation through Carstair's Planet; you may communicate with any non-Federated planet you choose. Since you lack subspace radio capabilities, all communications must be made via old-style radio waves. To simulate this, you may only contact other planets by written notes, passed from you to whomever you are contacting. You may not leave your seat.

OBJECTIVES: The Federation has the resources to alleviate many of Menak III's economic and health problems. All you want is a chance to speak, one-on-one, to a Federation representative.

Sulu nodded. Looking about, he saw a table near the main door, apparently stocked with props for their scenario: a painted scepter, assorted colored and numbered tokens, writing implements and a great deal of paper, the mother board from some electronic device (the Carstair's Planet Maori cadet took this), and a wheel. Sulu abandoned his seat to collect some paper and a pen, then settled in only a few chairs away from Carstair's—to facilitate communications. After a single nervous, unhappy glare, the cadet ignored him.

Sulu tucked his feet up under himself on the chair, until he was firmly seated, tailor-fashion. Licking the point of his pen with a flourish (and then deciding not to do that anymore), he composed his first communiqué:

Carstair's—Everybody's dying here, we aren't having a terrible lot of fun economically, and we understand you have some pull with the Federation Council; I'd desperately love a visit from a Federation representative. Any help at all would be appreciated.

Love,
Menak III

He smiled, resisted the temptation to line the bottom of the note with "hugs-n-kisses" *X*'s and *O*'s, folded it into a neat little square, and turned to the young woman next to him. "Would you hand this down to the planet on the end, please?"

Before she could reply, Coan interposed herself between them and plucked the note from Sulu's hand. "Foul, Menak," she informed him, grinning. "You can't talk to a neighboring planet—you've got to write."

Sulu took the note back from her, annoyed. "You mean I have to write her a note just to ask her to pass *this* note?" That struck him as ridiculously restrictive.

Coan only nodded. "That's what I mean. Try again."

Sulu's second note was short and to the point—
"Help! I'm being held prisoner in a complex Starfleet scenario! Please pass this note to Carstair's Planet (the social butterfly to your right) before it's too late!"—and the 'transmission' to Carstair's was quickly on its way.

Carstair's gawked at the note, stared in almost-horror at the cadet who'd last touched it, and finally directed a black-eyed glare down the length of chairs at Sulu.

Sulu waved again, and smiled. This was going to be a long game.

"I'll bet you've got quite a wait ahead of you."

Sulu craned a look over his shoulder, finding Coan still standing nearby, watching Carstair's. "Carstair's can't approach the Federation Council without at least one Federated planet to support him. That's not always easy under normal circumstances—Narv's lack of social graces isn't going to work in your favor."

Sulu sighed and glanced back at the cadet. Narv was already kneeling near one of the outlying Federation chairs, talking, quietly but gruffly, with the inhabitant. "What am I supposed to do in the meantime?" he asked Coan. "My planet's got a lot of problems!"

Coan leaned over to tap Sulu's pad of paper. "Sketch something. You can sell the art to other planets and upgrade your economy."

Sulu perked up at the suggestion. "Is that allowed in this scenario?"

Coan's laugh was cheerful, but not reassuring. "No. But you might be able to buy yourself lunch with the proceeds."

"What about paper airplanes?" Sulu twisted in his

seat to follow her progress as Coan started to move away.

"No!"

He flopped back into his seat with a sigh; he'd expected as much.

Seven minutes—and ten elaborate paper airplanes —later, Carstair's and Rigel V made their way up to the main Council table. Sulu sailed his last airplane in the general vicinity of an equally bored cadet (who'd been returning fire with clever, chittering paper constructions that reminded Sulu of kamikaze crickets), and settled in to observe Carstair's plea on his behalf.

Rigel and Carstair's waited another full minute before the Federation delegate finally turned to them and demanded, "What do you want? Can't you see we're trying to agree on negotiation formats?"

The cadet snorted noisily and thrust a piece of paper up at the Federation cadet's face. "A list of demands," he growled. "For my people."

"Who are you?" The Federation glanced at the list, then deposited it atop the table between himself and the two Empires. Perez-Salazar plucked it up and studied it in silence.

"Carstair's Planet," Rigel V volunteered. Then, flashing the Federation a ridiculously wide and stunning smile: "I'm Rigel V—already a member in good standing with the Federation."

"Great." The Federation's enthusiasm seemed limited. "We'll consider your requests and get back to you."

"All services are sorely needed," the Carstair's insisted when the Federation would have turned away. "I insist upon immediate attention!"

Perez-Salazar uttered something brief and sibilant. "These requests are ludicrous!" she exclaimed, pitching the paper back at Narv. The rumpled sheet caught the air and fluttered erratically off to one side. "You want missile technology, computer assistance, access to our data centers . . . !"

"The *Federation's* data centers," the Federation reminded her firmly. "They aren't asking for *anything* from the Klingons!"

Perez-Salazar twisted her mouth and narrowed her eyes. "Racism again? You don't feel the Klingon Empire has anything to offer?"

Sulu covered his smile with one hand. Perez-Salazar was the Klingons—he should have guessed.

"Nothing that *we* can't offer more safely!" The Federation handed Narv back his note. "Go sit down. We'll get to you."

"I ask little," Carstair's insisted. When the Federation didn't answer, the cadet turned to face Vulcan on the opposite side of the room. "If I cannot appeal to your less compassionate neighbors, then I appeal to you, logicians, for recognition."

The three at the main table uttered simultaneous inarticulate cries while Vulcan looked to Coan for direction. The monitor shrugged mutely.

"You *idiot!*" the Romulan Empire howled.

"Hey!" Coan barked. "There'll be none of that around here! This is just a game!"

The Romulan Empire wilted noticeably, weaving her hands into angry baskets in front of her. "Sorry, sir . . ."

Coan was still frowning as she nodded to Vulcan. "Start timing your half hour again."

"Aye, sir."

And that ended Carstair's first round of negotiations.

Sulu made sure a note was waiting for the Carstair's by the time he returned to his seat.

What happened to my requests? Fifty million more people have died around here! Don't I need food more than you need missiles?

Narv's lips moved through the message slowly. Once finished, he scrawled a brief reply across the bottom, crushed the paper into a ball, and threw it back at Sulu. Sulu untangled the note to read what he already suspected it said: *"NO."* He flicked the ball away from him, and started on his notes again.

Hi! I'm Menak III, a small, insignificant, and technologically underdeveloped planet in the Murasaki sector. Carstair's Planet is ignoring me, and I'm bored. Wanna start a war?

He folded the note into his most careful aircraft yet, and sailed it across the room into Orion's lap with the delicate precision only a born helmsman could command.

Orion's automatic reply was a chittering cricket. Sulu quickly folded a second plane, scribbling across the wings, *"Read the first airplane!"* and bounced the second plane against Orion's chest. Orion blinked twice, raised his eyebrows, then set about trying to locate the message plane among all the others. He found it, dismantled it, and read it. The reply arrived in Sulu's lap less than a minute after Sulu's secondary launch.

Sulu unfolded the plane and scanned the answer.

Sorry—Orion is officially hostile toward Menak III. If I get into ANY kind of war, it'll probably be with YOU! Better luck next time.

Orion II

A chittering cricket—bearing the proclamation, *"I am a primitive thermonuclear device. Ka-BLAM!"*— quickly followed up the note. Orion returned Sulu's startled look with an apologetic shrug, but didn't retract the mock bombing. Sulu dismissed him further, and Orion went back to folding his toys.

Carefully tearing off the bottom part of the page, Sulu eliminated Orion's negative response. Somewhat more tattered, but still flightworthy, the airplane looked like the only survivor of Orion's last message. He aimed it at random, hoping chance would help him find a sympathetic government on his own side of the room. The plane bounced into the lap of a stocky, redheaded female four seats away. Picking it up, she asked, "What's this?"

Sulu captured her attention with a friendly wave. "It's an old-style wave radio transmission—I'm reaching out to my fellow man."

She smiled, but sailed the plane back at him. "I'm tech level two—I don't have the capabilities to receive an interplanetary transmission. Sorry."

Sulu plucked the craft out of the air with one hand. Frustrated, he turned to the room at large and called,

"Is there anybody with a tech level four or better who isn't hostile to Menak III and wants to start a war?"

Even as the room burst into laughter, Coan called, "Foul, Menak!" from the other end of the room.

"But—!"

"Foul!" Coan was smiling, but didn't relent. "You have to pass notes, or you can't communicate at all."

Sulu fingered the nose of his aircraft unhappily, slouching into an exaggerated pout for Coan's benefit. "Do I even have to send notes to you?"

Coan snorted briefly with laughter. "You can't send notes to me."

"Why? Who are you?"

"I'm God. Now hush!"

Sulu had delivered his war offer to half the participants on his side of the room by the time Carstair's gained the Federation's attention for a second time. "We're considering!" the Federation irritably assured Narv before he could even speak.

"These are matters of much importance." Narv's tone of voice could have indicated anything from fury to pleasant neutrality.

The Federation collected Carstair's note, but didn't read it. "More missiles?" he inquired acerbically. Rigel V winced. Beyond him, a line of fidgeting delegates stretched nearly into Vulcan's lap.

"Consideration of Carstair's application," Narv persisted. "We wish to be as Rigel—Federated into your ruling body."

"Starfleet doesn't rule," the Federation began, and Perez-Salazar amended hotly, "Tell *that* to the Romulans!"

"Hey!" The Romulan Empire leaned across the table in front of Earth to scowl at Perez-Salazar. "The Federation *does not* have us henpecked!"

"I never said they did!"

And so ended Carstair's second approach to the Federation Council.

Sulu tore free a sheet of paper and began methodically shredding it into a pile at his feet. According to his time piece, he had approximately another hour and twenty-five minutes to kill before this scenario reached its less-than-climactic climax. He resolved to make a pile as high as his seat before that time.

"You're wasting your national resources." Coan appeared at his shoulder, still wearing that infuriating know-it-all smile. "You've got nearly eighty-five minutes yet, Ensign!"

"My stock market crashed," Sulu replied. He tried to keep annoyance out of his tone, but failed miserably. Shifting to face Coan, he hooked one foot over the chair's arm and propped his elbow atop the back. "It's pointless! I'm in a position where I can't do anything for myself, I'm paired with an antisocial Federation hopeful who isn't a great deal of help, and those three at the main table are still trying to decide what kind of china to use at their formals!"

When his comments only seemed to amuse Coan the more, he turned away from her again, grumbling, "And my cadet bloc monitor is a closet sadist that somebody gifted with commodore's bars."

Her hand took hold of his shoulder in warning. "Careful . . ."

Sulu felt his face grow red. "Excuse me, sir."

Once Coan was gone, he reevaluated what he'd said

to her. He didn't really want to quit—he didn't want to be a one-legged swamp crane who never learned to dance. What would Poppy say after spending all that time explaining about the silly dancing birds? Sulu smiled and glanced at the Federation Council on the other side of the room. Well, if the mountain wouldn't come to Mohammed . . .

He attracted Coan's attention by bouncing an origami crane off her shoulder. Expressing more irritation than he suspected she actually felt, she stepped through the assembly to squat by the arm of his chair.

"I want to go to the Federation myself." Before she could condemn or verify his plan, he elaborated, "I know I've only got the wave-radio capabilities, and I know they wouldn't be expecting my call. And I know it would take—" He tipped his eyes unconsciously ceilingward as he figured. "—nearly eighteen months for the call to reach them."

Coan grinned at him. "And you've only got eighty-five minutes to go."

"This is a scenario," Sulu pointed out. "Can't we compact time a little?"

Still grinning, Coan reached behind his chair and came up with one of his many paper constructions. "You seemed to be doing pretty well with these earlier." Sulu shrugged, and Coan went on: "If you can land a message on the main table, or even in the lap of a Federated planet, anyone who reads it can act for you. Just because they rely on subspace communication doesn't mean they can't hear what you send." She unfolded Sulu's paper plane as she stood, dropping it into his lap. "What if they won't read it, or they ignore you?"

Sulu shrugged, flattening the piece of paper. "Then I'm no worse off than I am right now."

She studied Sulu so intently it made him shift uncomfortably in his seat. "Only seventy-five minutes and eighteen months to go," she said finally, breaking her gaze. "You'd better start writing!" And, with an approving smile, she moved away.

Sulu considered his note carefully, knowing if he was to have any hope at all of Federation intervention it would be dependent on how effectively he could convey his plight in writing. He discarded Coan's unfolded plane in favor of a clean sheet of paper.

Dear Delegates of the Renowned and Honest Federation Council

He hated it immediately. Too wordy, too insincere. Scribbling out that line, he began anew, more thoughtfully.

Dear Champions of Freedom

"Yuck."

He scratched out his second attempt, and finally settled on a neutral, unimpressive:

Dear Members of the United Federation:

I send you this communiqué on behalf of the citizens of Menak III. Although not members of the Federation, we respect and appreciate the good your kind emissaries do throughout the galaxy. We appeal to you now for your aid.

Menak is being crushed beneath the weight of economic and health turmoils beyond our ability to control. We are mineral poor. We are neglected. We are dying. Please—all we request is the opportunity to speak with you regarding help for our people. You have knowledge of medicines, and safe power sources; without your assistance, we fear Menak will have no future at all.

Please.

> *The Governing Body*
> *of Menak III*

Satisfaction displaced the frustration of only a moment ago. Sulu tucked the rest of his papers into a pocket, and considered the best delivery method for his note. Paper wads were out, since they were too easily mistaken for a personal affront; origami cranes were more dense than airplanes (and so traveled better over short distances), but they had a tendency to tumble while airborne, so didn't frequently exercise much accuracy in attaining their targets; airplanes ran the risk of overshooting, and (for reasons Sulu failed to comprehend) it seemed no one ever thought to unfold the planes to find their message. Still, airplanes seemed the best of the three alternatives, and seventy minutes really wasn't enough time to get creative. He hummed to himself as he folded the plane.

The resultant vessel was hardly a work of art, but Sulu was confident it would traverse the distance necessary to deliver his plea to the Federation Council. He caught Coan's eye as he inspected the lines of his aircraft, and returned her conspiratorial wink with a somewhat embarrassed smile.

No wind disturbed the air in the spacious room, so Sulu knew nothing but satisfaction as he watched his courier float cleanly over the heads of half his classmates and dip sweetly to a landing over the Romulan Empire's right shoulder. Perez-Salazar was the only member at the table to even notice the landing; she made a face at the paper construct, then pushed it out of their work area.

Sulu was folding another plane before Perez-Salazar had even rejoined the heated discussion; he should have learned from his exchange with Orion. Scrawling a repeat of his "READ THE FIRST AIRPLANE" message, he tossed the second plane toward the main table.

This time, Perez-Salazar snatched the plane while it was still airborne, crushing it in her fist. She fixed Sulu with a disapproving glare as she tossed it to join the first plane. In an agony of frustration, the ensign called, "Read it!" only to be drowned out by Coan's stern, "Foul, Menak!"

"Of course . . . !" he grumbled, slouching low in his chair.

If this were indicative of galactic politics, Sulu was sufficiently convinced that he didn't want to be a councilor. He tore a sheet of paper into six rough squares, sullenly folding a crane from the first as he listened to the Klingon and Romulan empires argue about voting rights.

In the smallest handwriting he could manage and still be legible, Sulu started at the nose of the crane and wrote: THIS CRANE WILL SELF-DESTRUCT IN 5

SECONDS. Then he decorated the crimped wings with: . . . 4 . . . 3 . . . 2 . . . 1 . . . He was disappointed that there was no room left to write *BOOM!*

Widening the tiny hole in the bottom of the crane, he inserted the tip of his pen to launch it. He stopped himself just before sending the crane on its way. Terrorism wasn't the answer—not if he really wanted to establish some rapport with the Federated planets. He removed the little crane reluctantly, and set about writing another impassioned plea.

This note he folded as a crane (sufficiently discouraged with the responses to his airplanes). He mounted it on his pen like the first, then snapped it catapult-style toward the main table. The crane careened over the Romulan Empire's head, into the center of the table, and over the Federation's right shoulder. The Federation delegate growled something short and foul as he stooped for the paper bird; Sulu wondered if he were the only one to notice where the crane landed when the Federation tossed it offhandedly away.

Vulcan started quite satisfactorily as the crane bounced into her lap, staring at the origami avian as though uncertain if she should touch it. "Uh, Commodore Coan?" The hesitant summons caused everyone at the head table to twist about in startled dismay. "Is this a communication, sir?" the solitary cadet asked, holding up the little crane.

The Federation squeaked in indignation. "Where did you get that?" he demanded, frantically scanning the room proper. "Who sent that?"

Sulu wished desperately to be less than three feet tall.

"Well, you threw it to me . . . but it came from over

there." Vulcan pointed across the room toward Sulu; the young cadet waved. "Does this mean I should start timing my half hour again, sir?" Vulcan appealed to Coan again.

"No!" The Federation's insistence sounded more desperate than well-considered.

Coan stayed where she was against one wall, her arms folded across her front. "What do you think?" she asked with a shrug.

Vulcan studied the crane very seriously. "Well, it *is* a transmission from an outside source . . ."

"Oh, come *on!*" the Federation moaned.

". . . so I guess it's only fair . . ."

"Fair?" The Federation leapt to his feet to seize the crane from Vulcan. "Fair to drive the Federation to desperation just because some jerkwater planet is throwing *ducks?!*"

Sulu straightened in his chair. "They're *cranes!*"

The Federation slung the crane back at him; it only flew about halfway. "They *look* like ducks!"

"Stop acting like children." Perez-Salazar's Latin contralto cut through the beginning of Sulu's reply. "You're only complaining," she accused The Federation, "because you planned to use Vulcan as the solution to all your problems. This is what you deserve for not having the courage to act for yourself!"

"What I *don't* deserve," the Federation returned acidly, "is a bunch of war-mongering idiots grubbing up every planet they come to and then claiming they own the whole system!"

Sulu thought he had never before seen someone's soul truly catch fire. Perez-Salazar's face grew even darker as her eyes began to smolder; Coan started across the room for the head table. "Okay, people, I think that's enough for now . . . !"

"You are accusing my people of cowardly acts?" Sulu wasn't sure whether Perez-Salazar was responding from a sense of offended nationality or if she'd gotten too involved in the role-playing.

"Take it as you will," the Federation replied.

Perez-Salazar rocketed to her feet just as Coan reached the table. She spit on the table in front of the Federation. "Congratulations, *el jefe estupendo*—you now have a war!"

Coan physically sat herself on the table between the two, stopping the Federation's advance with a warning hand on his chest. "This is make-believe!" she reminded him, then turned to rake a meaningful look across the rest of the room. "Maybe you'll all appreciate the *usefulness* of make-believe in the rest of your training!" Waiting until the Federation had nodded his understanding and returned to his chair, Coan motioned that Perez-Salazar should sit as well. "I wish you could all just *listen* to yourselves! It's like recess with a bunch of kids!" Nobody laughed.

"I have never had a less cooperative, more selfish bloc of cadets in my life!" Coan continued through their guilty silence. "You were all chosen to be here because you're special—intelligent—because you display abilities common to good command officers!" She paced toward the middle of the gathering, turning slowly as she walked in order to rake an icy glare across them all. "Well, where did all those fine traits go?" Stopping just behind Sulu's chair, she leaned against the back of it. "I saw *one* of you use creativity and *cooperation* to solve the problems put to him. And everybody else either made fun of him or ignored him!" Sulu had a feeling he knew who was being singled out. "If this had been real life," Coan berated the rest of them, "you'd be lucky if Menak didn't bomb you all while you were busy squabbling among yourselves!" Sulu slipped the terrorist crane into his pocket as surreptitiously as he could manage. "In later scenarios, you won't get the chance to be so kind to one another, even if you feel so inclined."

She looked them over with coldhearted calculation one last time, then broke into a friendly smile and clapped her hands. The transformation was so complete, Sulu didn't know whether to respect her flexibility or resent her manipulations. "Okay, everybody," she cried, making herding motions toward the closest door, "time for lunch! Go put food in your stomachs—we've got a million things to do yet today!"

Sulu tossed his accoutrements into the growing pile on the head table, pocketing the last of his origami cranes. "I don't suppose you'd be interested in a housing deal on Menak III?" he quipped to Perez-Salazar.

She didn't dignify his comment with a reply.

Sulu barely noticed the passage of the next week. Class followed class followed drill followed meals. Sleep must have occurred somewhere between the busy days, but Sulu honestly had no memories to account for all the nights. What happened on Tuesday was as distant or as near as what commenced on Friday; Sulu took to dating his class notes and his private reminders just to keep the past in perspective. His future he didn't even think about as yet.

He recognized Monday when it arrived only because it was the very first day on which he had any inkling what would happen next: his class schedule was the same as that first Monday, and he had kept meticulous record. Somehow, the warp-driven pace seemed a little less grueling, the instructors and courses just a little less confusing with that time schedule as an anchor for reality. Sulu achieved the end of the day in much better humor than he had one week before.

No voices greeted him upon his return to the bunkard. He was somewhat surprised to have beaten everyone else back, but privately admitted that sprinting across the quad (the weather was far too exhilarating to allow mere walking) probably affected his time. He sailed his course notes at his bunk from three meters' distance, then swung into the adjacent concession by catching the doorpost with one hand as he danced past.

He stumbled to a stop when Poppy called cheerfully, "I was hoping you'd get here soon!"

Sulu dashed frantic looks in all directions, expecting Coan to appear like an avenging angel and shrivel him with a glance. "What are you doing here?" he demanded in a high stage whisper. "*How* did you get here? This is a restricted campus!"

The old man climbed to his feet, patting Sulu's cheek as though to soothe the ensign's distress. "Old Japanese men look distinguished," he explained. "I told them I was an admiral."

"Oh, good God . . . !"

Tetsuo followed amiably as Sulu dragged him toward the door. "They were polite before then, but they got *very* polite afterward. They said I could find you here."

"Poppy . . ." Sulu checked both directions before leading his great-grandfather out into the hall. "I think it's a capital offense to impersonate Starfleet officers!"

Tetsuo scoffed. "I didn't *impersonate* anybody," he insisted. "I didn't even give them my name!"

"I don't think that's the point." When the door at the end of the hall whisked open, Sulu tucked Tetsuo back against the wall until he had glanced around the corner to verify the presence of a guard. A bored senior cadet wandered back and forth in front of the doorway, occasionally glancing at the inviting weather outside.

"Where are we going?"

Sulu put his hand over Tetsuo's mouth; the old man fell obligingly silent. "You want to be an admiral?" Sulu whispered.

Tetsuo shrugged. "Not especially."

"Well, do what I do anyway—and don't *say* anything!"

Sulu didn't wait for Tetsuo's acknowledgment. Stepping through the doorway, he pulled his shoulders back, tucked his chin up, and strode purposefully toward the guard at the end of the hall. The cadet turned at the sound of Sulu's footsteps, waving a cordial hello as the other cadet approached.

Returning the security guard's casual greeting with a terse nod, Sulu barely glanced at the young man on his way by; Tetsuo's friendly, "Hello!" was almost lost under Sulu's stiff, "Carry on."

Once on the quad, Sulu relaxed his stance and turned to pull Tetsuo up next to him. "I told you not to talk!" he scolded, walking them further away from the building.

Tetsuo shrugged, grinning. "I forgot."

Sulu growled with feigned frustration and pulled the older man into a hug. "Maybe we can get you off on mental incompetence."

Tetsuo chuckled and returned his great-grandson's hug soundly. "I've always thought that wouldn't be hard."

"But, seriously, Poppy, *don't* sneak in again! You can get us both in a lot of trouble."

"If you say so." He pushed Sulu away and started them walking again. "So how is everything?"

"Okay," Sulu allowed. "It's only been a week—I've been too busy to have an opinion." The air gusted around them with the smell of ocean and late roses; it ruffled Sulu's hair like a warm, loving hand. "You could have called if that's all you wanted to know."

Tetsuo didn't answer. Sulu glanced over at his great-grandfather when the older man reached inside his jacket for a tiny square of colored paper. He folded a delicate crane as they walked. "Poppy . . . ?" The smile on the old man's face was sweet and happy, like the smell of fragile honeysuckle just before the frost. "Poppy, is something wrong?"

Tetsuo's eyes remained fixed on his tiny work. "I'm dying, son," he said without prelude.

Sulu wasn't sure how he was supposed to respond to that, so he only slipped his arm around his great-grandfather's shoulders and whispered, "I know, Poppy."

"No, I mean really," Tetsuo went on. "Right now." The crane finished, he tucked it gently into another pocket, and retrieved another slip of paper. "Doctor Kobrine says the tumor's bigger. He wants to operate on me."

Coldness swelled against Sulu's heart. "And?"

Tetsuo paused in his folding, smiling wanly at Sulu. "I came here because I wanted to talk to you. I wanted to explain."

The coldness closed into a painful fist. "Explain about what?" He didn't want to understand.

Tetsuo put away the half-finished crane to take both of Sulu's hands in his own. "The operation isn't really going to help anything. It'll make the tumor smaller, Doctor Kobrine says, but they can't take it completely away because of the way it grows."

Sulu nodded slowly. "I know that . . ."

"So operating could maybe kill me. It won't make the treatments unnecessary, and it may not even slow down how the tumor grows. All it does, at best, is make it all go on a little longer."

"Doctor Kobrine is the best in the world," Sulu insisted, wanting to speak before Poppy got too far—wanting to make him understand. "If he says you should do it, then you should! It's better than nothing."

Tetsuo squeezed his great-grandson's hands and smiled. "I'm not so sure about that anymore."

Panic swam counterclockwise to sorrow. "Why are you telling me this, Poppy?" Sulu demanded urgently. "What is it you're trying to say?"

"I'm trying to say," Tetsuo said gently, "that one-hundred-and-three is older than God ever meant people to be. Giving you something like a grade four glioma is His way of telling you to hurry it up—give the next generation a crack at the world." He reached up to touch his great-grandson's face. "I wanted you to understand why I told Doctor Kobrine to stop the treatments, because I know no one else ever will."

Sulu's stomach twisted in silent despair. "You can't stop the treatments . . ."

"I already have."

"No, Poppy!" He pulled away, out of the old man's reach, out of his grasp. "Don't you realize what'll happen? Don't you understand what you've *done?*"

"I've gained a month, maybe two, of feeling happy, healthy, and *alive* before I die," Tetsuo told him. "Whatever comes after that . . ." He shrugged. "Maybe nobody really knows. But it doesn't frighten me anymore."

Sulu felt tears wringing out of his ragged emotions. "You're giving up!" he accused, furious. "You're going to desert me just because you're afraid to—"

"No," Tetsuo interrupted sternly, "I'm not afraid. Not of dying. Not like this, at least. I'm afraid of dying *badly,* son. I'm afraid that if I wait . . ." Pain glittered in his stone-black eyes. "I have *loved* my life! I loved your great-grandmother. I loved all the children we had together, and all their children, and all theirs. I loved boating, and the ocean, and the way my face felt after the salt and wind dried it all shiny like the sand. I loved the animals at the gardens, and those plants you used to bring home all the time . . . " His voice trailed off into a gentle laugh. His eyes focused again, and he sighed. "I want to say goodbye to all that while we're still on speaking terms. If I stay, I'm afraid I'll learn to hate living . . . then I'd really have nothing to live for after all."

Sulu stared at his great-grandfather, ashamed of the cold tears on his cheeks, ashamed that shedding those tears should make him so afraid. "Doctor Kobrine will stop you."

"He won't," Tetsuo said with certainty. "I've thought a long time about this. And I've been folding cranes." He displayed the half-done crane, shiny purple in the afternoon light.

Sulu slapped the paper construct out of his hand. "I don't care about your damn cranes!" he cried, his voice choking on the pain gathered in his throat. "I care about you, Poppy! You said you'd come when I graduated! You said—"

"I'm sorry. But it has to be done—it has to be this way." Sulu jerked away when Tetsuo reached up to touch him. Lonely disappointment flashed through the old man's eyes. "I thought you, of all people, would understand."

"Well, I don't!" Sulu grated. "And I never will! How could you want to die? How could you want to leave me. . . !" He felt more tears rush to the surface, and turned away before his great-grandfather's gentle sorrow could make him cry. "Just go home and die if you want to!" he shouted. "Don't try to make me justify it for you!"

When he broke and ran for the bunkard, he didn't know if he wanted Tetsuo to stop him or let him go. As it was, his great-grandfather said nothing.

It was that image of Tetsuo, standing abandoned

and small in the middle of the windy quad, that Sulu would remember for the rest of his days.

"Ugh!" Sulu threw himself onto his bunk, not caring enough about the mud and pitch and detritus on his uniform to bother stripping out of his clothes. "I can't believe anybody actually *lives* in those mountains!" he moaned to the cadet in the next bunk over. "What did they say? Two and half million people in one of the smaller cultural centers alone?"

His companion's uniform and equipment were as filthy and sweat-soaked as Sulu's; he displayed the same lack of concern for his bed's welfare as he stretched out on his own bunk. Cadets all throughout the bunkard were engaged in similar pursuits.

"I feel like I haven't slept in weeks," Sulu replied. "After two months of midnight drills and six A.M. breakfast calls, you'd think I'd be used to this."

The cadet's only reply was a loud snore.

Sulu closed his own eyes, relishing the decadent feel of relaxation. After a week and a half on the other side of the North American continent, Sulu welcomed even San Francisco's damp, chilly autumn. They'd been dropped in ten degrees centigrade weather in the northern Allegheny Mountains and instructed to make their way to a predetermined base "as soon as you can." They'd had sufficient gear and food to keep them alive (Sulu had hoped), but it was a white-haired, smart-mouthed boy from upstate New York who saved them all. He reckoned directions by the stars better than anyone Sulu had ever seen; they reached their destination in record time, losing only a backpack and a sleeping tent in the process. Sulu, as commander of the excursion, was distinctly pleased.

He was also exhausted. Classes, duties, and drills demanded more time and energy than Sulu would have believed he possessed two months ago, and this trek through the Alleghenies was only the last on a long list. He took inspiration and stamina from every available source—invigorating conversations, newly formed friendships, frequent naps and frequent meals —but his greatest source of strength was his family. Communications from home—especially from Poppy—had formed the underpinnings of his endurance. He hadn't realized how much he would miss that support until it ceased.

Tetsuo had called twice after their argument on the quad. Sulu responded to neither recorded message, but the second made him silently cry himself to sleep. "I feel wonderful," Poppy had told him. "I feel *free.* If I can't make you understand why it has to be this way, at least be happy for me . . . I love you so much."

The worst part of it was that Sulu thought perhaps he *did* understand. His life and activity were always so important to Tetsuo; the same things were important to Sulu, as well. He couldn't imagine his own life without Starfleet, without windsailing, without fencing . . . But if he admitted to himself (and to Tetsuo) that there was dignity in choosing the time to die, it might seem as though he condoned it. And he didn't want Tetsuo to go.

Sulu rolled over roughly, uttering a guttural sound of frustration. The unhappy thoughts slipped to the back of his mind, following a route well-worn after two months of dismissal. He tried studiously to will himself to sleep before any more thinking could occur.

He didn't know how long he'd been dozing before someone jounced his bed. "Mail call! Rise and shine."

Sulu struggled into a sitting position, feeling as though he'd been bound up in cotton like a mummy. He held out a hand for the message tape the other cadet presented to him. "Oh . . . uh, thanks . . ." he muttered fuzzily.

But the mail carrier was already awakening the next cadet in line. "Mail call!"

Sulu squinted at the message's origin through a yawn. When he saw the California transmit code, the last of his tattered haze of sleep dashed away. He scrambled to his feet.

Sunside—as Sulu and the other cadets eventually discovered—was the recreation area for off-duty cadets. No one had ever discovered a reason for the enigmatic name, but, with time, no one seemed to care anymore, either. Along with the chairs, tables, and food services stations, Sunside also sported seven reader terminals.

The terminals were deserted now. Sulu slipped into the closest booth; no doubt everyone in this bloc was still recovering from the wild and frigid Alleghenies.

His name, rank, and serial number appeared, followed by a return transmit code that he didn't immediately recognize. He sat back in the padded seat and waited to see who was the originator.

Arthur Kobrine's face appeared on the screen, backed by a room Sulu didn't recognize, and accompanied by voices Sulu had never heard. All hope inside him paused, but he couldn't bear to banish it just yet.

"Cadet Sulu," Kobrine said, his voice low and strangely roughened. "I . . . They said you were gone on maneuvers. I hope those went well. I only wish I . . . I wish you were here, son. I'd rather tell *you* this, not some machine . . ."

Kobrine glanced over his shoulder anxiously, his eyes following something beyond Sulu's ability to see. When he turned back, his eyes were sad. "Your great-grandfather died today, son. I tried to call you, but they said you were gone. I didn't want to leave a message . . . a lot of messages for you to find when you got back . . . He was only sick for the last week, only really sick for the last few hours . . . He was really happy, son. And he missed you. He said to tell you . . ." Kobrine dropped his gaze, scrubbing at his eyes with the heels of his hands. "He said to tell you he loved you," he finally finished miserably. "That he always had and always would . . . He left a bunch of those paper cranes you and he used to make all the time. A thousand of them, he said . . . He said you'd understand . . ." Someone interrupted him again from behind; Doctor Kobrine nodded an acknowledgment, then raised his sad face again. "I have to go. I'm sorry I had to tell you like this. Call me at the hospital, if you'd like. I'm so sorry, son . . ." The transmission ended on a white corridor wall while a distant intercom called Doctor Kobrine away to care for some patient who was still among the living.

* * *

The rock upon which Sulu laid was bone-eating cold, smoothed by centuries of interplay with the ocean and by the feathery green plants that clung to it for support. Foliage draped in limp tendrils across muscles, stones, and mollusks to bob in the moonlit tidal pools like weary undines; Sulu felt them, cool and moist, beneath his stomach as he stared across the glassy sea. Like the kelp, ebb tide found the young cadet without the strength to stand.

The ocean seemed his only respite after Doctor Kobrine's horrible message. Sulu left Sunside without bothering to take the tape from the reader. Stopping in the bunkard only long enough to slide a bulky box out from its place in his locker, he walked away from the bunkard, the quad, and the Academy without speaking to another living soul.

The box cut into his chest now, pinned between his pain-racked body and the cold, kelp-wrapped rock. Sulu had emptied the contents of the box into the retreating tide; the last of the thumb-sized cranes floated beyond the limits of his sight over an hour ago. Silver, white, transparent, rainbow, blue . . . He'd folded them out of any material that fell into his hands. While high in the Alleghenies, he'd folded more than a dozen out of the scarlet-and-white protective strips on their rations. He'd folded them against the growing numbers he knew his great-grandfather collected—folded in desperate need of a miracle now that science and love had failed him—folded six-hundred-and-forty-four before Poppy finished his one thousandth and ended the silent race. Now, the evening breeze blew the little cranes out to sea like six hundred vanished souls, leaving only Sulu and an empty container behind.

It was moonless and full dark before Sulu was able to rouse himself and stand. He felt stiff, and sick, and tired—partly a legacy of the cold rock he'd been hugging, partly the emotional vacancy that ate at his heart like a dying fire. He walked with cottony, uncaring steps, up the jagged embankment, across the long green concourse, down the quiet, starlit streets. He deposited the box into a refuse container as he passed.

The Academy quad was warm and well-lit upon his return. Moving into the almost-daylight, something like embarrassment stirred in Sulu and made him brush ineffectually at the front of his singlet. A few pieces of kelp dislodged to fall wetly to the stones at his feet. Sulu wished he'd thought about his appearance before stretching out on the rock, but he couldn't truthfully say he'd thought about *anything* except somehow freeing the cranes he'd tried to contain. At that time, that had seemed so terribly important.

As he stepped through the student entrance, the guard on duty nodded a reserved, "Good evening." Sulu returned the greeting, but didn't pause; he heard the ensign open an intercom panel just before he passed into the hall.

Coan waited against the wall outside the bunkard. "Good evening, Commodore."

Even her dark eyes looked cold in the subdued light. "Congratulations," she said quietly. "You've just accrued a batch of demerits that'll take three years to undo."

Tears welled up inside him again, and he did

everything he could to keep them out of his voice. "I know, sir . . . I'm sorry."

"Save your 'sorry's for your parents," she countered. The disappointment and anger on her face hurt far worse than her words. "This is command school. I don't give a damn what you apologize for—I give a damn what you do!" She pushed away from the wall with a rough, angry movement, and started down the hall. "Go in and get to bed. We're running a scenario tomorrow that you're going to need your sleep for."

". . . thank you, sir . . ." He'd spoken so softly, he doubted she had heard. Even if she had, he felt sure she wouldn't care.

". . . including responding to computer-generated incidents such as any starship captain is apt to encounter," Coan continued, ceasing her pacing of the lecture hall to sit on the edge of the raised platform. "The commander of the *U.S.S. Exeter*—your ship for the course of this scenario—was chosen by our all-wise, all-knowing computer earlier this morning." She angled her chin upward to meet Sulu's gaze from all the way down the long hall. He didn't know if he should be horrified or flattered. "Are you ready to take your post, Captain Sulu?"

Everyone turned to look at him—some to smile, some to stare. Sulu only shook his head dumbly and said, "I don't want to be the captain."

Coan's look of disappointed anger from the night before flashed briefly into being again. "Then why are you in command school?"

"I meant—"

"I don't care what you meant. You're captain for

this scenario. You'll be in total and complete command, even over the line officers who have agreed to help us with this. Remember that, no matter what happens." She stood then, and announced to the class at large, "Be at the simulator deck in twenty minutes. Don't be late! Dismissed."

Sulu sat, staring down at his hands, as the rest of the class filed out the doors. His heart still ached from yesterday; he lacked the creativity to decide which pair of underwear to choose this morning, much less the quickness required to adequately command a scenario. He knew Coan would feel little sympathy for such sentiments, though; when the last of the class arrived at the simulators, Sulu arrived along with them.

The bloc was split into seven different groups of varying sizes and composition. Four officers (two commanders and two captains) greeted Sulu's bridge crew at simulator four and assigned them their positions. Sulu settled into the command chair hesitantly, feeling as though he were sitting somewhere he shouldn't and that someone would soon come to chase him away. No one did, though, and the simulator was soon sealed and ready to run.

Lights, smells, and sounds cocooned Sulu from all sides. He heard status reports from faraway sections of the nonexistent ship, unimportant flippancies over intercom channels, sensors cooing peacefully beneath the more strident computer prompts. It was all so active—so *real!* His heart awakened, ever so slightly, as though responding to some half-heard clarion; he gripped the arms of the chair for strength.

"Helmsman," he beckoned, trying for briskness

and instead achieving a sort of breathless anxiety. "What is our current heading?"

The cadet at the helm glanced at the officer manning navigations. Completely in character, the officer only raised an inquiring eyebrow and turned back to her own equations. Nodding, the helmsman reported the heading, then added of his own accord, "That will take us within fifteen point seven parsecs of the Klingon Neutral Zone, sir."

Sulu was certain that detail would matter. Swinging his chair about, he confronted his executive officer. He drew back slightly in surprise and alarm to see Perez-Salazar seated in the exec's station by the turbolift doors; he didn't know why her presence hadn't registered before. "First Officer Perez-Salazar," he said, recovering, "what is the nature of our mission in this sector?"

Apparently much more at ease with her position in this scenario, she consulted her computer briefly. "Routine scouting," she reported. "We are due to take on supplies at Station F9 in four days."

"Is F9 on the neutral zone?"

Perez-Salazar smiled grimly. "If we could *cut through* the Neutral Zone, we could reach F9 in twelve hours."

"I see . . ." Sulu rotated his chair back toward the front, only just remembering to say, "Thank you, Mister Perez-Salazar."

The helmsman and navigator both looked at him expectantly. Sulu flashed them a confident grin and instructed, "Navigator Janda, plot a course around the Neutral Zone for rendezvous with Station F9. Helmsman, ahead warp three."

"Course plotted and laid in, sir."

"Warp three, sir. Aye, aye."

Sulu settled back in the chair a bit more comfortably. "Very good. Carry on."

He'd barely had the chance to adjust to his newfound status before the communications officer started in her seat and called, "I'm receiving a transmission . . ." She touched her earpiece and frowned. "It's very garbled, sir . . . and it's on the distress channel . . ."

Sulu uncrossed his legs and sat forward in his chair. A distress call! This was working up to be an interesting scenario indeed. "Put it on audio."

The communications officer complied; a broken wall of static filled the tiny bridge. ". . . *Maru,* nineteen periods out of . . . six . . ." The voice was British, thin with both distance and concern. ". . . Mayday! Mayday! . . . neutronic fuel carrier *Kobayashi Maru,* nineteen . . . out of Altair . . . We have struck a gravitic mine . . . all power, many casualties . . ."

"Gravitic mine. . . ?" one of the cadets whispered.

The captain at navigations nodded bleakly. "I don't know who lays them, I just know they tear the hell out of passenger ships and freighters."

"They do a good number on starships, too," an engineering cadet added.

". . . hull breach . . . Do you read? . . . Mayday! Mayday! . . ."

Sulu signaled communications to ready them for reply. *"Kobayashi Maru,"* he declared, "this is *U.S.S. Exeter.* What is your position?"

". . . read you, *Exeter* . . . Sector ten . . ."

Sulu glanced at the navigator, who winced. "In the Neutral Zone, sir."

Sulu stopped the next words he planned to say.

". . . *Exeter,* we're losing air . . . can you help us? . . . Over."

"Sir," communications finally prompted, "do you wish to reply?"

The Neutral Zone. "Helm," Sulu said, more softly, "give me a long-range scan on that sector. What do you get?"

The helmsman gnawed at his lower lip, then finally shook his head. "Dust, gas . . . I'm getting a lot of interference . . ."

"Is there a ship out there?"

"I . . . I *think* so, sir . . ."

That didn't help with the decision. "You *think* so?"

The helmsman opened his mouth as though ready to commit more fully, then scanned the readings again and sighed. "I don't know, sir."

When Sulu said nothing for several moments, Perez-Salazar pressed, "Captain, the *Kobayashi Maru* is awaiting your reply."

Sulu nodded, slowly, stiffly. *"Kobayashi Maru* . . . You are a civilian freighter?"

"Neutronic fuel carrier . . . three hundred passengers. *Exeter,* what's the problem?"

"What are you doing in the Neutral Zone?"

The answer this time was long in coming. ". . . don't know . . . must have slipped course . . . *Exeter,* can you help us . . . ?"

Sulu swallowed, feeling a sickness in his stomach

that told him everything he was about to do was wrong—only something else inside him knew this was his only choice.

"Kobayashi Maru," he answered calmly, "I'm . . . sorry. We can't help you. I'm afraid you're on your own." He felt his small crew stir like agitated bees, but no one said anything to him. "Breaching the Klingon Neutral Zone with a *Constitution*-class starship could be considered an act of war. An interplanetary conflict with the Klingons would result in millions of lost lives, and . . . that's a risk I am not prepared to take for the lives of so few . . . I'm very, very sorry."

". . . you *daft?* We're *dying!* . . ."

"I'm sorry."

"Captain, I'm—" The communications officer recoiled slightly when Sulu turned. "That's really lousy," she said, dropping out of the scenario. "I think we ought to go in."

"She's right," the helmsman intervened. "You can't just leave them out there."

"We're leaving them." Sulu couldn't believe his voice sounded so calm and assured. "You've got your course, Mister."

"Uh . . ." The navigator, laughing slightly, turned away from her panel. "You can't do this," she began.

"I'm the commander," Sulu reminded her firmly. But his insides quivered, and he didn't dare let go of the command chair, lest they see how badly he was shaking. "I have total control over this vessel, and I have made my decision." *A hard decision—a horrible decision—a decision that means all of those people will die!* The navigator nodded, and turned back to her post.

"Listen, Sulu," the cadet at the security station interjected, "we're supposed to be in Starfleet. We're supposed to guard, and protect!"

"Avoiding a war—"

"Is cowardice! *Kobayashi Maru* is less than fifty parsecs into the Neutral Zone—we could be in and out before the Klingons even knew we were there!"

"They may already know." No one interrupted, so Sulu went on. "What is *Kobayashi Maru* doing in the Neutral Zone, anyway? Why can't we clearly scan her coordinates?"

"The ionization factor—" the helmsman began, but Sulu cut him off.

"Possibly. Or a Klingon trap. There may be no ship out there to rescue."

The cadet at the science station threw his hands up in disgust. Sulu noted with some irritation that it was the Federation from the Galactic Politics scenario on their first day. "That's so damn paranoid!" the cadet exclaimed. "Do you mean to say that, as a starship captain, you would couch all of your decisions in terms of 'maybes'?"

Sulu looked at him, unsure how to respond. "What else is there?"

Protests erupted from all across the bridge, some of them in favor of his decision, most of them emphatically opposed. Sulu kept expecting the floor-to-ceiling viewscreen to crack like an oyster and return them all to Coan and the outside world; he studied the stars displayed on the screen and waited.

"Ladies and gentlemen!" a voice cut in sharply from behind him. "This is *mutiny!*"

The uproar cut off like a transmission that had

suddenly lost its signal. Every thought in Sulu's brain simply ceased, and he turned the command chair slowly as Perez-Salazar queried, "Should I contact security, sir, and have these miscreants thrown in the brig?" He only blinked at her.

"Calm down, Maté," the security cadet grumbled.

Her eyes splashed him with prideful fury. "If we are to treat this scenario as reality for the purposes of rescuing *Kobayashi Maru,* then we should treat our officers realistically, as well." She turned to all of them, scowling her disgust. "If this is how you would truly respond to your commander and peers, I never want to serve on a starship with *any* of you!" Her dark gaze glanced off Sulu, and he felt the implicit, *Except you,* in that look. Pride and shame, strangely inter-mixed, thickened his throat beyond his ability to respond.

"How *dare* you!" she went on, stepping down to stand by his right hand. "How dare *any* of you assume his decision is an act of cowardice! You!" She stabbed a finger at the cadet manning communications. "Save your starship, or save yourself. Choose! Now!"

He opened his mouth, shut it, then opened it again and stammered, "I . . . my . . . my ship!"

The scowl that twisted Perez-Salazar's dark, Latin face betrayed her opinion of his decisiveness. "Do you say that because you really wish the ship to survive, or because you are afraid of the repercussions should you choose the more selfish option?"

The cadet didn't volunteer a reply.

"No matter how noble that choice may seem to you or to others, *that* was a decision of cowardice," she told him. "For it to be truly noble, you must choose death because to live any other way is unthinkable."

Sulu sucked in his breath abruptly, feeling as though he'd been kicked, deep and hard, from inside. "Mister Perez-Salazar . . ."

She turned, straight and proud, at his summons.

"That will be all . . . Thank you."

He didn't look away when she paused to study his eyes with painful candor. "Yes, sir." Passing her muster left him somehow strangely pleased.

"Communications," he said, turning back to the front, "contact the nearest Starbase with details on the *Kobayashi Maru*. If Starfleet can locate a Klingon representative in time, it might still be possible to save the freighter. In the meantime, we have a supply run to make. Helm?"

Only the navigator uttered a cool, "Aye, aye, sir," in acknowledgment. But they all turned back to their stations without complaint.

"I hope he knows what he's doing," the science officer whispered to someone beyond Sulu's sight.

The ensign remained fixed on the stars, and pretended not to hear. *What has to be done,* he told himself gently. *I understand that now, Poppy . . . I honestly, really do . . .*

Brutal. He decided that was the best word to describe the lecture and review following the *Kobayashi Maru* scenario. Coan replayed the events on a large-scale monitor (embarrassing Sulu as well as everyone else in the bridge crew), then the class discussed their opinions and suggestions regarding the young ensign's course of action. While the commodore was studiously nonpartisan throughout the debate, the bridge crew wasn't quite so hostile by the time class let out; Sulu felt he had a pretty good idea what Coan's view of his decision had been. The knowledge made him proud.

The wind through the quad was brisk and chilly, but sunlight leapt from one granite-flecked square to the next as Sulu crossed the white stone plaza. It seemed somehow sinful to be so lighthearted less than twenty-four hours after hearing of Tetsuo's death, but Sulu thought Poppy would understand, and maybe even approve.

He caught sight of Perez-Salazar walking alone, as always, a half-dozen running steps ahead of him. Oscillating only briefly between approaching her and pretending not to see, his feet solved the dilemma for him by lengthening their strides until he found himself matching her stiff, determined gait. "Hi!"

She glanced at him pugnaciously, and he continued before she could speak, "I wanted to thank you for standing up for me during the simulation. It was a big help."

She looked forward again and shrugged. "I didn't do it for your benefit." Her eyes almost glanced at him, but she seemed to remember herself and directed them away again. "You were simply in the right, that's all."

Sulu smiled. "I had a good teacher." She didn't prompt him for further information; he considered letting that mean she didn't want to talk to him further, but decided he didn't want to play this game by her rules anymore. "My great-grandfather had a lot of understanding about responsibility, and things that just need doing." The pain inflicted by the subject was barely overbalanced by the love he would always feel for the old man. "You'd have liked him," he told her. "He was a very strong man."

"And a wise man," Perez-Salazar allowed. "A very wise man, if he taught you these things so well." Her voice was just as cold as always, but Sulu still felt warmed by her words.

"Yes," he admitted. "A very wise man. He taught me the difference between playing hero and being responsible . . . and how sometimes the two can be the same." He continued matching her pace as they approached the main building, not wanting to break this newfound rapport with Perez-Salazar, yet not sure how to continue it. As they entered the building's long, gray shadow, he asked abruptly, "Have you ever seen Old San Francisco?"

She paused in her walking, and so surprised Sulu that he almost overshot her position. "No," she said warily. "Why?"

"Well, I'm a *great* native guide," Sulu informed her with a wink. "We could get passes for this evening, and I'll show you Golden Gate Park, and Fisherman's Wharf, and the Palace of Fine Arts." He saw something like panic move in her eyes, and amended, "No strings. Just a thank you . . . Really."

The panic subsided, leaving only a vestigial smile on her face; the smile made her very pretty. "All right. I shall meet you here after supper."

"Great!" Sulu dug into his pocket and drew out the crumpled paper crane he had folded during the class debate over his *Kobayashi Maru* decision. He presented it to Perez-Salazar with a flourish. "Redeemable for one dynamite tour."

She took it as though it were a soiled sock. "This is one of those ducks," she complained, but not so severely as her expression suggested. "You folded these all through our first scenario."

Flattered that she'd even *noticed* him during the turmoil of Galactic Politics, he hid his embarrassment behind an expression of resignation. "They *aren't* ducks! They're *cranes!*"

"Cranes?"

Sulu closed her hand about the tiny construct and explained patiently, "In ancient Japan, cranes were revered for their grace and beauty. It was believed that if you folded one thousand paper cranes while meditating, you could create a miracle."

Perez-Salazar opened her hand only long enough to sneak a look at the origami bird, then smiled more stunningly than before. "Does it work?"

A swell of pain and love overwhelmed him again, and Sulu thought of Poppy and nodded. "I believe it does," he told her sincerely. "I really believe it might be true."

Chapter Seven

HALLEY

WELL, HE WAS RIGHT, Kirk reflected unhappily. *It wasn't funny.* He stared at the airlock door and willed Scott to hurry.

"Your great-grandfather must have been a very exceptional man," McCoy finally said softly. "I would have been honored to meet him."

Something reminiscent of a smile tugged at Sulu's lips. "Hang in there, Doc," he confided weakly. "You might still get your chance."

"Captain? Shuttle?"

Scott's voice from the front cabin drew everyone's attention. Chekov slid from his seat behind Sulu and trotted into the front as the engineer reported, *"I've got . . . some bad problems out here, Captain—a dust storm, or a cloud, or something . . . I just busted my tail to repatch a conduit that's been shredded by dust, and—"* The channel didn't waver; Kirk heard Scott swear softly before continuing. *"I'm hurrying as fast as I can,"* the Scotsman finished grimly. *"But I think . . . Well, it's best you not wait on me."*

McCoy threw Kirk a frightened glance. "What's he saying? What does that mean?"

Kirk gripped the back of his seat and wished for the millionth time that he wasn't injured. "Get him back in here," he ordered tightly.

". . . I *knew* it . . . !" Chekov hovered in the doorway, looking pale and shaken. *"I should be out there, not him!"*

"Chekov!" Kirk snapped. The lieutenant started, flushing with embarrassment. "Get him in here! Hurry!"

"With what?" McCoy insisted. "Jim, we haven't got a radio!"

Chekov bolted for the suit locker by the exit. "Yes, we do!" he gasped. "My God, we have six of them!"

Kirk couldn't believe none of them had thought of the helmet radios sooner. "Good, Chekov!"

"Scott?" Chekov held the locker door open with one foot as he triggered the radio in one of the helmets with his hand. "Mister Scott! Do you read?"

"Keep out of my ear, Chekov!" Scott's voice returned peevishly. *"I'm trying to concentrate!"*

"No," Chekov countered, "come back in. You can finish when the dust storm has passed."

Scott's warm, rich laughter was thinned by stress and distance. *"I can't wait that long, lad, and you know I can't. Now shut up and let me work."*

"Didn't you listen to Sulu's story?" Chekov asked the engineer. "Heroics don't always help!"

"What are you prattling about?"

Kirk waved for Chekov's attention, shaking his head. "Let him be . . ."

Chekov looked up in response to Kirk's voice, and a skirl of keening feedback tore through the front of the shuttle. McCoy swore caustically; Chekov twisted away from the helmet in his hands. As the clamor peaked and slid away, Scott's voice pierced the resultant static with a sharp, frightened cry.

Chekov clutched the helmet to him again. "Scotty!"

"I've got a suit breach! Ah, DAMN! Chekov! Listen, lad, you've got to—"

Silence engulfed the open channel. Chekov's suit helmet clattered to the deck as the lieutenant began hastily stripping off his duty jacket. He slung the jacket onto the front row of seats and dragged a full suit from the locker without even asking permission to go.

The shuttle groaned and shuddered slightly, echoed by a short, ringing report along the starboard hull, and a muted thump. An almost imperceptible sensation of movement made Kirk's head spin. He realized then that *Halley*'s tumble had shifted; Scott had cut the cylinder free.

"Where do you think *you're* going?" McCoy's voice brought Kirk's attention back to the room. "Chekov, don't be an idiot!"

The lieutenant was half-suited, hastily checking his pressure and seals. "Stay inside, Mister Chekov," Kirk ordered sternly.

Chekov didn't look up from his work. "I won't leave the lock," he promised. "If I can't see him, I'll come right back."

"Chekov . . ." But the thought of abandoning Scott turned Kirk's stomach; it could hardly do more harm to let Chekov salve his conscience by checking.

"We need *someone* in this shuttle besides me who isn't incapacitated . . ." McCoy sat with Chekov's jacket in his lap, twisting the garment into a thick rope with his nervous hands. "Chekov, didn't *you* listen to Sulu's story? Sometimes you have to sacrifice—losing *both* of you won't help anyone!"

"I *know* that!" Chekov shouted, slamming the locker door with one suited hand. "Do you think I didn't know that *before* we sent him out there?" He calmed abruptly; Kirk watched him take four deep, measured breaths before stooping for the fallen helmet. "But we can't afford to lose *him,* either," Chekov finished quietly. "That's the difference between classrooms and reality."

"Go on, then." Kirk intercepted whatever McCoy had been about to say. "But be careful."

Chekov only nodded. Running his hand across the overlarge controls beside the airlock door, he inspected the seals on his helmet one last time as he waited for the door to open. Kirk was just about to question the delay when Chekov looked up with a frown and touched the clumsy panel again.

Something almost like pain crossed the lieutenant's face as he stared at the panel. Kirk's heart wrenched inside him. "What is it? What's wrong?"

"I . . ." Chekov shook his head slowly. "I can't access!"

McCoy straightened in his seat. "What?"

"It won't let me in!" Chekov cried in delight. He

tossed the helmet back behind him again. "The airlock—it's cycling! He's alive!"

McCoy was already on his feet beside Chekov by the time the status light on the airlock door flashed green. Chekov yanked off his own gloves as the doors sighed open; it was all the two men could do to catch Scott as the engineer stumbled through and started to fall.

"Scotty, move your hand!" McCoy ordered, trying to pry loose the hand Scott had clamped just above his left elbow. "Move your hand!"

The hand moved, but not in response to McCoy; Scott caught at Chekov's wrist as the lieutenant reached to break Scott's helmet stays. A six-centimeter-long tear marred the arm of the suit, revealing Scott's blood-stained tunic beneath. McCoy thrust his hand into the opening as Scott motioned Chekov frantically to his left shoulder. The lieutenant nodded comprehension.

"Whoa! Hold on a minute!" the doctor protested when Chekov shouldered him out of the way. "This man's hurt!"

"He also has a suit breach," Chekov answered shortly. "There are joints in these suits that lock down to minimize air loss. They also cut off circulation." He angled his eyes up at Scott's visor and asked loudly, "Ready?"

Looking thoroughly miserable, Scott merely nodded.

Chekov twisted something at the shoulder of the suit, and the seal gave way with a popping gasp. Scott threw his head back with an expression of profound pain, then slid bonelessly to the floor between Chekov and McCoy.

"Is he all right?" Kirk asked anxiously.

McCoy nodded from where he was still bent over Scott's arm. "Looks that way. This is long, but clean, and not too deep." He flashed Scott a rueful grin as Chekov removed the engineer's helmet. "So much for the heroics, eh, Mister Scott?"

Scott's grin looked weak and sad against his pale face. "No more heroics, Doctor—*that* I can promise you . . ."

"Did you sever the nacelle?" Kirk wanted to know.

Scott nodded. "I was hit at a good time—just when I was ready to go. She's severed and on her way." He chuckled. "She ought to produce a bonny fireworks display when she hits home, too."

"Well done, Mister Scott," Kirk told him, smiling. "I'll get you a promotion for this."

"I'd settle for a week off with pay," the engineer replied.

"Done."

"Sir . . . ?" Sulu stirred slightly, but didn't open his eyes. "Do you really think the *Enterprise* will see the flash?"

Kirk sighed, afraid to hazard a promise. "I don't know, Mister Sulu," he admitted at last. "We'll just have to wait and see."

White-blue light bathed the shuttle nearly an hour later, blinding Kirk and Chekov, who happened to be watching out the starboard windows for the event. "Do you think that did it?" McCoy wanted to know.

"It did something," Chekov replied cynically. "We just have to hope it hit the right asteroid."

Scott stretched out to rest in a row of rear seats; when a lightning show of sparks and flashes commenced precisely a half hour following the explosion, the engineer only commented, "I'd say we hit the right asteroid," and went back to sleep.

An hour of tense inactivity followed, but the *Enterprise* didn't appear. "Maybe Spock wants to be sure before he commits to coming this close to the planet," McCoy suggested halfheartedly.

Scott was the only one moved to respond. "More likely, not enough of the explosion's energy made it through this system's gravitational mumbo jumbo to register as noteworthy on the *Enterprise*'s sensors," the engineer explained sadly. "We didn't look any different than anything else that's going on out here."

"Meaning?" McCoy pressed.

"Meaning nothing," Scott told him. "Nothing at all."

No one else cared to speculate further on the *Enterprise*'s absence. Kirk's stomach embarrassed him by occasionally punctuating the silence with voluble grumbles; he soon gave up apologizing. They were all hungry, and tired, and depressed. He tried not to remind himself that all these conditions would end far too soon.

"How are you feeling, Scotty?" he asked, just to break up the silence.

Scott looked up from his impromptu couch and rubbed at his bandaged left arm. "Good enough," he said. "But I'm not going EV again!"

Kirk smiled. "I don't think you'll have to."

"Do you have a *Kobayashi Maru* story?" McCoy wheedled from the front row. "We still have time to fill."

Scott pushed himself upright with a sigh, wincing when his injured arm brushed against the back of the seats. "I suppose I could take up a wee bit of time with the story."

Chekov looked honestly surprised. *"You* took the *Kobayashi Maru?"*

Scott scowled at him. "No, they just let *any* engineer take the bridge when the captain is gone!" He softened his words with a smile. "I had my share of command school. I just didn't take to it so well."

"With the destructive tendencies the *rest* of this crew has displayed," McCoy commented, "I would think anything *you* did as a cadet would be exemplary."

Scott shook his head and settled in for the tale. "Doctor, when it comes to destructive tendencies, these bairns have *nothing* on me . . . !"

Chapter Eight

IN THEORY

"IF THIS WERE GRADE SCHOOL, Mr. Scott, I'd have to take those drawings away."

Scott hastened to conceal his papers beneath splayed hands, scratched a meaningless line along the left-hand margin of his diagram in the process. Admiral Howell smiled indulgently from the front of Scott's desk; that's when Scott realized the rest of his classmates were long gone. He felt his face begin to warm. "Oh . . . Sorry, Admiral, sir . . ."

"Somehow," Howell commented with a sigh, "I doubt you are." He plucked the bottommost paper from Scott's pile and turned it about for study. Scott tried hard to withhold a wince when Howell frowned at the drawing, rotated it another ninety degrees, then lifted one eyebrow in uncomprehending curiosity. "Schematics?" he finally queried, glancing at Scott.

The young Scotsman knotted his hands together in his lap. "Aye, sir . . ."

"Mister Scott, this is *history* class, not design!"

"Oh, I'm not *designing* it, Admiral!" He leaned halfway across the desk, bending the edge of the paper back to peer at the scribbling upside down. "I'm *re*designing! See, it's part of a defective coolant system at my cousin's station. I was helping her trace a fault, and we got as far as here—" He tapped one complex tangle of lines and symbols. "—before I had to leave for command school." His attention caught on a mismatched circuit reference; the stylus was in his hand, scribbling at the paper before he took the time to consider that Howell probably wasn't interested in the drawing's accuracy. "What I can't figure out," he went on, returning the stylus to his desk, "is how this coupling—" He circled yet another portion of the sketch with one finger. "—fits into it all. I mean, it fits—right here—but it doesn't *fit in,* if you see what I mean. And I think that's the problem. See, if you look right here—"

"Mister Scott . . ."

"—you can see where the current—"

"Mister Scott!"

Scott clamped his mouth closed on his blathering, forcing his mind to shut down all technical thought. Stopping thinking was never easy for him, but it was something he figured he'd have to get used to. Captains were supposed to depend on other people for cleverness. That's why they were captains.

Howell kept glancing from the paper, to Scott, to the paper again. "You drew this from memory?" he asked, brown eyes busy with thought. "All of it?"

"Well . . ." Scott pulled down the corner of the sheet again, just in case they'd somehow begun discussion on another sketch without his knowing it. The same drawing filled the crumpled sheet. It was no wonder Howell felt the need to verify the blueprint's authenticity; Scott was ashamed of his own sloppy handiwork. "I only tore the system down the once," he was forced to admit abashedly.

Howell snorted once with amusement, then dropped the schematic back among Scott's other things. "What's your major area of study, Mister Scott?" he asked as Scott shuffled his drawings into some order.

"Engineering, sir." He wished Howell would excuse him before remembering to turn this talk into a formal reprimand.

"And you studied engineering before the Academy?"

"Yes, sir . . ." Smoothing his crumpled drawings with one hand, Scott tried to ignore the despair slowly twisting his stomach. "I've always studied it."

"I see." Howell leaned back against another desk and folded his arms. "Why are you here, Mister Scott?"

"I . . ." Scott cursed aloud when he realized it was 11:13 and he was more than just a little late for his next class. "I don't know!" he cried. "I was due in tactics—"

"No, Scott . . ." The admiral caught at Scott's arm as the engineer pushed to his feet in a flurry of books and loose paper.

"But, sir, I—"

"I mean what are you doing in command school?" Scott's mind shied away from all thoughts of captaining a starship; he didn't want to give fear another chance to tear up his peace of mind. "I . . . I'm learning to be a starship commander."

"Do you want to be a commander?" Howell asked him, still holding on to his arm.

Scott shrugged (a bit stupidly, he thought), all the while wishing his mouth hadn't gone so dry. "I don't know, sir."

Howell nodded. "I take it that means no?"

"Yes, sir," he admitted timidly. "I guess it does."

"So why are you here?"

Scott sighed and sank back into his seat. "My family, sir . . ." He spent a moment casting about for words that wouldn't misrepresent the situation back home. "I've been helping my cousin, who's a bonny engineer," he finally sighed. "But the rest of them . . . well, they think I'm being wasted by not being in command . . . I got tired of fighting them, that's all . . ."

"Didn't your cousin have anything to say?"

Scott laughed as he remembered the string of voluble profanity Cheryl had launched at the family when she heard of Scott's "decision." "Aye, she had *plenty* to say. But the folks figure you can buy fine engineers through the mail." He caught a flash of disapproval in Howell's eyes, and leaned forward to insist, "They mean well, Admiral—they truly do! They're *good* folks, and *good* people. They just don't understand the calling—they most of them don't know what it *means* . . . !"

"But it's *your* life, Mister Scott." Howell tugged at Scott's diagrams but didn't pull them free again. "It's *your* career! If you really don't want to be a starship captain, *tell* me! I'll go to Admiral Walgren and see if I can have you transferred to Engineering School."

The very thought made Scott's stomach wrench with worry. "Please, sir, don't do that." Pushing to his feet, he pulled all his books to his chest and hoped they would hide his unsteady breathing. "I got in here, after all, so I must have something. If I've really got the ability Starfleet seems to think I do, I figure it would be a crime not to use it. Besides, it would break my poor mother's heart if I just walked out now."

Howell sighed and partially turned away. "Have you thought about what you're going to do when they finally push you up to your own command?"

Scott stepped past Howell and headed hastily for the door. "I'll make do," he assured the admiral. "I always do."

Scott rubbed at his eyes and slouched lower at his workstation. The coupler he'd been designing rotated slowly through all three dimensions on the computer screen in front of him. He paused it wherever he felt necessary, but there were few alterations to make at this stage; he'd been working on the coupler for several hours.

At three in the morning, the computer lab was predictably empty. Scott didn't mind the solitude; in fact, he preferred it to the noisy, pointless evenings enjoyed by his fellow cadets. Listening to the others speculate on their future careers, their future commands, ate at Scott's already fragile sense of self-worth; his own lack of ambition hung around his neck like a stone, marking him as unworthy of the attention and encouragement he'd already received in Starfleet.

He felt guilty that he'd allowed himself to be pressured into coming to command school—guilty that he didn't *want* to be here at all. Scott would have been happy repairing and designing ships' systems forever, and, for some reason, he felt guilty about that, too.

Stopping the coupler display's rotation, Scott leaned forward to speak into the computer. A few notes to Cheryl, then he'd batch the entire design off to her before cutting off to bed. He'd already have a rough time slipping into the barracks unnoticed; he wished he worried about curfew violations as much as he worried about his future.

The technical notes to Cheryl only took a few seconds. Scott hesitated briefly over whether to include personal hellos to the family; he decided against it when all he could think to say was, I DON'T WANT TO BE HERE! over and over and over again. And then, I MISS YOU ALL.

He'd only just sent the transmission on its way when the computer screen flashed black and the coupler design vanished. Scott paused, his hand hovering over the power switch, wondering who he would report a malfunction to at this time of night. Of course, he could always pry the equipment apart and track down the problem himself. Before he could slide the terminal about and set to work, an amber trail of print danced across the screen.

I THOUGHT THIS MUST BE YOU. NICE DESIGNING, 'SCOTTY'.

"What in . . . ?" He pulled his hands down into his lap, not sure if he should power down the terminal or encourage this peeper by responding. The fact that some computer wizard had managed to "peep" into the Academy's system at all troubled Scott mightily. There were more important data than Scott's engineering designs in the Academy computer; all it took was one careless peeper, and the whole system could come crashing down. Then it occurred to him that the peeper might very well be *within* the Academy, and not an outside source at all. That calmed his mind a little. "Where are you?" he asked. "Don't you know it's after curfew?"

AMUSING. I NEEDN'T WORRY ABOUT CURFEW. BUT YOU SHOULD—IT'S AFTER 03:00. WHY RISK SO MANY DEMERITS FOR SUCH A SILLY PROJECT?

Labeling Cheryl's coupler "silly" wounded Scott's pride. He'd promised Cheryl a finished design before he left; he was delivering nearly three months late, but he was confident enough in his abilities to believe she'd think the wait well worth it. He wasn't about to try and explain his affection for design to some peeper whose very hobby made clear that he didn't give a damn about the pride people took in their systems. "Who are you?"

PERHAPS I'M YOUR FAIRY GODMOTHER. I AM WILLING TO GRANT YOU ONE WISH.

Send me home! Scott thought, all unbidden. He shook his head to scatter such dreams, afraid to even mention them, much less wish for them.

YOU ARE A FINE ENGINEER, BUT AN UNHAP-
PY CAPTAIN. IF YOUR FAIRY GODMOTHER
WERE TO OFFER YOU A CHANCE TO LEAVE
COMMAND SCHOOL AND RETURN TO
ENGINEERING—WITHOUT SHAMING YOUR
FAMILY OR REQUIRING YOU TO BE REMISS IN
YOUR DUTIES—WOULD YOU ACCEPT?

Scott touched the screen with wondering fingers.
The coupler design sprang up beneath them, rotating
a slow, silent waltz.

YES OR NO, MISTER SCOTT?

the peeper pressed impatiently.

THE ANSWER IS THAT SIMPLE.

"Yes."
It was done. He couldn't take the word back now,
no matter what happened. The genie was out of the
bottle and promising his fealty.

VERY WELL. SIMPLY BE YOURSELF, SCOTTY.
LEAVE THE REST TO ME.

The coupler vanished, along with the glowing
words, leaving Scott all alone in an empty computer
lab. He thumbed the power switch with one numb
hand, then sat for a long time after the faint hum of
the machinery faded.
Early the next morning, as Scott pulled on his boots
in a crowded, brightly lit barracks, he realized it all

must have been a dream. You just didn't get second chances of such magnitude—Cheryl would get her coupler design, Scott would get his captain's stripes, and all these silly wishes would be left far behind. Unknown peepers just didn't come in and fix everything without being asked. That just wasn't how the real world worked.

He tried not to let the incident bother him anymore.

"Tell me again—*how* did I get to be in command of this scenario?"

"Computer selection. I always thought the computer picked the best commander for any scenario based on student records." The other cadet glanced Scott quickly up and down, shrugging more to himself than to his companion. "I guess it's just random draw, though."

Scott was inclined to agree. In a previous scenario, he'd been assigned the position of chief engineer, and the annoyance of having to tell a half-dozen other cadets what to do (as if engineers couldn't think of enough duties for themselves) nearly killed him. Now the computer was saying that Montgomery Scott was the best it could do for a starship commander from this class; if that were the case, Scott was heartily concerned about the rest of Starfleet.

The simulation chamber—so startlingly like a real starship's bridge that Scott kept expecting the *real* captain to chase him out of the command chair—rumbled shut like a monstrous clam. How could they lock him in here like this, responsible for so many people? It was only make-believe, true, so any decisions he made couldn't *really* affect the whole Federation. Still, no one had even *asked* Scott if he wanted to be the captain, and he most emphatically *didn't!* Oh, Admiral Howell had asked, "Are you ready?" just before steering Scott off for the bridge, but Scott knew that was only a polite question, not a real question wanting a real answer. So Scott had replied, "I'm ready," in a voice whose steadiness lied about his trembling hands. Smiling a little sadly, Howell had clapped him manfully on the back and sent him on his way. Scott would rather the admiral had banished him to the outer Pleiades.

The first part of the scenario passed in a haze. The *U.S.S. Saratoga* didn't appear to be doing anything important in this simulation—just a routine training cruise to Gamma Hydra, without even supplies to drop off or passengers to coddle. Scott mouthed meaningless course changes, responded woodenly to questions and comments. He couldn't completely divorce knowledge of the simulation's falseness from everything that happened, so he tried to convince himself that nothing impressive would be expected from him. When asked about rescuing a damaged neutronic fuel carrier, Scott responded with an automatic affirmative, then turned back to the discussion he'd been conducting with *Saratoga's* nonexistent engineering staff.

The red alert siren startled him out of a dissertation on circuit rerouting and energy dispersal. "What's the matter?" he asked, realizing belatedly that he probably should have directed that question to his exec.

"Three Klingon cruisers, dead ahead," the science officer reported, just as helm exclaimed, "They're readying their weapons!"

Scott's stomach turned to hot water and started to crawl about his insides. "Communications," he summoned evenly, "try to explain to these . . ." Mindful of the monitoring officers, he tempered the label he'd intended to employ. *". . . people* that we're here on a rescue—"

"Incoming!"

"Full power to screens!" The command had barely cleared Scott's lips when the first barrage of disrupter fire expended itself against *Saratoga's* deflectors. Scott's teeth clacked together as he was flung back into his seat by the impact.

"Screens four, seven, and eight are down," the executive officer, bent over his viewer, reported stonily. "Screens three and sixteen are damaged. They won't last another round, sir."

Scott stared at the exec in stunned disappointment. "Were our deflectors *up?"* he sputtered. Intellectually, he knew they were; instinctively, he just couldn't believe a simple disrupter could wreak that much havoc, even through only partial shielding.

"We've also got premature detonation in four of our six torpedo tubes," the exec continued.

"What?!"

"And a complete loss of power in the starboard warp nacelle." The young officer raised his head from his viewer like a doctor pulling away from a dying patient. "We're just about done, sir."

Scott would have been less confused if the man had started speaking in tongues. *"That* much damage . . . ?"

The exec nodded. "That's the whole tally, sir."

"How?"

"Disrupters, sir," the helmsman sighed, a bit irritably. "They can do a lot of damage to a ship."

"Is that so?" Scott grated softly, feeling the blood rise hot and angry into his cheeks. He lifted his chin to the Klingons who closed on the viewscreen, suddenly not caring that this was just a damn scenario. "Well, not to *my* ship, they don't—not with a single damn barrage!" Any computer that thought otherwise deserved whatever Scott could throw at it. He slammed his fist onto the command chair's intercom button. "Phaser bay!"

"Aye, captain?"

"Yes, sir?"

"Sir?"

Another blast rocked the ship. Scott felt each rumble like fire in his blood. "Number three screen, down!" the exec called. Scott ignored him.

"I want all phaser bays to fire on my command, each of you aimed at one of those bedeviled crafts," Scott instructed the phaser chiefs grimly. "Continuous fire—start at your lowest possible frequency—"

Another disrupter hit. And another.

"Number three screen is *down,* sir!" the exec repeated loudly.

Scott wished the beggar would quit interrupting his thinking. "—range upward until you match their interference pattern and cut through those shields like butter!"

"Aye, aye!" all three bays responded in unison. Scott smiled the smile of a satisfied hunter.

The navigator was already plotting an escape course as the *Saratoga*'s bays opened fire with a chilling, climbing wail. "I can't signal Starfleet," the communications officer interjected from behind Scott. "The Klingons are jamming my signal."

Golden-red light burst across the viewscreen like a nova, burning Scott's eyes with its brilliance as *Saratoga*'s phasers finally reduced the Klingons to atoms. "Not anymore, they aren't," Scott told communications. "Contact Starfleet. Helm—get us out of here."

"Working on it, sir." The helmsman swore suddenly, punching at his panel. "But we've got company again!"

The five blue-gray cruisers hove into view even as the helmsman reported.

"That's it for the phaser banks, sir," the science officer reported as the *Saratoga* began her limping retreat. "Bay crews report all cells exhausted beyond our ability to recharge."

Scott waved off the report, dropping back into his chair. He wanted to feel weak and wasted after that first adrenaline surge. All he felt was sere and angry—angry at the monitoring officers for making him captain in a scenario he patently had no business commanding, angry at whoever had programmed this fatalistic computer in the first place. "Don't worry about the phaser bays. We aren't going to need them again, anyhow."

"Klingons closing!"

"Cut all rear shields," Scott ordered. His brain raced about like light in a mirrored box, searching his memory for any ideas at all. "I want everything we've got up front." *Especially with a computer that so overestimates Klingon firepower!* He punched at the intercom again as a course of action began to take form. "Engineering!"

"Aye, sir?"

"Pull me a canister of antimatter—"

The engineer sputtered. "Sir?"

"Don't question, just listen!" He didn't have time to explain every step of his plans to these nervous nellies. "It should take you just under three minutes, if you hurry. Pull me the whole thing and run it to the closest transporter room!"

"But—I—"

"Move! Bridge out." He thumbed another button as the helmsman announced that the first Klingon torpedoes were on their way.

"Torpedo bay," a nervous male voice replied to Scott's brusque summons. "You called, bridge?"

"Aye. You're dead down there, right?"

"Meaning the bays, sir?"

Scott dropped his head into his hands and counted quickly to three. "Yes, the bays. You don't function?"

Light, white and flashing, sprayed across the bridge as the Klingon torpedoes impacted with the forward screens and detonated.

"Everything's completely dead down here, sir," the weapons tech answered when the explosion was past.

"All right, then," Scott continued decisively. "Pack up every torpedo you can get your hands on and get 'em to the transporter rooms."

"Everything?"

"Everything! Six torpedoes to each transporter room! Now go!"

"Transporter room to bridge!" The call came immediately upon the torpedo bay's sign-off. "We've got that antimatter canister, sir. What now?"

Scott held the channel open, turning to the helmsman. "Pull us back. *Keep* pulling us back as fast as impulse drive will allow."

"Aye, aye, sir."

"Navigator?"

"Sir?"

"Start a continuous reading on the crux ship's position, and transmit your data down to the transporter room." He bent to the intercom again. "Prepare to receive coordinates."

"Incoming," the helmsman announced, with somewhat less concern than before. Scott nodded his acknowledgment, already working equations in his head for the next fleet of ships he knew the computer would send.

"Coordinates received, bridge," the transporter room responded after a moment. Then: "Uh, sir? Which should we use?"

Scott grinned. "Give me less than two kilometers in front of the crux ship—"

The second barrage hit with considerably more force than the first. Scott clung to the command chair while half his bridge crew was thrown to the floor; the lighting dimmed sharply before climbing again on emergency power.

"—less than two kilometers," Scott picked up again when the systems had stabilized, "from whatever its coordinates are when you energize. Then I want you to *immediately* beam back the canister."

"But—"

"*Just* the canister," Scott stressed. When would these bairns learn to shut up and just *listen?* "Leave the antimatter behind."

"Holy cow . . ."

Scott listened while transporter techs scurried about like busy ants. The distance was too great for the bridge crew to see when the antimatter was delivered, but everyone knew when the crux ship struck the antimatter's area of affect: all five cruisers flew apart into white noise and molecular wind just as they leashed another assault. Scott was grinning like a fool when the ship bucked him out of the chair and onto the deck.

"Screens are *down,* Captain!" sounded on top of someone else's frantic, "Hull breach! We've got a hull breach in section six hundred!"

Scott climbed back into the command chair without bothering to ask the science officer if any trace of the enemy ships remained (the velvet emptiness beyond the viewscreen rendered such questions extraneous). "Navigator! Are we out of the Neutral Zone yet?"

"We *have* been!" the navigator replied. "They're *following* us!"

"Ah, hell . . . !"

"Nine!"

Everyone on the bridge jerked about at the science officer's broken squeak. "What?" Scott demanded, irrationally annoyed at the man's interruption.

"*Nine!*" the officer replied, still looking shocked. "We've got *nine* Klingon ships closing on our port bow!"

"Coming around!" helm announced even as Scott stabbed at the intercom to call, "Transporter room!"

"We've got them!" the main transporter room proclaimed. "Six torpedoes in every room. Orders, Captain!"

It won't work, Scott realized suddenly. He checked the equations in his head again, and wondered if a computer would let mathematics outprove experimentation. Shaking his head, he admitted that he had nothing to lose. "Take your coordinates from navigations again—" The navigator nodded understanding and started to scan. "—and from the science station." The science officer whirled to face her panel. "Lock on the juncture points in the Klingon screen system and beam six torpedoes to each juncture point on my command."

Scott studied the sleek ships on the viewscreen as he awaited the transporter rooms' readiness. The monitors would stop the scenario, he was sure of it. Someone would blast open the screen and rail at him for dishonesty—for cheating! His career would end in ruin!

"Transporter room, here." The voice at his elbow made him jump. "All rooms ready for beaming."

Scott licked dry lips and nodded at the approaching ships. "Transport at will."

The resultant explosion was beyond deafening; Scott's ears rang in painful symphony with his aching heart as atomic fire consumed the nine Klingon war dragons less than a thousand kilometers beyond his bow. He ducked his head against it, hearing the navigator bark a startled curse. He was still staring at the floor as the world faded from white, to ephemeral pastels, to gray-speckled normalcy again. *They're going to kill me,* he thought with sick resignation.

"Fifteen war dragons, on the way." The helmsman began to laugh a little manically. "Jesus Christ! *Fifteen . . . !"*

Scott couldn't make himself look up to watch the ships close. The knowledge that this was not reality—and that he could pay dearly for taking advantage of that fact—had been driven home again with gale force when those nine ships cleared the screen. Suddenly, he'd lost interest in defending the honor of a ship that wasn't even really there. He would do his best until this travesty was all over, but he knew better than anyone else at this Academy just how pitiful his best would be. "Engine room, unlock the warp drive main control. You'll need somebody from weapons, but . . ."

Scott kept his eyes carefully focused on the wall above Admiral Walgren's head. He didn't know whether or not this private conference room was really colder than the rest of the Academy, but it certainly felt like it now.

"Do you know why I've called you here?" Walgren asked the engineer stiffly.

"Aye, sir," Scott answered softly. "I . . . I think I do."

"Could you state that reason, please?" Commodore Hohman glanced sidelong at Walgren, evincing more than just a little annoyance. "For the benefit of those of us who aren't entirely certain."

Scott looked at Walgren for confirmation. The tall,

gray-haired Englishman seemed the only one of the four monitoring officers who fully understood what Scott had accomplished in the simulator. Too bad—if Walgren hadn't known, either, Scott might actually have gotten away with it.

The two commodores continued to look politely uncertain, and Admiral Howell wouldn't raise his eyes from where he played with the ice in his water glass, looking guilty and ashamed. *You SHOULD be ashamed of me,* Scott ruefully thought to the admiral. *It was a crime against physics. I deserve to be punished.*

"Mister Scott . . ." Walgren's sharp tone recaptured Scott's attention. "Explain, please, what you did."

"I used the Perera Field Theory to destroy that last squadron of war dragons." It was the last squadron he'd *destroyed,* at least—the last fifteen dreadnoughts had atomized *Saratoga* without taking a single hit. Scott was still convinced he could have taken the last fifteen, if there had *really* been an engine room, and if he could have run down there to demonstrate to the engineers what he was trying to explain when *Saratoga* was destroyed. "You see," he continued when no one save Walgren looked any more enlightened, "Klingons run in packs so they can link their shields into a multiship field system. That way, any shield hit hard enough can draw power from other parts of the system to keep from buckling." He paused to glance between the two commodores. "Should I go on?"

Hohman's lips quirked into a half-scowl, half-grin. "Please."

"Well," Scott continued, "the Perera Theory hypothesizes that a photon torpedo placed at any juncture point in such a screen system will detonate due to the forces exerted by the complex energy exchanges. All the math and prior theorems support Perera's conclusion."

"Sounds good," Hohman allowed. "So what's the problem?"

"The problem," Walgren cut in, "is that Perera's Field Theory is wrong."

"It doesn't work in practice," Scott added for purposes of clarification. Noticing Walgren's icy glare, he quickly returned his attention to the wall.

"You mean," Howell asked carefully, "that when you do it in real life—nothing happens?"

"Precisely." Walgren nodded. "No one's entirely certain why, but it's been proven through experimentation. And hard data override mathematics every time."

Commodore Shoji politely raised one hand to gain Walgren's attention. "Are you objecting to Mister Scott's use of the theory because it is not applicable in real life?"

"Certainly!" the Englishman replied. "This is supposed to be a *simulation,* not a fantasy!"

"But the students are expected to use everything they have at their disposal," Shoji returned. He glanced at Scott with an inquiring tilt to his head. "You understood that this Perera Theory did not truly work?"

Considering his knowledge of engineering—not to mention his experience with the Perera Theory—Scott found the question surprising. "Of course!" he asserted. "But I also figured the *computer* would let me do it, because any mathematics it worked out would support Perera's findings."

The Japanese commodore shrugged. "I believe Mister Scott acted well within the parameters of the scenario," he concluded. "He recognized the avenues open to him, and utilized them."

"But this is *supposed* to be real!" Walgren argued, even as Hohman growled, "I *still* don't understand what the problem is!"

"Well, I sort of cheated, I guess," Scott volunteered in response to the commodore's complaint.

"More than 'sort of,' it would appear," Howell admitted.

"Are you *sure* this Perera thing doesn't work?" Hohman pressed. "I mean, even Scott's introductory lecture sounded okay to me."

The British admiral uttered a distinctly superior snort and refused to even look at Hohman. "You, Commodore Hohman, are *not* an engineer."

Admiral Howell sighed. "And neither are Commodore Shoji and myself. In the hopes of reaching some consensus regarding Mister Scott's solution, Admiral Walgren, do you think you could find your way clear to produce some definitive source of information on this subject?"

Walgren offered the other admiral a haughty glare. "As if the word of two engineers weren't enough!"

"Uh, Admiral?" Scott shuffled uncertainly from his place at the center of the room. "Sir, I could—"

"Keep your peace, Mister Scott," Walgren suggested sternly. "We haven't finished with you yet."

But I can explain! Scott wanted to plead. Still,

Walgren's steel-gray eyes didn't look interested in producing a "definitive source" other than his own, so Scott merely uttered a doubtful, "Uh . . . aye, sir . . ." and fell silent.

Walgren buzzed his own yeoman to bring the appropriate references from his library. Scott twiddled his fingers behind his back and tried to recognize constellations in the speckled tile on the ceiling.

"Ah! Here it is!" Walgren was already deep into one of the manuals, keying past pages so fast Scott was surprised the man could identify the contents. "In the *Encyclopedia of Engineering Development and Design,*" the Englishman recited. "Under *A,* for 'Aberdeen Solution.'"

Hohman made a face. "The engineer's name was Aberdeen?"

"That's the city where the theory was tested," Scott volunteered quietly. Howell flicked a quick glance at the cadet, but no one else seemed to hear.

Walgren ran a finger down the reader screen, tracing the lines of type. "'Aberdeen, Scotland, Earth . . .'" he muttered, his voice without inflection as he scanned ahead of what he read. "'. . . in which Earthborn engineering student Montgomery Scott constructed seven separate field generators in order to simulate the current Klingon design, based on data obtained . . .'" Scott saw Walgren's eyes dart back to the top of the screen, then the older admiral's hand stopped its tracing. "Montgomery Scott?"

Everyone turned to stare at Scott. Blushing, the ensign offered them a small shrug. "Aye," he admitted, grinning. "That's me."

Hohman looked as if he'd lost the ability to breathe. "How *old* were you?"

Scott shrugged again, uncertain why this mattered. "About sixteen, I suppose, sir."

"Good God . . . !"

"Do you tinker with engineering as a hobby, Mister Scott?" Walgren asked seriously. His eyes bore into Scott intently, as though this were the final question on some test Scott hadn't known he was taking.

"I majored in Engineering, sir," he answered honestly. "And I thought about being a starship engineer before I came to command school." Walgren's steady scrutiny was beginning to bother him.

"So you didn't want to attend command school?"

"No, sir," Scott asserted, deeply sincere. "I respect what captains do, sir, and I appreciate that Starfleet thinks I'd make a fine one. But . . ." He sighed and shook his head. "I think my heart's meant more for commanding machines than commanding people. I'd rather I had a captain who appreciated that—one who didn't feel the need to make me what I'm not inside." *There—it's said!* The results of his admission would no doubt quickly follow.

A certain distant tenderness settled onto Walgren's weathered features, and the Englishman nodded slowly. "I think we can arrange that, Mister Scott, if you don't mind."

Scott frowned. "Sir?" His heart labored under a hope he didn't dare tender.

"I'm removing you from command school," Walgren stated brusquely. "You performed inadequately during the *Kobayashi Maru* scenario, and you have been found to display an attitude and disposition not suited to a command officer in Starfleet." At Scott's delighted gasp, Walgren almost smiled.

"I . . . Well . . . Thank you, sir!" It seemed such a ludicrous response; Scott didn't even care if the older man understood just what he'd done.

"Make good use of your failure, Mister Scott," the Englishman advised as he gathered his tapes and turned to go. "We don't all get a second chance."

Scott stared at Walgren in admiring gratitude as the admiral headed for the door. "I'll do that, sir," he promised. "And I'll never forget you for this!"

The door slid aside, and Walgren paused only briefly, surprised. "Don't thank me, Mister Scott. Thank your coupler." He smiled at Scott's startled stare. "I couldn't very well let the engineer who could piece that together slip away. Good designing, Mister Scott. And God go with you."

"God go with *you,* Admiral Walgren!" Scott called as the hatchway whispered closed.

He never saw Walgren again after that, but Scott kept track of the older engineer until Walgren's death at age seventy. During that time, Scott always hoped that grand luck did, indeed, follow the admiral to the very end.

Most of all, he wished he could tell Walgren just how much that one decision had meant to his life. "The difference between living and just hanging around," he would have told the admiral. "You understand that, don't you?"

Scott couldn't help but believe the admiral did. Any real engineer would have.

Chapter Nine

HALLEY

SCOTT SMILED AT KIRK from across the shuttle's narrow aisle. "It *has* been grand," he sighed with a placid smile. "Hasn't it, sir?"

The captain nodded, pained and warmed by all the memories he and the engineer shared. "Yes, Mister Scott, it certainly has . . ." There was nothing more to say, and volumes left unspoken. Kirk closed his eyes, listening to Chekov reconstruct the radio from Scott's hastily wired alarm in the front hatch.

"Come on," he heard McCoy cajole the engineer softly, "lie back and get some sleep. We've had enough yarning for one day."

"There's no such thing as enough tale-telling, Doctor," Scott replied, but there was no real protest in his voice. "We still have the whole realm of *fiction* to address!"

McCoy must have pulled some spectacular face, because the next thing Kirk heard was Scott's deep chuckle. "Save it for some other time, Scotty," the doctor chided. "You need your rest, and so does our brave leader."

"Aye, Doctor."

McCoy knows, Kirk thought, without any great alarm. *He knows Spock didn't see us. He knows not to hope anymore.* Kirk had come to this realization an hour after the severed nacelle's explosion; sharing that knowledge with his old friend lifted some of the burden from his own conscience, but didn't help him to accept the defeat. Some part of his mind still rooted for a solution, like a terrier after a particularly wily fox. He felt as though he were only digging at stone now, though; there was nowhere else to look for that fox within the confines of the real world. Still, the terrier wouldn't stop trying.

A touch on his knee brought his attention back to the present.

"How're you doing?" McCoy asked when the captain opened his eyes. Kirk suspected the question probed for information on more than just his knee.

"As well as could be expected," he replied, truthful on all accounts. "How about Sulu?"

Aborting a glance over one shoulder, the doctor shrugged and continued loading a hypo. "Asleep. He'll be all right, I think. I've done everything I can." The hypo filled, he injected the contents into Kirk's swollen knee. "That should dull the worst of the pain," he explained with professional detachment as he returned the last of his gear to his pouch, "although it might tend to make you a little sleepy. Just try to be comfortable, and call me if you . . ." The doctor's hands hesitated in stowing the equipment away. ". . . if you need anything."

Kirk caught McCoy's wrist, switching his grip to the doctor's hand when the older man looked up to meet his gaze. "Thanks, Bones . . ." He hoped McCoy would understand all the other things he didn't have the words to say.

The doctor only smiled wanly and squeezed the captain's hand. "No charge," he said softly. "Now go to sleep." McCoy dimmed the overhead lights on his way back to his own seat.

Dancing on that dividing line between emergency lamplight and darkness, rest proved too elusive for Kirk's agitated state of mind. The pain in his knee, just as McCoy promised, dampened to nonexistence, but only a dryness in his mouth and a muzziness in his head hinted at the sleep that should have accompanied that respite. One by one, all movement from Scott and McCoy stilled, both men's breathing drifting into the childlike susurrus of exhausted sleep. Sulu's harsh, strained breathing blended with the quiet white noise from the damaged radio up front.

I've done it, Kirk thought, oddly fascinated by the realization. *I've failed.* He tried to reject the thought, but couldn't; so far, the only way they'd kept themselves safe was by exhausting every available avenue. Now, there was nothing left to hope for. Nothing left but the waiting.

I WON'T give up! Kirk insisted. He valiantly wanted to dig for just *one more try,* but exhaustion crept in too close, and he felt his eyes begin to close. *I don't believe in the no-win scenario!* Still, try as he might, he sank into a restless sleep to the melody of the radio's distant static.

And awoke in a fever, certain of what they must do.

Kirk pushed himself upright, delighting in the swell of anguish that engulfed his knee, in the giddy, dizzy darkness that lingered all about him. Only one emergency lantern still burned—in the main cockpit, where it illuminated only the front quarter of the passenger area; Kirk could just make out the somnolent forms of his four crewmen as he rolled over and started to rise.

Slapping at the lighting control as he hobbled past, Kirk even reveled in the sleepy confusion that reigned as the others struggled into wakefulness.

"Jim, I—"

"I've got a plan," Kirk interjected, cutting off McCoy's protest. "I think we can still get out of this."

No one said anything for a heartbeat. Sulu stirred slightly; Chekov placed a protective hand on the helmsman's shoulder as Sulu asked faintly, "What's all the excitement about?"

"You'd better be damn sure about this," McCoy warned the captain grimly.

Kirk turned instead to Chekov; he couldn't promise McCoy certainty, so he wouldn't promise anything at all. "Mister Chekov—the navigation computer's permanent memory keeps track of *Halley*'s location in relation to all the pertinent beacons and markers. Correct?" The security officer only nodded. Kirk shot the next question at Scott: "Is there anything wrong with that permanent memory?"

"Not a thing," the engineer replied.

"Then we know precisely where *we* are." That was hurdle number one. "All right," Kirk continued. "Sulu, can you recall the *Enterprise*'s coordinates when you left the bridge?"

"Yes, sir. 896-448-009 mark 24, and holding."

"So we know where the *Enterprise* is," McCoy picked up. "But I still don't understand."

Kirk grinned at him. *"You* don't have to." Shifting position on his good leg, he braced himself more firmly against the bulkhead. "The problem with waiting for the *Enterprise,"* he addressed them all, "is that the *Enterprise* doesn't know where to look. It doesn't help that the sensors are half-blinded by what's going on in the system around us. You said it yourself, Scotty—we don't look any different than everything else the *Enterprise* can read. So what we need to do is *make* ourselves look different, then aim that difference at the *Enterprise* so she can't help but notice."

Delighted by the prospect of rescue, Scott's face still betrayed some reservation. "How?" he wanted to know. "We've barely got life support!"

"But we've got the radio." Kirk waited until he saw understanding begin to dawn in the engineer's eyes. "Can you make it receive *everything* aimed in our direction—radio transmissions, light, sensor scans, the works?"

"A portable black hole . . ." Scott muttered distantly.

Kirk nodded. "That's the idea."

"Well, aye . . . but what good does that do us?"

"That's where Chekov comes in." The young lieutenant stiffened in his seat, immediately wary and insecure. "Let's presume Spock started running a logical, by-the-book search pattern as soon as the *Enterprise* lost track of us . . ."

"*That* should be a safe assumption."

Kirk ignored the doctor. "I want you to use that assumption, and the coordinates Sulu remembers, to plot out where the *Enterprise* is now—in relation to us." He returned his attention to Scott. "If we can direct your black hole at the ship, a routine scanner sweep should pick it up. I'm trusting Spock to do the rest."

Scott nodded absently, his fingers twitching on nonexistent circuits as he plotted through his construction. "We'll have to coax that remaining engine into action," he mused, not fully turning his attention away from his thoughts. "With the bad converter, we'll have to suck off all our life support and lighting power if we want to beat this tumble long enough to do any good." Then his eyes focused abruptly, and he shot an anxious glance at Sulu. "Assuming we've got a pilot, that is . . ."

A brave but weak smile tugged at Sulu's lips. "That's where *I* come in," he croaked. His dark eyes flicked to one side in search of McCoy. "Better get me off these drugs, Doc," he advised blithely. "It's going to be bad enough trying to pilot when I can't turn my head!"

Blue eyes clouded with apprehension, the doctor shook his head. "Jim can do it."

Kirk almost laughed. "No, Jim can't."

Before McCoy could protest further, Sulu explained, "The captain can pilot a fully functional ship all right, but this isn't the same thing. It would be kind of like trying to ride a unicycle when you only know how to ride a bike. Same principle, different skill." He tried to flash McCoy a reassuring grin. "I'll be okay."

"Sulu, you start messing around with that shoulder, you'll . . ." McCoy's voice trailed off as he saw the look on the lieutenant commander's face.

Kirk nodded.

"We have a problem . . ." Chekov's dismal voice brought everyone's attention back to him. He stared up at Kirk in mixed amazement and dismay. "The equations we need," he explained, looking at the others as though in apology. "Mister Spock might be able to do that kind of mathematics in his head, but *I* can't. Not without a computer."

Kirk felt his hope slip away.

"Can you work out the equations by hand?" Scott called from the rear; the engineer had already bounded out of his seat to begin collecting various equipment and tools.

Chekov considered for a moment. "I *could*," he allowed. "But—"

Grinning smugly, Scott reappeared in the doorway with a slender rod in one hand. "How about on deck plates?"

Frowning as Chekov rose to study the offered tool, Kirk asked, "What is that?"

The engineer pulled the rod down the wall by his head, leaving a shiny dark streak behind it. "A deck marking tool," he explained. "You use them for marking circuit information on bulkheads and decks." He handed the little tool to Chekov with a triumphant flourish. "Where do you want to start?"

Thinking ahead, Scott tore up all four rear seats while Chekov was still occupied on the back wall. The seats Scott jettisoned out the airlock; the Russian carried his figuring down onto the floor without pause.

Excitement built in Kirk like a coiled clock spring, ticking away at his patience with every line of equations scribbled across the scuffed deck and walls. Across the aisle from him, Sulu's bright humor slowly faded as more and more of McCoy's pain-killing drugs washed out of his system. "I'm going to be okay," he kept assuring no one. "We're all going to be okay."

McCoy paced until Chekov explained (somewhat irritably) that he was going to have to start writing on the doctor's feet if they weren't kept out of the way. The suggestion moved Sulu to laugh, but McCoy was somewhat less amused; he retreated sullenly to his front-row seat—tucking his feet protectively beneath him as he watched Chekov work along the floor. Kirk did his best to encourage everyone to remain calm, despite the fact that he'd have outpaced McCoy if his damaged knee allowed. Only Scott gave the captain no headache throughout the planning; however, watching the engineer disappear into the back with an increasing amount of the forward hatch finally caused Kirk to quip, "Leave Sulu something to pilot with, Scotty!"

The burly Scotsman laughed with pleasure. "The toilets go before the helm does, Captain! Don't you fret!"

But Kirk fretted anyway.

McCoy kept an equally worried eye on his patient, occasionally reaching across the seats to touch Sulu's uninjured shoulder. "You all right?" he asked, time and time again.

"Sure," Sulu always assured him, adding the last

time: "I need to be clear-headed if I'm going to pilot this wreck."

The doctor snorted. "Are you going to be clear-headed while you're in this much pain?"

Sulu made a tiny sound that reminded Kirk more of a sob than a laugh. "More than I would be on your drugs," he replied thinly. Then, after a minute pause: "Just keep talking to me . . . okay?"

"Sulu!" Chekov called from the rear of the shuttle; he was out of sight behind the remaining seats, guarded over by a wall of navigational graffiti. "What are the *Enterprise*'s last coordinates?"

"Pavel," the helmsman sighed, "didn't you write them down?"

"Tell me!"

"896-448-009 mark 24."

Chekov finally sat back on his heels with a weary sigh. Cramped black writing sketched a cobbled path down the length of the main aisle. He stretched, stood, and stretched again, then turned and jotted several lines of numbers on one of the front walls. "Pry this loose for me," he instructed Scott on one of the engineer's trips.

"All finished?" Scott asked with a smile.

Chekov nodded, not exuding quite the same level of optimism. "That's our course."

"I'm ready to fly," Sulu insisted. His voice was stretched as thin as fine wire. "But I need help getting up front."

Scott paused by the helmsman's seat. "We don't need you yet," he told Sulu, displaying the increasingly complex device in his hands. "I've got to get this outside first. Hang on a while longer."

"I'm fine," the helmsman answered faintly. "I love my job."

Scott smiled. "I know you do, lad . . . I know."

The extravehicular duty fell to Chekov this time. Scott double-checked every seal on the lieutenant's suit, clucking and scolding like a maiden aunt as he pressed the hodgepodge contraption into Chekov's hands. "Belay to the lock *before* we crack the doors," he stressed sternly. "And keep this thing tied fast to you—lose it, and I'll see you busted lower than you've ever dreamed!"

Chekov tugged at the cable fixing Scott's device to the suit. "I won't lose it," he assured Scott. Then he pulled on his helmet before the engineer could harangue him further.

Scott caught the lieutenant's helmet in both hands just before Chekov turned away. "Be careful!" He stared hard through the thick face plate. "You hear me?"

Kirk saw Chekov nod once, then the lieutenant stepped into the waiting lock and was swallowed by the closing doors.

No radio chronicled Chekov's progress along the shuttle's hull. Scott tried to reassure Kirk: "He's only going a little way—not even as far as the nacelle. There's a service hook-up that the gadget will fit right nicely." It didn't help. Kirk finally insisted McCoy and Scott move Sulu into the front hatch just so there would be something else to do.

Every step proved agony for the young Oriental; as the pain increased, so did his breathing, which only tore at his damaged shoulder more. By the time they situated him at the front console, his sobbing gasps had almost torn Kirk to shreds.

The captain hobbled into the front doorway to find McCoy kneeling by the helm. "Let me just give you something!"

Sulu couldn't even command the breath to object, he simply clutched at McCoy's wrist with his good hand and refused to let go.

"Damn it, Sulu—!"

"No . . . !" the helmsman whimpered. ". . . Doc, *please* . . . I'll be okay . . ."

The doctor clung to his hypo as though afraid to try and cope without it. "You're sure?"

". . . sure . . ."

McCoy retreated into the passenger area without even commanding Kirk to sit down.

Chekov returned less than five minutes later, flushed with excitement over the successful placement of the beacon. Stripping off his helmet and gloves, he joined Kirk and Sulu in the front hatch as Scott went aft to fire up the engines. "You have the course?" Chekov asked Sulu as he stepped out of his e-suit.

"Sure," Sulu whispered. He pointed shakily to the marked bulkhead plate before him on his panel. "But . . . why don't you read them off to me? . . . So I can just think about piloting . . ."

Kirk plucked the square of metal off the console and handed it back to Chekov. The security officer took it with a wan, worried nod; but his voice was calm and confident as he reported to Sulu, "Bring us about to heading 896-448-887 mark 3 . . ."

". . . aye, aye, Mister Navigator . . ."

A resonant *clunk . . . clunk . . . clunk . . . clunk* passed down the length of the shuttle as Scott killed the main lighting. Kirk heard McCoy rise wordlessly in the passenger cabin and begin snapping on the emergency lamps once again; the captain clicked on the inset lantern above the main console without interrupting Sulu and Chekov's dialogue.

"I'm slipping! . . . Are we slipping off course?"

Chekov leaned over Sulu's shoulder to look, touching the helmsman reassuringly. "You're fine—right on course."

No lights, no air, no heat . . . Kirk whirled the tally around in his head as he studied Sulu's pain-creased face. Back to exactly where they'd started, their lives depended on the performance of Scott's tiny construction outside, on Chekov's hastily prepared navigational equations, on the viability of Kirk's original plan. If any part of the complex structure failed, they would all die, just like in the *Kobayashi Maru.*

But we all BEAT the test! Kirk's mind insisted. *We proved you don't have to accept defeat gracefully!* You could reroute it, like Kirk; or carry on despite it, like Chekov; or avoid it, like Sulu; or fight it to the last like a Scottish bulldog. They would do all those things before giving up now, if Kirk had to sacrifice his own soul in the process. "Heading, Mister Sulu?" he requested in his most composed captain's voice.

". . . 896-449-678 mark 89 . . ."

"Very good . . ." He glanced up at Chekov for verification; the Russian simply nodded. "Carry on."

Almost precisely an hour later, Sulu collapsed. He simply didn't respond to Chekov's course correction, then slid slowly sideways until Kirk was forced to lunge out of his own chair to catch him. Chekov and Scott carried the helmsman back to the passenger cabin. This time, they laid him gently in the center aisle, atop a layer of heavy uniform coats; Chekov spread his own jacket across his friend's torso.

"Do you think it worked?" the Russian asked quietly as McCoy administered a series of injections to Sulu's lifeless form.

"If the black hole worked," Scott tendered glumly. "There was really no way I could test it."

"And if Spock happened to search in this direction," Kirk added.

"And if my equations were correct . . ."

"Listen to all of you!" McCoy grumped crustily. He stomped back to his own place and seated himself with determined confidence. "It worked. Now shut up and wait."

It was cold again, and dismal. Kirk hoped they wouldn't have to wait for long.

"Ah, Jim, *look* at her! She looks like—like an *angel!*"

Relieved almost to the point of tears, Kirk didn't respond to McCoy's enthusiastic commentary; the *Enterprise* filled his eyes and heart beyond his ability to react to anything else, and all he could think was that, to him, the great ship looked like a fairy-tale swan.

McCoy's shining, blue-white angel had flickered into view a mere fifteen minutes after Sulu's collapse. Growing in the starboard ports like the rising sun, the point of light rapidly took on the shape of their salvation. Kirk hadn't seen the big ship from the outside for a long time; he'd almost forgotten how beautiful she could be.

Scott dashed about *Halley,* closing up equipment lockers, battening down the cannibalized panels. "What a bloody mess!" he kept exclaiming. "If I let my lads see a work area I've been in while it looks like this, I'll *never* get 'em to put their gear away!"

"What are you going to tell them about the seats?" McCoy wanted to know.

Scott groaned. "I'll say we built a drive engine out of them—it'll keep up their respect."

"Tell them the truth," Kirk suggested. "That should build enough respect."

"You don't know my engineers," Scott said. "Bigheaded, all of 'em. It's best if they think I can build a ship out of scrap wire, believe me!"

By the time the *Enterprise's* rear shuttle bay engulfed their wayward craft, Scott was trying to decide if he should dismantle the defaced interior walls or keep them for posterity. Chekov stalwartly refused to voice an opinion.

McCoy sprang to his feet the moment *Halley* bumped to a cockeyed standstill at the center of the shuttle bay. Punching at the airlock controls, he complained, "Scotty! These things won't open!"

"That's because we've got no power," the engineer replied.

McCoy slapped at the closed doors with his hand. "Well, we've got injured people in here, damn it! How are we going to get out of here?"

"Spock will open the doors," Kirk assured him. "Now sit down, Bones—they've got to pressurize the bay first."

"That damn Vulcan thinks we've got all day . . . !" The doctor struck the door a second time before starting to pace. "It probably never occurred to him we might have casualties! Hurrying is no doubt an 'illogical' activity!" He swung about abruptly and pummeled the doors again. "Spock, can you hear me? Open this damn door!"

As if inspired by the doctor's vehemence, the airlock slid open, releasing warm, sweet-smelling air into *Halley*'s central cabin, revealing Spock framed in the doorway.

"Good afternoon, Doctor McCoy," the science officer greeted him. "I am pleased to learn that eighteen hours of unnecessary confinement has not adversely affected your social skills."

"Oh, get out of my way," McCoy ordered brusquely as he shouldered past the tall Vulcan. "Nurse! Get a litter in here! Have sickbay prepare for surgery!"

Spock moved calmly out of the doorway, coming to stand by Kirk's shoulder as McCoy hurried back in with a stretcher and a small team of medics. Sulu tried to struggle upright as he was lifted from the floor. "What's going on?" he murmured fuzzily. "Where are we?"

"Home," Chekov told him, smiling. He caught at Sulu's arm to hold the helmsman down when Sulu sat up to hug him.

"We did it," Sulu said. Joy at finding himself still alive seemed to override any pain he might be feeling. "We actually pulled out of this! We should get some sort of medal."

Chekov laughed and pushed his friend flat again. "I'm satisfied with being alive."

McCoy grumbled from the head of the stretcher. "That can be rectified, Lieutenant." When the security chief only looked startled, McCoy elaborated, "I'm taking this patient to sickbay. Now, either get out of my way or walk alongside, but quit holding up the wheels of progress."

"Sorry, Doctor." Chekov stepped meekly aside. "I'll be down later," he promised Sulu as the stretcher passed.

"I'll wait with bated breath."

Chekov followed the medical team out the door, and Kirk watched a swarm of chattering engineers take their places. "Don't touch the walls!" Scott bellowed at the tech who scratched at the equations with a thumbnail, seeing if the script was permanent. "I haven't decided what I'm doing with 'em yet."

"Jesus, Mister Scott," the tech commented, startled. "They're a little heavy to frame, don't you think?"

Kirk suspected Chekov was glad he wasn't around to hear all this.

"A full record of my activities since your misplacement is on file on the bridge, Captain."

Spock's voice caught Kirk's attention, reminding him of his first officer's presence. "Very good, Mister Spock—very efficient." He shifted position on the seat, angling his gaze up at Spock as though they were discussing a recent chess game. "I take it everything went well?"

The captain detected a mental shrug in the tilt of the Vulcan's head. "With the exception of *Halley*'s misfortune, everything has transpired acceptably. We are still endeavoring to reestablish contact with the Venkatsen Group, however." Kirk didn't have the heart to tell Spock that he'd all but forgotten about Venkatsen.

When the Vulcan swept a cool look about the interior of the shuttle, Kirk glanced about as well, seeing the destruction as if for the first time. "Kind of made a mess, didn't we?"

"I *shall* be interested to read your own report regarding the last eighteen hours," Spock admitted at last.

"A report couldn't do it justice, Mister Spock," he chuckled, pushing himself to his feet. "This is something better left to tales than records." Spock surprised Kirk by offering the captain an arm for support; Kirk tried to refuse, but relented after only two stumbling steps. Leaning heavily on Spock's arm, he quipped, "Well, Mister Spock—should you lead, or shall I?"

"Captain?" Which meant Spock didn't entirely understand.

Kirk smiled. "Let's just say you haven't got much of a career in dance."

"Indeed."

The bright bay lights made Kirk blink as he trudged slowly down *Halley's* inclined ramp. He wondered if he'd truly believed he'd never see the *Enterprise* again, or if some foolish part of him maintained faint hope. He suspected the grateful ache in his heart was the answer. "Nothing's ever impossible."

Spock glanced down at him curiously. "I beg your pardon?"

"Did I ever tell you about my solution to the *Kobayashi Maru* test, Mister Spock?"

"I think not, Captain." Spock raised an eyebrow.

"By *solution,* do you mean to imply that you beat the scenario?"

"Oh, yes." Kirk nodded.

"Your solution . . ." Spock asked, "it has some bearing on what occurred on board *Halley,* I presume?"

"All the bearing in the world," the captain answered softly. He rested his hand against the *Enterprise*'s cool ivory bulkhead for a second, then allowed Spock to guide him out into the corridor.

THE STAR TREK

PHENOMENON

more on next page...

THE
STAR TREK
PHENOMENON

____ **THE KOBAYASHI MARU**
65817/$4.50

____ **SPOCK'S WORLD**
66773/$4.95

____ **TIME FOR YESTERDAY**
70094/$4.50

• •

____ **STAR TREK– THE MOTION PICTURE**
67795/$3.95

____ **STAR TREK II– THE WRATH OF KHAN**
67426/$3.95

____ **STAR TREK III–THE SEARCH FOR SPOCK**
67198/$3.95

____ **STAR TREK IV– THE VOYAGE HOME**
70283/$4.50

____ **STAR TREK V– THE FINAL FRONTIER**
68008/$4.50

____ **STAR TREK: THE KLINGON DICTIONARY**
66648/$4.95

____ **STAR TREK COMPENDIUM REVISED**
62726/$9.95

____ **MR. SCOTT'S GUIDE TO
THE ENTERPRISE**
70498/$12.95

____ **THE STAR TREK INTERVIEW BOOK**
61794/$7.95

**POCKET
B O O K S**

Simon & Schuster Mail Order Dept. STP
200 Old Tappan Rd., Old Tappan, N.J. 07675

Please send me the books I have checked above. I am enclosing $_____ (please add 75¢ to cover
postage and handling for each order. N.Y.S. and N.Y.C. residents please add appropriate sales tax). Send
check or money order—no cash or C.O.D.'s please. Allow up to six weeks for delivery. For purchases over
$10.00 you may use VISA: card number, expiration date and customer signature must be included.

Name_____

Address_____

City_____ State/Zip_____

VISA Card No._____ Exp. Date_____

Signature _____ 118-23